Devil's Knock

DOUGLAS SKELTON

Luath Press Limited

EDINBURGH

www.luath.co.uk

RENFREWSHIRE COUNCIL	
197075521	
Bertrams	22/12/2015
	£9.99
CEN	

First published 2015

ISBN: 978-1-910021-81-1

The paper used in this book is recyclable. It is made from
low chlorine pulps produced in a low energy, low emissions manner
from renewable forests.

Printed and bound by
Bell & Bain Ltd., Glasgow

Typeset in 11 point Sabon
by 3btype.com

January 1995

FRIDAY

AS MUCH AS Dickie Himes wanted to get up and dance, his bladder told him it was not possible. He loved techno, and the DJ had been raising the roof all night. He was now giving the crowd a string of numbers from TTF. He'd begun with 'Retribution' and, like the rest of the half-cut clubbers, Dickie had joined in with the line 'punish the guilty' that ran right through the song. Dickie's heart swelled when he heard the band's tracks blast from the speakers. They were Scotland's first techno band and the bloke who formed it was from Glasgow, too. Apart from that, he didn't half fancy the female singer. Shame they'd stopped performing. Now 'New Emotion' was pounding through the club and Dickie really wanted to show his moves, but his heart wasn't the only thing swelling.

He'd been drinking rum and coke all night and the mixer tended to run right through him. So he leaned in close to Skooshie Thompson's ear and yelled over the thudding beat that he was going to siphon the python. His mate Skooshie dragged his eyes from the jiggling backside of the diminutive brunette he'd been checking out all night and nodded in acknowledgement. Dickie weaved his way through the pulsating crowd then glanced back to see his pal heading in the lassie's direction, his shagtime grin on his face. He'd nip her. He always did. Skoosh case, that.

It was the last time he saw his mate.

As Dickie made his way to the Gents, he reflected on how much of a dump this place was. It looked okay at night, with the lights going and the beat belting. But he'd been in it during daylight, when the glamour was diluted, and calling it a shithole gave it class it didn't deserve. The walls were black, all the better to hide the damp patches, and when it was rocking, as it was tonight, the heat generated a layer of condensation on the lowered ceiling which dripped down onto the crowd. They didn't mind, though.

Most of them were out of their head with drink, drugs or just high on the sounds. Despite that, Dickie loved the place. Even though, technically, he and Skoosh should not have been there. Big Rab would go off his nut if he found out.

The pressure on his bladder built as he pushed through the heavy double doors into the corridor and he hoped to Christ there wasn't a queue in the toilet. There was nothing worse than waiting in line with the pish just about to flood your shoes. The doors swung shut behind him but he could still hear the music pulsing, as if it were part of the fabric of the rundown building. A quick jimmy, then back in there and he'd show them what dancing was all about. He was drunk, but not so drunk that he didn't know he was drunk, so he held onto the rail as he stepped down the two flights of stairs to the toilet on the ground floor. He needed to get there fast, but not too fast.

He reached the Gents without suffering injury and shouldered his way through the first door, then the second one. He pondered, and not for the first time, why they always have two doors, like an airlock. With a mixture of despair and irritation, he saw that the six urinals on the far wall were all in use, while the three cubicles were all occupied. He was experiencing very real pain now, and if he didn't get rid of some of this, there was going to be an accident. He tried to wait patiently, but found he couldn't stand still as he watched the six backs lined up along the urinals like the rear view of an ID parade. He was seriously considering going in one of the sinks when a cubicle door opened. Dickie brushed past the bloke coming out, urgency now the name of the game, closed the door behind him, unzipped and let go. The sensation of the fluid erupting from his body was almost sexual, and a satisfied sigh slid through his smile. He heard the voices of the guys outside, laughter, the blow of the hand dryers, then the sound of the doors opening and closing. Then there was silence. It was cool in the toilet, which was also a pleasure, given the heat upstairs. He could still feel the music vibrating, although he couldn't say what the song was. He gave himself a final shake and zipped up his trousers. Then he opened the door.

And stepped into hell.

There was only one guy left at the urinals, but that was not what worried Dickie. It was the other three blokes waiting outside the cubicle that made his balls shrivel. He knew the one in the middle well. Scrapper Jarvis was not tall, but he was powerfully built, thanks to years working in his father's scrapyard, which was how he got his nickname. He lived up to it, too – his broad face bore the marks of his other activities, two scars down one cheek, left there during a fight in a pub owned by his mother, the formidable Maw Jarvis. He had taken exception to some drunk who had made the mistake of calling the Jarvis matriarch a scabby-faced auld harridan. It was a bit harsh, for Mrs Jarvis had been something of a looker in her day and still retained a certain appeal. However, the then 17-year-old Scrapper ended up with his face opened, as the drunk turned out to be pretty nifty with the razor he carried in his pocket. Two quick slices and Scrapper was bleeding all over the sawdust and the man was off into the night, never to be seen again. Some say he fled the city, for Maw Jarvis's wrath was not something you wished to behold. Scrapper bore his battle scars with pride, for he had defended his family honour, which was a bedraggled thing, but still something the Jarvis clan guarded zealously. Now, ten years later, Scrapper had dished out many a scar of his own and, it was rumoured, put at least three men in the ground as his family clawed their way out of their council house by way of the veins and noses of the city's drug users. Paw Jarvis had dropped of a heart attack in 1993, so it was Maw who took the family business onwards and upwards. They still lived up Possil, but their house was bought and paid for, even though it remained resolutely unostentatious. It was rumoured they had millions salted away in offshore bank accounts. It was also rumoured that one of those millions was the first pound Maw Jarvis ever earned, her not being exactly free with her cash.

And now here was Scrapper Jarvis standing in front of him with his two mates, who Dickie had seen around but couldn't immediately put names to. It could only be bad news. Dickie looked past the three blokes, wondering if he could nip round them and away out the door, but that was a forlorn hope. There was a slapping coming his way, he could feel it in the air, which had turned from cool to clammy. He felt himself sobering up fast as he slipped his hand into his trousers pocket and wrapped his fingers round the flick knife he always carried with him.

Scrapper jerked his head towards the urinals and his two mates moved to stand on either side of the boy relieving himself. He had been studying his flow as if he had discovered the secret of life down there, but looked up when he became aware of their presence, then glanced over his shoulder to see Scrapper and Dickie facing each other. He understood there and then that he was surplus to requirements and he tried to stop peeing. But whatever it was that had opened was not for closing again. His body was determined to flush itself out and there was nothing he could do about it.

Dickie couldn't keep his mouth shut any longer. He said, 'Scrapper, give us a break, eh?'

Scrapper raised his finger to silence him and glared across at his two mates and said, 'What the fuck, Marty?' Marty Bonner, that was the tall one's name, Dickie remembered now. His mate was Stewie Moore.

Bonner shrugged and said, 'Fuckin Niagara Falls goin on here.'

'Tell him to finish or I'll finish it for him,' said Scrapper in the curiously high-pitched voice that never ceased to surprise Dickie. Looking at him – at the scars, the broken nose, the puffy skin over the eyes where he had been punched once too often, at the muscles that bulged at the sleeves of his t-shirt – Dickie always expected him to have a voice as rough as a badger's bum, but he was almost girlish when he spoke. Not that he – or anyone for that matter – would ever say that to his face.

The boy at the urinal finally finished and zipped up. He turned and, with a last look at the four of them, darted towards the door. Scrapper grinned at his pals and said, 'Dirty bastard didn't even wash his hands.'

His boys dutifully laughed, but fell silent as Scrapper's own smile froze and he turned his attention back to Dickie. His eyes, though, were dancing, and it had nothing to do with the muffled beat pulsating upstairs. Dickie didn't know what Scrapper was on, but he was certain it would make him even more unpredictable. More dangerous. Scrapper's reedy voice was little more than a whisper when he spoke. 'What have I told you McClymont boys about the Corvus?'

'Scrapper, we're only here for a night out...'

Scrapper raised his hand impatiently and repeated, '*What* have I told you?'

Dickie sighed and said quietly, 'Not to come here.'

Scrapper leaned forward, his hand to his ear. 'What? Can't hear you, son.'

Dickie said louder, 'You've told us not to come in here.'

'Yeah. I've told you not to come in here, that's right. And what did I say would happen next time one of you boys showed your face in Jarvis territory?'

'You said there'd be trouble.'

Scrapper nodded like a teacher working with a none-too-bright pupil. 'I said there'd be trouble. So, the question is, if you know that, if you know Club Corvus is off limits, what the fuck are you doing here?'

'Scrapper, we're no here for trouble, we're only here for a drink and a dance.'

'And to sell some gear as well, eh?'

'Naw, we're no workin the night, straight up. Just out for a night, you know?'

Scrapper's eyes narrowed. 'That right? That gen up, son? Just out for a night?'

'On my mother's life, Scrapper, mate...'

'Just out for a drink and a dance?'

'Aye, a bit of fun, an that...'

Scrapper smiled and Dickie thought maybe he would get out of this toilet in one piece after all. 'A wee bit of fun, aye. Maybe pick up some fanny an all, eh?'

'Aye, if we're lucky.'

'Oh, you'd get lucky, son, no doubt about it. Wall-to-wall fanny out there, fuckin muff carpeting we've got here, eh?'

Scrapper laughed and his boys laughed and Dickie joined in,

but his was a nervous giggle. He wasn't out of the woods yet. He would only relax once he was out of this cludgie and away from the club altogether.

Scrapper was still smiling when he spoke again. 'So, okay, you and your mate, whatsisname again?'

'Skooshie.'

'Aye, Skooshie.' He pulled a face at his sidekicks, 'Stupid fuckin name, that. How'd he get it?'

'Cos nothing ever puts him off, everything's a "skoosh case" to him.'

'That right? Well, we'll see about that, eh?' Scrapper jerked his head to Bonner, who pushed past Dickie and went out of the door. Only two with him now, the odds were levelling. Stewie was a hanger on, not a tough guy. Dickie took his hand out of his pocket, the flick knife hidden in his palm.

Scrapper was talking again, his tone even, his voice friendly, but Dickie wasn't taken in by it at all. 'See, here's what puzzles me, Dickie, son. If you and your mate are just here for a night out, and you're not puntin gear to my customers, how come we saw your mate Skooshie selling blaw to a coupla lassies? Eh?'

Dickie felt his skin chill, even though the atmosphere in the toilet had turned tropical. He had told Skooshie not to shift any gear, not in Jarvis territory. Even if Scrapper or one of his brothers didn't find out, then Big Rab McClymont might have, and the last thing Big Rab wanted was trouble with Maw Jarvis and her clan. Relations between them were always edgy, but there was, for the moment, an uneasy truce that Big Rab didn't wish to undermine. Dickie was not stupid, he knew what an *entente cordiale* was, but he knew that this particular *entente* was far from cordial. However, it was an *entente* all the same.

He thought Bonner had gone to fetch Skooshie, but he was back in seconds, dragging a skinny drink of water with the bleached-out look of a junkie. Dickie's heart sank, not just because he'd missed his moment to make a break for it, but because he guessed what was coming.

'And if puntin blaw wasn't bad enough, Dickie son, your mate sold some gear to this guy here.' Scrapper turned his head towards the lean-faced addict. 'That right? You cop some gear off his mate?'

The junkie nodded and Dickie thought to himself, *Skooshie, what have you got me into here?*

Scrapper asked, 'What'd you get off him?'

The junkie swallowed hard and said, 'Some jellies.'

'Some jellies? That right? What flavour?'

The addict looked blankly back at Scrapper, who was laughing at his own joke, his pals joining in. Dickie was thinking, *Skooshie, we were told not to sell anything, and here you are selling Temazepam.*

Scrapper's face suddenly turned serious. 'And did you see anyone else makin deals with him tonight?'

The junkie nodded again and Dickie knew his chances of escaping without some level of chastisement was unlikely.

A crowd of four laughing young men burst in and headed for the urinals. Irritation clouded Scrapper's face and he jerked his head to his boys. Dickie felt a pair of hands grab him by the shoulders and he was propelled out of the toilet towards the emergency exit. His grip tightened on the blade. This might be a good thing, get outside, get a bit of room. Maybe he could buy himself some time, enough to leg it into the night.

Scrapper punched the bar to release the fire door and led them into a narrow lane that linked Buchanan Street to West Nile Street. Dickie knew it widened a few yards away into a tiny courtyard where grilled back doors led to the shops. They had brought the junkie with them and he was pushed across the lane to cower against a dirty brick wall opposite. The door swung shut behind them, but Dickie could hear the music throbbing above them. Another TTF track. He recognised the sound of 'Real Love'. He wasn't feeling much of that in the lane.

It was snowing heavily and lying thick on the ground. There was no light in the lane, but there was a tiny neon sign above the door leading back to the club, a flickering light in the shape of a crow. Its blinking gave the snow an intermittent red glow.

Dickie knew he would have to move first and it was now or

never. His right hand shot up and the blade snapped out. He swung it towards Bonner, who was closer, and sliced a furrow from chin to ear. The boy screamed and staggered back, both hands covering the wound, blood streaming through his fingers. Dickie crouched, his attention more on Scrapper than Stewie, who was looking in horror at his pal. He'd been right, not a tough guy at all. Scrapper had produced a blade of his own and he was smiling as he waited for Dickie to make another move.

'Scrapper, this doesn't need to get any worse,' said Dickie, his words trembling.

'Dickie, son, this is going to get a whole hell of a lot worse, believe me,' said Scrapper. 'You cut one of my boys. Can't let that pass, know what I'm saying? I mean, puntin gear in a Jarvis place is one thing, cuttin a Jarvis boy, that's something else. Can't be allowed.'

And then Scrapper lunged. Dickie swung his knife up, but Scrapper was an old hand at this and he easily blocked it with his free hand, stepped in closer and plunged his blade deep into Dickie's belly. Dickie felt the white heat of the thrust and his lungs sucked in air sharply, his weapon tumbling from his nerveless fingers as he stumbled back a couple of steps. When he slumped to the ground, Scrapper followed him down, his knife darting in and out. Dickie felt the pressure of the hits but not the pain. He heard Bonner's voice, thin with his own pain, yelling at Scrapper to stop, but there was no stopping him. Dickie couldn't move now, all he could do was lie on the cold snow as Scrapper knelt over him and stuck him over and over again.

Then it was over and Scrapper was jerked away. Through layers of muffling, Dickie heard Bonner yell, 'Fuck's sake, Scrapper, that's enough! We need to get the fuck away from here.'

Another voice, Dickie didn't recognise it, then a scream, a girl, and Scrapper cursing. Another scream and the sound of feet slapping away through the snow but the sounds merely drifted around Dickie. He felt so very tired as he lay there and all he wanted to do was sleep, just sleep, that's all. His eyes were open and he watched the flakes of snow floating towards him as if they had hidden parachutes. He felt their cold kiss on his cheeks, but he could not move to wipe them away. All he could feel was the chill penetrating from below and the soft caress of the snow from above. There was no pain, so maybe he wasn't hurt that bad. He could feel the music now, a pulse, a beat, vibrating below him. He didn't want to dance now. He was too tired. At one point he was aware of faces looming over him, then they, too, were gone. Somewhere a girl was sobbing, he didn't know who. Didn't matter, he was just going to have a wee nap and when he woke up, he'd see Big Rab and they'd talk about what was to be done about Scrapper Jarvis. After he'd had a wee nap he'd be fine.

And as he lay there, his life staining the snow red around him, he felt the music end.

Davie McCall could see the waiter looking at them in the reflective sheen of the metal doors, wondering just what the hell they were doing there. The guy had a small trolley with two trays on top. Delivering room service, Davie decided. He'd never had room service. Never stayed in a hotel, come to that. Unless you count Her Majesty's Hotel Barlinnie, where room service was a piss pot in the corner. He couldn't blame the guy for giving them the eye, because neither he nor his companion looked like the hotel's regular clientele, who paid more for a manicure than Davie spent in a week. He saw the look in the bloke's eye that said *you don't belong here*, but he held the gaze. The guy looked away. Davie was unsurprised. They always did.

A bland, electronic version of 'Moon River' eased softly from hidden speakers, all life and charm squeezed out of it in the process. Lift music. Davie hated lift music. A sniff from his companion caused the waiter to shift position in order to study him in the door. Freddie Armstrong was a picture, right enough. He had a stocky, powerful frame, a broad face with skin so smooth it belied his 34 years and hair long and straggly, tied back in a ponytail. He was wearing a heavy parka to ward off the January cold and thick cargo pants, his booted feet leaving wet traces of snow on the lift's plush carpet. That was not what was distinctive about him,

though. It was the sniffing. He wasn't making a wordless comment
on the quality of the music. Winter or summer, he seemed to have
a cold and constantly sniffed, snorted or blew. His hands were
thrust deep into the pockets of his parka and Davie knew they
would be filled with paper hankies. As if to emphasise the point,
he treated the lift to a long, rattling inhalation that contorted his
face, as if he was drawing the mucus right to the top of his head.
It was for that reason they called him Kid Snot. Davie knew the
man would have preferred Freddie the Ponytail, but he'd long ago
given up trying to argue the point and now accepted the nickname
with some degree of pride. In their crowd, it was good to have a
nickname. It showed acceptance.

Davie McCall did not have a nickname. He didn't require
acceptance. Those who knew him well called him Davie, but that
was a small group. Most everyone else called him McCall. Often
preceded by the words 'that bastard'.

The lift stopped on the fourth floor and Davie and Kid Snot
eased past the trolley.

An arrow pointed in the direction of the room they sought, but
they both turned the other way. When they heard the lift doors
sliding shut again they reversed, walked wordlessly down the corridor and stopped in front of room 403. Kid Snot gave another long
sniff and rattled his knuckles on the door. He took out a clean tissue
and blew his nose. Davie wondered where he kept all the phlegm.

The door swung open to reveal a woman for whom the word
gorgeous didn't quite make the grade. She was in her mid-twenties,
with cropped platinum-blonde hair, a slim frame wrapped in a
voluminous sweatshirt, its wide neck slipping off one carefully
burnished shoulder, and cut-off denim shorts showing off long,
straight legs with good muscle tone. When she smiled, she revealed
a dazzling array of perfect white teeth. Right away, Davie knew
she wasn't from around here.

'Hi, guys, can I help you?' she said in a voice that carried with
it the sunshine and surf of Malibu.

'Lester sent us,' said Kid Snot, hastily thrusting his used tissue
in a pocket and automatically straightening his stance as his free

hand reached up to smooth down his hair. She smiled, used to that reaction from men, and switched her gaze to Davie. He didn't react. She didn't seem to mind. When a girl was that attractive, one guy being immune to her was no great tragedy.

'Cool,' she said and stepped to one side. 'C'mon in, guys. Mickey'll be right out.'

Davie didn't know who Lester was, but he suspected it was some kind of code word. It wasn't Lester who had sent Kid Snot but Big Rab McClymont, Davie being there for protection. Davie was not sent, or told, or instructed. He was asked. Rab didn't order Davie around.

The suite was large and plush and probably bigger than Davie's Sword Street flat, given that he could see two doors leading off the sitting room. He suspected they opened onto two bedrooms, each no doubt having their own en suite facilities. There was a large heap of muscle sitting at a glass-topped dining table, his body about to erupt from his white t-shirt. His head was shaved into the wood and his broad face was impassive as he regarded the newcomers. His skin was light brown and his features Hispanic. It didn't take Sherlock Holmes to peg him as a bodyguard.

The blonde was walking ahead of them, giving the Kid the opportunity to appreciate her tanned thighs and pert behind. She turned. 'Get you guys anything? A soda, maybe? Or a drink? We got wine, scotch, bourbon, beer.'

'I'm fine, hen,' said Kid. Davie merely shook his head when she looked in his direction.

'Cool,' she said again, treating them both to another wide smile before she threw herself onto a couch big enough to sleep a family of four and picked up a magazine. She crossed her legs, all the better for them to see her perfect tan. Kid Snot couldn't take his eyes off them. Davie leaned against the wall beside the door, from which vantage point he could see the entire room and all entrances, while being ideally placed for a swift exit if needed. It wasn't a conscious act, it was just something he did, like breathing.

There was a lull in which Davie was perfectly comfortable. Silence did not bother him. Kid Snot, though, was restive. He stood in the centre of the room, looking like a pile of clothes that had once been dumped there and forgotten about. He scanned the suite appreciatively.

'Some place, this,' he said, obviously feeling the need to fill the void.

The blonde looked up from her magazine and cast her eyes around her, as if for the first time. 'Yeah,' she said, 'it's kinda cool. Don't like your weather, though. I mean, how can it be so cold all the time?'

'Welcome to Scotland, hen,' said the Kid. 'Where even the polar bears get frostbite.'

Her mouth twitched and she gazed at him through narrowed eyes. 'Come on – you don't have polar bears in Scotland.'

'Too bloody cold for them, that's why.'

One of the bedroom doors opened and Kid Snot's eyes bulged as he recognised the man who walked in. Even Davie was impressed. *Mickey*, he thought, *the girl said Mickey*. He hadn't expected Mickey to be Michael Lassiter. But then, why would he expect a Hollywood A-lister to appear in a Glasgow hotel room, even one as pricey as this?

Lassiter wasn't as tall as he appeared on screen, but he was almost as good-looking. On set, make-up would have filled in the lines around his mouth and disguised the slight discolouration beneath his eyes. Like the girl, he had a deep tan, but his dark hair was beginning to go grey. Davie knew all about that, for his own hair was already turning. It looked good on the actor, just as it had on his father James, who had been a star from the 1960s and '70s. But the flesh on his cheeks and jowls was puffy, as if the lifestyle that Davie had read about in the tabloids was taking its toll. Drink, drugs and women, the Hollywood cocktail.

'You're Michael Lassiter,' Kid said, just in case the guy had forgotten who he was.

Lassiter was dressed in a long bathrobe and was drying his hands on a towel so thick it could be used as a mattress. He tossed it to one side and gave Kid Snot his best west coast grin. The girl rose from the couch – in the fluid way of someone who exercised regularly –

to retrieve the towel from the floor. Davie guessed that was part of her duties. He wondered what else she did for her boss.

'That's right. Pleased to meet you,' he moved to Kid Snot, his hand outstretched.

The Kid gave Davie a glance and a nervous smile, then shook the proffered hand. 'Freddie Armstrong,' he said, then felt the need to inhale some wayward slime. This acted as a reminder. 'But they call me Kid Snot.'

Lassiter retracted his hand hastily and said, 'No kidding.' He looked across the room at Davie, expecting him to volunteer his name. Davie remained silent, so the Kid stepped into the void again. 'That's Davie, Davie McCall.' Lassiter nodded in Davie's direction. Davie nodded back. Lassiter stared at him for a second, a bemused smile on his lips, as if he expected some kind of verbal response. He was disappointed.

'You got something for me?' Lassiter asked.

The Kid unzipped his parka and fumbled around in an inside pocket to retrieve a plastic bag filled with white powder. 'Your medicine, Mister Lassiter, right there.'

Lassiter took the bag and barely looked at it as he dropped it onto a low table in front of the couch. 'Mannie'll settle the tab,' he said. Prompted, Mannie hauled himself to his feet and dug around in his trouser pocket before producing a wad of notes. He held them out, obviously not prepared to deliver. The Kid crossed the room and plucked the cash from Mannie's large hand.

'Cold out?' Lassiter said to Davie, who had not moved from his position against the wall, hands in the pockets of his thigh-length woollen jacket, collar turned up. Davie nodded. Amusement crept into Lassiter's eyes and he turned to the Kid, who was indelicately counting the notes. Starstruck he may have been, but if he went back to Rab a pound short there'd be hell to pay.

Lassiter jerked his head towards Davie. 'He say much?'

Kid Snot stopped counting and looked first at the actor, then at Davie. He shrugged and returned to fingering the bills. 'Not that you'd notice.'

'Okay,' said Lassiter, thoughtfully, studying Davie again. 'Okay.'

Then he picked up the bag and turned to the bedroom door again. 'Thanks for coming, guys. Have yourself a good night, okay? Coco will see you out.'

And then he was gone. The blonde, still holding the wet towel, led the Kid to the door, giving him another chance to enjoy the view. 'Nice to meet you, guys,' she said, giving them that smile again.

'You too, hen,' said the Kid, politeness itself, as he thrust the bundle of notes into his jacket and zipped it up again. Davie followed him through the door.

In the hallway, Kid Snot said, 'Can you believe that? Can you fuckin believe that? Michael fuckin Lassiter! Fuckin hell, wait till I tell the lads. And did you see the size of that boy Mannie? I mean, c'mon to fuck, man! Tell you what, I wouldnae like to clean out his cage. You think he's on steroids?' The Kid didn't wait for a response. 'I think he's on steroids. Stupid bastard. They'll shrivel his winkle.'

Davie remained silent as he punched the button to summon the lift. The Kid wasn't normally that excitable, but he was hopped up on star juice. 'Hey, you know what? You kinda look like him, you know? Michael Lassiter, I mean, no Mannie Mountain. Same size, same build, hair's kinda the same. You've both got blue eyes, fuck sake, you could be brothers. He hasn't got that scar, though – you never did tell me how you got that.'

And I never will, Davie thought.

'Don't say anything about tonight, Kid,' said Davie, flatly.

The Kid gave Davie a wide-eyed stare, unable to believe this. 'What? How no?'

Davie sighed. 'Not a word.' If Davie had been one to explain things, he'd've told the Kid that the money tucked away in his jacket bought more than a bag of medicine, it also bought discretion. However, he doubted if the Kid even knew what discretion meant.

'Don't see how no, Davie. I mean, it's Michael Lassiter. Did you ever see him in that picture? She was a cop, he was a male prostitute? Fuckin magic, so it was.'

'Keep your mouth shut about it, Kid. I'm telling you.'

Kid Snot grumbled about it all the way down in the lift. For the first time in his life, Davie McCall was grateful for lift music.

Frank Donovan stood under the flashing light and surveyed the alley. The uniform keeping the incident log had told him it was a bloodbath, a killing ground. He was right.

Donovan's churning stomach had nothing to do with the blood and death before him. He'd thrown up in the station toilet just before the shout came in and he could still taste the bitterness in his throat. He'd had a couple of drinks ahead of his shift, but that wasn't what had caused him to speak to God on the big white phone. Mind you, it hadn't helped. He had things on his mind, lots of things on his mind, and an extended period of disturbed sleep, fluttering nerves and too much drink had knocked his body out of whack. Now, with the young boy spread-eagled at his feet, he forced himself to focus.

His name was Dickie Himes, according to his pal, who was being interviewed in the club's office. He was 19 years of age.

Just a kid, thought Donovan sadly. *They're all just kids.*

Blood had seeped into the snow around the body like dark wings. Donovan could not tell how many wounds there were, the exact number would be determined at the post mortem, but whoever did this was in a frenzy. One of the wounds must have severed an artery, for there was a blood spray across the narrow alley. There was a series of deep gashes on Himes' face, too, while his hands were lacerated with defensive wounds.

Donovan squatted closer to the body, being careful not to touch it, even though he was covered from head to toe in a white coverall, his hair encased in a plastic bonnet, his feet wrapped in disposable slip-overs. There was a time when detectives would have attended the scene in their overcoats, dropping fag ash and picking their noses all over the place. Donovan dredged up a quote about the past being a foreign country where they did things differently. That should be the motto of coppers everywhere, he thought, because change was a way of life in their business. Forensic was king, now. The scientists with their white coats and their microscopes and their major mass spectrometers, whatever the hell they were. Now detectives could look but not touch. Somewhere on this body there might be a contact trace, something that would link the victim to the killer. Hair, blood, saliva. The strictures extended to the scene, but the snow around the corpse was scuffed and slushy thanks to the combined trails of dozens of feet, so that wouldn't be much use.

He studied the dead boy's face, trying to place it but coming up blank. That did not mean anything in particular, except that their paths had never crossed. If the late Mister Himes had ever been in trouble with the law they would find a record, even if only a memory from a uniform somewhere.

'Don't think the kiss of life's going to help that one, Frankie boy,' said a voice behind him and Donovan sighed inwardly.

'What you doing here, Jimmy?' He didn't turn. He didn't want Jimmy Knight to see the look of distaste that had creased his face.

'I was in the area, thought I'd drop by, see what was what.'

Donovan straightened and faced the big detective. Jimmy Knight, now a Detective Inspector with the Serious Crime Squad, working out of Force Headquarters at Pitt Street. His large, muscular frame was encased in an expensive black overcoat, his dark features framed by his thick black hair and a heavy shadow on his chin and jaws. No matter how close he shaved, Jimmy Knight could never lose that shadow. Some people thought that was why they called him the Black Knight, but Donovan knew better. The man standing before him with that cocky grin earned his nickname for being an out-and-out evil bastard who would as soon batter shite out of a suspect than interrogate him. The bosses loved him, though, because he brought in the bodies. That was why, despite them being on the Job for the same length of time, Knight was a DI with Serious Crime while Donovan was only a Detective Sergeant with Stewart Street CID. Some things hadn't changed.

Knight kept his distance from the immediate area around the body, but Donovan could still see surprise flash across his face. 'Jesus, Frankie boy,' said Knight, sounding genuinely concerned. 'You lost weight? You on the F-Plan diet?'

'I'm fine,' said Donovan, curtly. He'd been telling colleagues that he was on a diet, but it wasn't true. However, he was not about to discuss his problems with Jimmy Knight.

'Just as well. All that fibre makes you fart like a young thing, I'm told. I'd need to make sure I was standing upwind.' Donovan didn't register any emotion because he knew it would only encourage Knight to further conversation. He saw Knight shrug before giving the body a cursory once over. As he did so, he asked, 'Where's your gaffer?'

'Inside.'

'In out the cold, eh? Privileges of rank, eh, Frankie boy?'

Detective Chief Inspector Bolton was talking to the victim's pal, but Donovan didn't see any point in enlightening Knight.

'Someone else copped it, too, I hear,' Knight said as he gazed up the lane towards West Nile Street, where the second corpse lay. Two other CID officers were standing over it, just as Donovan and Knight were standing over Dickie. 'Connected to this boy, you think?'

'Don't know. Doesn't seem so, though,' Donovan replied. 'Way we hear it, the guy was out in the lane with a girl and got in the road when the scroats ran off.'

Knight smiled. 'Was he gettin a wee feel? At least he went out with a smile on his face, eh? Got any clue who the scroats were?'

Donovan shook his head. 'Junkie was out here when it happened, but he says he can't identify anyone.'

'Believe him?'

Donovan shrugged. 'He's a junkie, who the hell knows what's the truth?'

'Want me to talk to him?'

Donovan shook his head. The last thing they needed was Knight scaring the shit out of the already traumatised addict. 'Nah, we've got it under control. What's your interest here anyway, Jimmy? Thought you Serious Crime boys had more to do with your time than turn out for a stabbing.'

'This place is on our list. The Corvus is a Jarvis set-up.'

That was news to Donovan. 'Maw Jarvis owns it? I thought it was a George Fisher place.'

Knight shook his head. 'Aye, Fisher's name's on the license and if you search the deeds you'd think it was his, but it's Maw Jarvis's club, lock, stock and beer barrels. So, when something like this goes down, it blips on our radar and we have to come out to see the score. Gentleman Jack insists on it.'

Jack Bannatyne used to be their old boss at Baird Street CID, now he was Detective Super at Serious Crime. Gentleman Jack, they called him, not so much because he was a dapper dresser, which he was, but because he reputedly kept his gloves on when he battered a suspect. That was in the old days, of course, when neds expected a good hiding while in custody, back when the beat cop used to fight petty crime with a firm slap across the back of the head, back when there *were* beat coppers. It was different now. Now the neds had human rights, no matter what they'd done. Someone forgot to tell the Black Knight about that, though. He was known for dishing out a slap or two. Sometimes more.

'You got a name for the stiff?' Knight asked, sensitive to a fault.

'Dickie Himes, according to his mate.'

Knight searched his memory, accessing his encyclopaedic knowledge of Glasgow scroats, scruffs and scumbags. That vast database he carried around in his head was something Donovan envied. In any other cop it would be something to be admired, but Donovan sensed that Knight used it for activities that, if discovered, would have the rule book hurtling towards him at 100 miles per hour.

'Nah,' said Knight, 'not ringing any bells. Who's his mate?'

'John Thompson.'

Knight's eyebrows raised. 'Skooshie Thompson?'

'You know him?'

'Oh, aye. Devious wee shite, punts anything that'll make him a few quid – blaw, jellies, eggs, smack. You name it, if it gives you a buzz, gets you high or puts you in a fuckin coma, he'll sell it. So this boy's his mate? Interesting.'

'Does Thompson work for the Jarvis clan?'

Knight shook his head and looked down at the body thoughtfully. 'Nah.' That was all he said, but Donovan sensed his mind clicking away. There was something the big cop had decided not to share. That was how he worked, keeping stuff to himself, for his own reasons – and sometimes not in the interests of justice, Donovan was certain. He had long thought Knight had his fingers in more pies than a bent baker, but no evidence. Even if he did, there was little he could do about it, for grassing was just not done in the Job.

However, Donovan could guess a little of what Knight was thinking – if Skooshie Thompson and Dickie Himes were selling drugs in the club and said enterprise was not sanctioned by Maw Jarvis, then that could be the motive for murder.

A second scenes-of-crime team pushed into the narrow confines of the lane, dressed in similar style to Donovan, making Knight stand out like a sore thumb in his made-to-measure suit and black coat. It was turning into quite a crowd scene, so Donovan and Knight left the experts to their photographs, swabs, smears and tags.

'Who *is* your gaffer?' asked Knight as they moved closer to the door to give the technicians room.

'Scott Bolton.' He was a good boss, straight as they come and thorough in his methods. Bannatyne had been the best boss Donovan had ever had, but DCI Bolton came a close second. Knight's face wrinkled and with some satisfaction Donovan recalled there was little love lost between them.

'Fuckin by-the-book Bolton. The only thing he does outside the envelope is write a fuckin address.'

Donovan covered a grin by sliding the covering from his head. He liked Bolton even more now.

Knight sighed. 'Better go and see him, I suppose. You get on with him okay, Frankie boy?'

'Aye, he's a good boss.'

A thin smile flattened Knight's lips. 'Aye, but you never were one to push the envelope either, were you?'

'Jimmy, there's pushing the envelope and there's ripping it apart.'

Knight's face folded into a slight sneer. 'That's why I'm a DI and you're still a DS, working CID. Sometimes the envelope gets in the way of good police work.'

'Yeah,' said Donovan, drily, just as the fire exit door behind them swung open and DCI Bolton appeared, talking to a uniformed inspector. When he caught sight of the Black Knight, Bolton's face darkened. He finished his conversation and the inspector walked off towards the Buchanan Street end of the lane while Bolton stepped closer, his expression grim.

'What you want here, Knight?' He snapped.

'Good to see you too, Scotty,' said Knight with a grin. 'How's the wife?'

When Donovan saw his boss glare, he recalled a canteen whisper that Knight had gone out with the girl who later became Mrs Bolton. The fact that Knight was married himself did not stop him from going over the side more often than Jacques Cousteau. Apparently the break-up had not been pleasant, something to do with Knight's inability to keep his trousers zipped and her catching him with a redhead at a send-off for a retiring officer. Donovan often wondered where he got the energy. Knight and Bolton had both been stationed in 'C' Division, after Knight got his promotion and left Serious Crime for a period. *That must've been a fun time*, Donovan thought.

'I asked why you're here, Knight,' said Bolton, not rising to the bait. 'This isn't a Serious Crime Squad case.'

'*Au contraire, mon frère*,' said Knight. 'In fact, it's as *au fuckin contraire* as it's possible to get.'

'Apparently the Jarvis clan own the Corvus, boss,' explained Donovan.

'That right?' Donovan knew Bolton was taking this in, giving the murders a new perspective. If the Jarvis family were involved, then this was no simple pub fight gone wrong.

'And John Thompson's a dealer, but not for them,' added Donovan.

Bolton looked at Knight. 'Who for, then?'

'Beats the hell out of me,' said Knight, his face blank.

Bolton grimaced. '*Au contraire, mon frère*,' he said, 'I think you do know and if you're playing any stupid Serious Crime Squad games with me, Knight, think again. I've got two dead lads here and I want the bastards who killed them.'

Knight was unimpressed by Bolton's show of authority. He looked past him to the second body being photographed, the dark lane illuminated by the flash like snatches of lightning. 'You got a name for him yet?'

'Aye, Ronald James Ross, an electrician with Glasgow City Council. He was out here with a lassie, winching, when three boys came piling out the exit there, did the first lad, then ran right into them. Young Mister Ross there ended up getting his carotid sliced open, bled out within minutes. Name mean anything to you?'

Knight shook his head. 'What about the lassie, she give you a description?'

'Nothing we can use. She's in a bit of state. I've sent her home with a wpc.'

Knight's head tilted towards the night sky. 'Pretty dark out here, which makes it the ideal place for a kneetrembler. Not so good for making a description, though.'

Bolton grimaced. 'Thanks, Sherlock, we wouldn't have been able to work that out for ourselves, being mere plodding officers and not a super sleuth like you.'

Donovan suppressed a smile and Bolton went on, 'So, unless you have any more stunning insights, Knight, or are willing to tell me what I'm certain you're keeping to yourself, I suggest you bugger off and do whatever it is you and the Brylcream Boys at Serious Crime do and let us get on with the day-to-day slog of real police work.'

Knight gave him an easy smile. Despite his brutal nature, he was very slow to rile. 'Always a pleasure, Detective Chief Inspector Bolton. Give my best to your wife. I know I did...'

Bolton lunged forward then, but Donovan stepped in the way. 'Leave it, boss, it's not worth the aggravation.'

Bolton hauled his gaze from Knight and glanced around him. The exchange had been witnessed by the team working the alley and a few of them had stopped what they were doing to watch. When they saw him looking their way they went back to work.

Knight's smile broadened and he nodded to Donovan. 'Frankie boy, always good to chew the fat,' he said and then wandered off down the alleyway towards Buchanan Street. Bolton watched him go, his eyes burning, and Donovan sensed his body was tense. He knew how he felt. Knight affected him that way, too.

'I don't know what Jack Bannatyne sees in that bastard,' said Bolton quietly.

'He gets results, simple as that.'

'Aye, but what else does he get? Off the books? You neighboured him, Frank, you know what he's like.'

'Aye, boss, but going for him in the middle of a locus isn't recommended, not for by-the-book Bolton,' said Donovan, despite his own worries feeling a smile growing. His boss knew what guys like Knight called him and treated it as a mark of respect. Donovan often ribbed him about it, though.

Bolton threw him a glance and said, 'Fuck off, Sergeant.' His face was set in stone but his eyes were smiling.

Donovan's smile grew. 'Fucking off, sir,' he said before his attention was diverted by a shout from further down the lane, where a couple of uniforms were waving their arms and pointing at something out of sight. Donovan and Bolton joined them.

'What've you got, Constable?' Bolton asked the nearest uniform.

'Up here, sir,' said the cop, a fresh-faced youngster, eyes bright with excitement. *Maybe he's found the Holy Grail*, Donovan thought, but instead the young PC led them into a small square that jutted off the lane. There were large rubbish bins here alongside a couple of skips and between two of them and the wall of the building was a collection of a cardboard boxes, old bits of carpet and felt, and even some tarred paper to keep out the rain. 'Somebody's been skippering here, sir. Been here for a while by the looks. He's nested.'

Donovan stuck his head into the crude doorway and looked around. It wasn't much, but it was better than dossing in the street. A ratty sleeping bag stretched out on top of a thick stack of flattened cardboard boxes, a wooden crate with a cracked saucer and a candle fixed in place by its own melted wax. Health and safety was clearly not a concern for whoever slept here.

Bolton also took a look inside then said, 'I want every office and shop in these buildings contacted and asked if they know who built this shelter. Somebody must have given whoever's sleeping here permission, or at least turned a blind eye – it's been here for a while. Chances are this dosser saw something, or heard something, or knows something. We need him found and we need him questioned, understood?' Bolton jabbed his finger at the two PCS. 'You two go and check now. Never know, there may be someone in somewhere.'

They nodded and sprinted down the lane. Bolton smiled. 'Remember when you were young and green, Frank?'

'I'm still young and green, boss.'

Bolton laughed, stepped from the small square and stared back at the crime scene. His voice turned sombre. 'This is going to be a bad one, Frank. I can feel it in my bones. The Jarvis clan's a nasty bunch. This is the sort of thing that can get out of hand faster than the speed of light. We need a result. And we need it sharpish.'

'We'll sort it,' said Donovan, confidently.

Bolton looked sceptical. 'I hope you're right, Frank, I really do.'

Scratchy wanted to run, but he didn't. Scratchy contented himself with scuffing through the snow as fast as he could. Scratchy didn't want to raise anyone's suspicions. But he had to get away, far away, keep moving, put distance between him and the lane. Maybe if Scratchy could get far enough away he'd forget what he saw.

He knew that boy, Scrapper, they called him. He was a bad one, right enough. Scrapper hadn't seen Scratchy, he'd been too busy with what he was doing, but Scratchy thought one of the other boys might've. Or maybe they'd been too busy trying to stop Scrapper from doing what he did. He saw them trying to hold him back, but Scrapper kept plunging and plunging.

Scratchy closed his eyes, trying to blot out the memory of what he'd seen. He pulled his threadbare coat tighter into his skinny frame, arms folded to ward off the cold that had settled in his bones. But it had nothing to do with the weather. He knew that, Scratchy knew he could withstand the Glasgow winter, he'd done it for years, so he had, but this was something different. This was a cold that nothing could keep out.

Scratchy had to keep moving, maybe that would melt the ice in his belly. Keep moving, get away, tell no-one what he'd seen.

He muttered to himself as he walked alone through the night and he barely noticed the snow as it began to fall once more.

Knight had told the Detective Constable driving the motor that he was going to walk back to Pitt Street because it was a nice night for a stroll. The young DC looked at the flecks of snow but said nothing. He was used to the DI's ways and he knew better than to question him. Knight ensured he was well away from the carnival that was the murder investigation before he slid the mobile from his pocket. The brick-shaped black phone tended to weigh his coat down, spoiling the line of its expensive cut, but the growth of mobile communication had proved to be a godsend to him. He stepped into the shadow of a shop opening where Buchanan Street met Bath Street and punched in a number he knew by heart. He had phoned it often. It took a few rings but then he heard a sleepy voice answer.

'Whit?' said Rab McClymont, his voice made ever rougher by having been awakened. Always a charmer, Knight thought.

'Sorry for disturbing your beauty sleep, big man.'

There was a slight pause and Knight knew McClymont's sleep-fogged brain was processing the sound of his voice. 'Knight? Fuck's sake, do you have to phone in the middle of the fuckin night?'

'No,' Knight said, 'it's just more fun. You sound so cute when you've just been woken up.'

'Fuck off,' said Rab, then broke into a barking cough.

'You need to lay off the Woodbines, big man,' said Knight. 'They'll be the death of you.'

'Gave up smoking,' said Rab and Knight recalled that there was a new kiddie on the way in the McClymont household and his wife had insisted he give up the fags. 'What's up?'

'You've got trouble. Right here in River City.'

He heard a woman's voice and knew it would be Bernadette, because Rab was a one gal guy. Knight had only seen her once, never been formally introduced, but she was an attractive piece. Knight wouldn't have minded a go at her, but she was well out of bounds. Rab's voice muffled as he held his hand over the phone, telling her to go back to sleep, then became clearer as he said to Knight, 'Hang on till I go in the other room.'

Knight smiled, knowing he had grasped the man's attention. He lit up a small cigar and blew a cloud of smoke at the flakes of snow drifting past the shop doorway. He listened to the rustle of movement and associated grunts and visualised the big guy hauling himself out of bed and padding across the room. He wondered what McClymont wore at night, his smile broadening at the notion of his thick black hair tousled, his chin – like Knight's own – stained by a permanent five o'clock shadow, and his powerful frame enclosed in an old-fashioned nightgown. If that was the case, he'd love to get a photograph. *What would happen to your tough guy image, then, big man?*

'Right, what's up?' he heard Rab say.

'You know a boy called Dickie Himes?'

'Aye.'

'He's pan bread.' Pronounced 'breid', as in 'deid'. Dickie was a ghost.

There was silence broken only by the sound of Rab breathing heavily through his mouth. 'What happened?'

'Ended up on the wrong end of a blade. He's lying in a lane right now behind the Corvus.'

'The Corvus? What the fuck was he doing there?'

'Don't know, but whatever he was doing it looks like the Jarvis clan caught him doing it. He was there with Skooshie Thompson.'

There was small groan on the other hand, then Rab said, 'I told that wee bastard to stay away from there.'

'Well, maybe you need to keep your people in line, 'cos the boys from Stewart Street have Thompson. He likely to burst?'

'Skooshie? Nah, he's brand new that way. No worries on that score.'

Knight nodded, satisfied. 'This going to be the start of something between you and the Jarvis clan?'

'Maybe,' said Rab and fell silent again. Knight could hear the gears working in the big man's brain, even if he was away over in his fancy house in Bothwell, far to the east. Rab McClymont had learned a lot from his mentors Joe Klein and Luca Vizzini, one of them being the need for respect from your peers. Mind you, that didn't help them much, for both ended up shot to death, neither murder solved. However, if you didn't have respect in The Life, you had nothing. The Jarvis clan bumping off one of Rab's boys was not exactly a tug of the old forelock towards Big Rab. Something like this could tip the delicate balance between his team and the Possil crew. Not that Knight cared – as long as he kept getting his cut from Rab, they could fire nuclear warheads at each other.

'Anyway,' said Knight, 'thought I'd give you a heads up.'

'Aye, right – thanks,' Rab still sounded thoughtful.

The connection went dead in Knight's ear and he returned the phone to his coat pocket. He sauntered up Bath Street slowly, savouring the chill night air and allowing the cigar smoke to billow around his mouth before he drew it into his lungs. There was not a soul on the street at this hour and that was the way he liked it. The snow was really coming down now, but it didn't bother him. As he walked back towards Pitt Street, Knight realised how much he loved this city and these streets. Hail, rain or shine, this was his town and he was master of all he surveyed. There used to be a music hall performer who did a drunk act, used to sing that Glasgow belonged to him. The old bastard was wrong.

Glasgow belonged to Knight.

Bernadette watched Rab from the doorway of the room he used as a home office as he stared at the mobile phone now resting on the desktop in front of him. A bookcase ran the length of the wall behind, filled with books he'd never read and was never likely to. Most of them were Joe Klein's at one time, his old boss. They were leather-bound editions of classic novels, but Rab's tastes ran more to pulp crime. She could see he was troubled, even in the half-light from the desk lamp he'd switched on. He looked up as she moved across the room and edged in behind him, one hand running through his hair, the other snaking down his chest and under his dressing gown. She kissed the top of his head.

'What's up, babe?' she said as he leaned his head back into her breasts.

'Trouble,' he said. 'Boy's just been killed, down the town.'

'Who?'

'Lad called Dickie Himes, don't think you know him.'

She didn't, but that wasn't unusual. There were a lot of people who worked for her husband, she didn't know them all. She knew the ones who mattered, though. The ones who were important. Or the ones who were a possible danger. She knew them all right. 'What happened?' she asked.

'Stabbed. Outside the Corvus.'

Bernadette stopped stroking Rab's head and laid her cheek against his hair. The Jarvis clan, it had to be. 'Does this mean something?'

Rab considered this. She knew what he was thinking, they were so much in sync. That was why they worked so well together. She knew what he was going to say before he said it. 'I think it has to be.'

He couldn't see it, but she was smiling. She had been advocating some kind of action against the Jarvis clan for some time because they had been growing more and more out of order. When they limited their operations within Possil, Milton and Saracen, they were tolerable, but Maw Jarvis had ambitions. Bernadette didn't hold that against the woman unduly, for she had a long-term plan for her own family. And that family was growing. She wasn't showing yet, but she was pregnant with their third child. Another few years, maybe another couple of kids, and Bernadette believed they would have enough salted away to give up The Life, to start fresh somewhere far away from Glasgow. Southern Ireland perhaps, a house on the West Coast, overlooking one of those beautiful beaches. The problem was Maw Jarvis's ambitions could mean loss of territory and income for Rab's operation and that Bernadette could not tolerate. She had been trying to push Rab but he had been unwilling at first to destabilise the delicate peace that existed among Glasgow's criminal families. He came round, though, he always did, for Bernadette had her ways. Action had been plotted, a target chosen, they were merely waiting for the right moment. A catalyst. A reason. An excuse.

Now they had one.

Davie was glad he wasn't driving. He'd passed his test the year before, but he'd never handled snow like this and he wasn't certain he'd be up to it. Kid Snot, though, had been behind the wheel since his late teens and appeared unconcerned. The wipers were working hard to keep the windscreen clear, almost keeping time with Gary Moore singing 'Over the Hills and Far Away' on the CD player. The Kid would have preferred something more up-to-date, but he kept the disc in the car because he knew Davie was partial to the old guitarist. Davie had become a fan when he'd heard him at Big Rab's house, years before. He'd been in the Barrowland audience the previous May to see Moore play with Jack Bruce and Ginger Baker. He also enjoyed swing band music and the songs of the Rat Pack, but that would have been above and beyond for the Kid.

Kid Snot had given up grumbling about keeping his mouth shut over their medicine delivery and began to talk about the blonde. He had an eye for the ladies, but seldom much luck, his nasal activity often proving off-putting. But he kept trying and was currently working his meagre charms on a grass widow, her husband doing time for cultivating and selling a large amount of cannabis.

'She was a real honey, right enough,' the Kid said, his eyes fixed on the road, both hands on the wheel. He was confident, but not reckless. 'You think maybe she'd want me to show her the sights while she's here?'

Davie's mouth tightened in what passed for a smile. 'Out of your league, son.'

The Kid nodded. 'Aye, right enough but, hey – a man's reach must exceed his grasp or else what the fuck's a heaven for?' The quote was punctuated by a lengthy slurp, during which Davie gave the boy a surprised glance. The Kid noted the turn of Davie's head and said, 'What?'

'Where'd you pick that line up?'

The Kid shrugged. 'Some picture, I think. Someone said it, dunno who, but I liked it.'

Davie looked away again, constantly amazed by what could come out of a Glasgow ned's mouth.

The Kid brought the car to a slow halt outside a tumbledown tenement on the Gallowgate that should've been torn down years ago and was unlikely to be spared the wrecking ball for much longer. The blank windows were dark and lifeless, the entrance-way covered by a wooden barricade through which Davie could almost feel the dampness and decay seeping. The Kid peered through the car's side window, which was already caked with a layer of snow, and said, 'Think Paddy'll be there?'

Davie nodded. Paddy was a low-level dealer who flitted from skipper to skipper but who had made the mistake of owing Big Rab some money. Rab took a dim view of people owing him money, no matter what their station in life. He believed it was bad business for anyone to get away with not paying their bills – let one person off with a debt and others will think they're free to take a liberty. So the Kid was ordered to find Paddy and either get the sum due or explain to him forcibly the error of his ways. That would be Davie's job, no doubt. Paddy would be here, Davie was certain. No-one with any sense would be out on a night like this, unless they had to be.

Their feet crunched in the fresh snow as they crossed the pavement and pushed open the wooden doorway, which they knew would be loose. Davie had been correct – the unmistakeable stench of dampness was the first thing to hit him. Then something else, something out of place even in this dying building. He stopped outside the door to the first flat, the one they knew Paddy had been staying in for some time.

'Smell that?' Kid Snot sniffed, but shook his head. Davie was unsurprised, for it was well known that the Kid had very little sense of smell.

'What?' said the Kid.

Davie did not reply. He used the knuckles of his left hand to push the door. It opened freely, revealing a long, dark corridor. The Kid thumbed a lighter to life and they saw that, apart from two boards in the centre still attached to rotting joists, the remainder of the floor had long since been removed. The plaster on the walls had crumbled to reveal strapping like sinews and bone left when the flesh has rotted away. The smell was stronger now and Davie knew what they were going to find in the room at the far end of the corridor. He led the way, eyes focused, in the flickering light in the Kid's hand, on the precarious walkway below. He moved slowly, silently, even though he was convinced there was no-one to disturb or alert. The same could not be said for the Kid, who was sniffing like a hay fever sufferer in a flower shop.

The door to what had once been a living room was hanging on one hinge and Davie pushed it gingerly in case it came off altogether. The smell was overpowering now and even the Kid had caught a whiff, for he placed one hand over his nose and said, 'Jesus Christ, what a ming.'

The source of the stench lay on a foldaway camp bed in the corner. Paddy was on his back, one leg crooked, the foot lodged under the other leg. His head was stretched to the side, as if he had been craning to see something, his jaw slack and mouth open. One arm dangled from the edge of the cot, the rubber tubing still wrapped round the upper arm but the hypodermic, which had delivered the heroin to his system, had long since dropped from the vein and now lay on the grimy floor. His face was swollen and blackened, his belly blown with gas, the veins of his neck marbled. Liquid drained from his nostrils and mouth, while his open eyes were turning milky. Davie was no doctor, but he knew Paddy had been dead for days, well over a week.

Kid Snot stared at the sight, all thought of sniffing banished from his mind. 'Fuck me,' he said, his voice a little hoarse. In the dim and flickering light cast by the lighter, Davie could see his face was pale. There were some things that could disturb even a Glasgow ned. Sudden violence, open wounds, broken bones he could take,

but the sight of a rotting corpse in a decaying tenement made him
queasy. Davie understood how he felt. There was a sour taste in
his own mouth and his saliva had turned waxy.

A scrambling noise from under the bed made them both start.
The Kid stepped back, dropping the lighter, which guttered and
died as it fell. Davie tensed, ready for an attack, eyes narrowing in
the darkness, compensating for the dim glow filtering through the
strapped up windows from the street light outside. He relaxed
when he saw what was hauling itself from the darkness.

The dog was a mongrel, a touch of collie and something else,
he guessed, and it looked in a bad way. Davie had no way of
knowing exactly how long ago Paddy had succumbed and perhaps
it had lain under the bed all that time, waiting for him to awaken.
The dog pulled itself out fully and stood still for a moment, staring
at them. It tensed when the Kid stooped to retrieve his lighter but
did not move, did not snarl. It merely blinked at them and waited.
Davie slowly lowered to one knee and held out his hand carefully.

The Kid rasped, 'Davie, what the fuck you doin?'

Davie ignored him and said to the dog, his voice low, soft, soothing. 'Easy, boy.' He had no idea what sex the dog was but he didn't
think it would mind even if it were female. 'Come and see me.'

The dog did not move. It looked at Davie's outstretched hand,
then at Davie. Davie could see that its hair was matted, the eyes
caked with hard matter. 'Come on, pal. It's okay.'

'Davie, fuckin thing could take a bite out of you...'

'He's not gonnae do that, are you, pal?' Davie edged forward,
his hand still before him, his other in plain view. He sensed the dog
was not dangerous, just hungry, confused. 'Come on, chum, come
see me.'

The dog's head strained forward, nose testing the air between
them, picking up his scent. One front paw moved forward, then
another. It came to a halt again. Davie had come to a standstill,
knowing that the dog had to approach him.

'Leave it, Davie, we've got to get out of here,' said the Kid.

Davie wanted to snap at him to keep quiet, but he knew it
might spook the animal. He slowly turned his face towards the

Kid and let his eyes do the talking. The Kid was not stupid, he read the look and decided to shut up sharpish. Davie looked back to the dog and motioned him to come closer. 'It's okay, pal, we're not going to hurt you. It's okay.' The dog, though, was not for moving. Davie did not know whether it was through fear or if it was protecting his master in some way. Another approach was needed. 'You got anything to eat on you?'

'What am I? Fuckin Safeway?'

Davie scanned the room quickly, spying an unopened tin of dog food on the mantelpiece. An empty tin lay on the floor below it and he knew that would've been the last thing the dog had eaten, whenever that was. He'd probably knocked the tin down, licked it out. 'Open that tin there, bring me it.'

The Kid sighed again but did as he was told. He swung the lighter in front of him, looking for the tin opener, found it lying on the floor beside the empty tin, and then brought the food to Davie, a filthy, matted fork stuck in the spongy meat. The dog watched with wary eyes as Davie dug out a forkful of the food, smothered with jelly.

'Take it, pal, it's yours,' said Davie, his voice still low, still soothing, as he held the fork out at arm's length. 'It's good.'

The dog tested the air again, catching the scent of the food, and edged forward, one pace, two, then when he was within reach, stretched his neck and sniffed the edge of the fork. He retreated again, still unsure. Davie held his breath, trying not to move, even though his crouch was growing more uncomfortable by the second. 'Come on, pal,' he coaxed, 'not going to hurt you…'

The dog crept forward again, body low, but hunger getting the better of him. He gave the food a final sniff before, still cautious, he opened his mouth and gently eased it off. He stepped back again, licking his lips, eyes on the fork as Davie carved more food from the tin. He held the fork out again, keeping all movement easy, his hand not as stretched as before, trying to draw the dog ever closer. The dog kept his eyes on the food end edged forward. It had had a taste now, it wanted more, and that overcame his fear. Davie let it take the second piece and he moved his hand to the dog's head, gave it a gentle rub. The dog let him, his focus totally on the food. 'That's it,' said Davie, 'not going to harm you. Not going to harm you.' He fed it some more and said to the Kid, 'There must be a leash somewhere, bit of rope, anything.'

'You're not going to take it with you, are you?'

Davie was rubbing the dog's ear now and he was enjoying it. 'Not leaving him here.'

'Is that a good idea? I mean, it's evidence or something.'

'I'm not leaving him here,' Davie said again and the Kid knew not to argue further. He liked McCall but he was not the kind of bloke you wanted to get on the wrong side of. He saw a weathered leather lead and a chain collar hanging on a hook behind the door so he fetched it and handed it to Davie, who carefully looped the collar over the dog's head. The dog did not flinch, did not move. Davie scooped another two forkfuls of food out and let the dog snatch it. He didn't want to feed him too much, though. He'd been hungry for a while and he didn't know what effect the heavy dog meat would have.

'What about Paddy?' The Kid asked, nodding to the rotting body in the corner.

Davie straightened and looked back at the corpse. He had known Paddy slightly, never much cared for him. Had never known he had a dog. His initial revulsion had passed. He felt nothing now as he gazed on the dead man. 'Nothing we can do for him.'

'So ... what? We just leave him there?'

Davie turned to the door, still carrying the open tin of food. 'He's beyond caring.' He gave the lead a gentle tug and the dog followed him from the room. He'd be fine, Davie thought, he just needed something decent to eat, some care, and he'd be fine.

Davie knew as soon as he walked into the Sword Street flat and saw the suitcases in the hall. He'd also seen the man sitting in the car outside. It was no great feat of deduction, for he had sensed that Vari had been building up to this for a couple of weeks. She hadn't discussed anything with him, but that would be his fault. He knew that. Davie McCall did not discuss feelings.

Kid Snot hadn't said anything during the journey from the Gallowgate but Davie could tell he was unhappy with the animal being in the car. He gave the dog sidelong glances and then looked at the car seats. The Kid kept his vehicle spotlessly clean and even Davie was aware of the dog hairs, and God knew what else, flying off its mid-length coat. The dog sat up all the way, watching the street lights slip by, and Davie had his arm around it, running his fingers through its hair. It felt dirty and matted and the first thing to be done, after something light to eat – scrambled egg, some toast maybe – would be a bath.

Vari sat in darkness in the living room. He stood by the door and looked at her. She had been crying, he knew, but he didn't comment on it. He waited. It was what he did. She looked at him then, at the dog by his side. He knew she loved dogs, they had often talked about getting one, and would ordinarily have ran across the room to pat it, but she sat where she was. She didn't want anything to weaken her resolve. He knew this. He'd seen the suitcases. He'd seen the man outside.

'Where did you find him?' Her voice was soft, husky. He'd always liked it, but maybe not enough. Sometimes, it was another voice he heard, another face above his in the dark, another body he stroked.

'On his own,' he said, which was as close to the truth as he'd take it. Even though she knew what he did for a living, he shielded Vari from much of it.

She nodded, slowly. 'You keeping him?'

'I'm keeping him.'

'Good,' she said and he knew she meant it. 'You'll not be alone, then.'

From anyone else that might've sounded harsh, but not Vari. Davie knew her, knew that this made it easier for her, somehow.

'I'm going to stay with my dad,' she said. He'd expected that. She and her father had reconciled the year before, following the death of her mother. Vari had left the family home after she told her parents she had been systematically sexually abused by her uncle, her father's brother, for years. The man, the proverbial

pillar of the community, denied all her claims. He was a God-fear-
ing man, a good man, he would never do anything like that. Vari
had slipped from virtue, he said, and he'd tried to help her and this
was his reward, to be labelled a pervert and a predator. Her
mother, also devout, believed him and called her daughter a
whore. Eventually the teenage Vari could take it no further and left
home. There had been no contact from her mother until cancer
took her. Her father had called Vari after the funeral, told her he
was sorry. He had believed her about his brother, but his wife had
been adamant. To his shame he had gone along with it, let Vari
leave, let her out of their lives.

'What about your uncle?' Davie asked.

'He's not been round since he got out of hospital,' she said.
After Vari had told Davie about her past, he paid the uncle a visit.
The conversation had been brief, but pointed. The uncle spent
four nights in hospital.

They fell silent again. Davie looked at the dog, who was still on
the lead but had settled on the floor, one front leg stretched out in
front of him, the other curled up against his chest. He was watching Vari as she turned her attention to a paper hankie she was
rolling around in her hand. Davie tried to find words, but they
eluded him. He had little to say at the best of times. When
emotions were involved, he had even less.

'I can't take it any more, Davie,' she said, softly.

'Okay,' he said.

'You're not here, not really. Even when you're sitting right
there, even when we're in bed, you're not really there, are you?'

Davie didn't answer. He couldn't. He didn't think she expected
one.

'You've been good to me, you really have,' she said. 'Ever
since... well, your dad.'

Davie shifted his feet, suddenly acutely uncomfortable. The dog
sat up as he moved, his head raised, watching him. Davie leaned
down and gave him a reassuring rub behind the ear. His hand
shook slightly. Mentioning Danny McCall always hit him like
that. It was his father who had beaten and raped Vari, just to draw

him out. She had moved in with him the following year. It was something that just happened and he didn't oppose it. Sometimes it was good to come home to someone.

'And I've tried to be happy and sometimes I really was. But I kept coming back down to earth when I realised that you weren't with me, you were just in the room.'

The sound of a car horn in the street made her look towards the window.

'That's my dad,' she said, standing up. 'He's been waiting out there for ages, so he has. For you to come home. I didn't want you to come back and find me gone, you know? Didn't seem right.' She paused, looking at her hand, and Davie could see the tissue had been reduced to little more than a pile of fragments. A slight smile plucked at the corners of her mouth and a soft breath slid from her nostrils. Perhaps she was wondering what that mound of shredded paper signified. She closed her fingers around it and thrust her hand into her pocket. She crossed the room and stopped to pat the dog's head.

'What's his name?' She asked.

He hadn't thought that far ahead. The name Abe came into his head first, but Abe had died two years before. He'd spent most of his life with a family in Easterhouse, who had taken him while Davie was in jail, and he'd never had the heart to take him away from them. But Davie still thought of him as his. He wouldn't call this dog Abe, though. That wouldn't be right. 'I don't know yet.'

'He needs a name. All dogs need a name.'

She straightened and gazed steadily into his eyes. She laid a hand on his face.

'Davie, I love you and part of me always will,' she said quietly, moisture filling her eyes. 'But you'll never love me. Because you can't. You can't let go, can you? And I can't compete with a ghost.'

She held his gaze for a moment, then brushed her fingers along the side of his face, caressing the scar that ran from his cheek to his chin. 'These run deep, don't they? He cut more out of you than just skin that day.'

And then she was gone, brushing past him at speed. He heard a sob break from her in the hallway as she hefted her cases and then the front door closed. Davie listened to the footsteps hurrying down the stone steps. He still had not moved. He stood in the darkness of the living room, the dog waiting for him to do something as he listened to the silence that had taken Vari's place. He thought about watching her climb into her father's car from the window, but what would be the point of that? So he stood there, letting the silence and solitude wrap around him like old acquaintances.

SATURDAY

'He's a cokehead,' said Davie, his voice flat.

'I know he's a cokehead,' said Rab, his mouth full of toast, 'but he's a cokehead with loads of dosh.'

Rab faced Davie across the table in the kitchen of his Bothwell home. It was a big house set in expansive gardens, situated among other big houses with expansive gardens. Rab liked Davie to come over and drive him to the pub on Shettleston Road he used as a base. The Black Bird had been one of Joe's places back in the day and Rab had always liked it. When Joe was murdered, his old pal Luca Vizzini had taken over, but he tended to stick to his café on Duke Street. When Luca was, in turn, shot to death – the grip of Glasgow's underworld figures on life often proving tenuous – Rab adopted the pub as his headquarters. His name did not appear on any paperwork connected to the site for, as with his other legitimate enterprises, there were intermediaries. The only traceable source of income he had was a builder's yard in Springburn. Davie doubted that the declared profits from that small business covered the price of this six-bedroom house. But then, that's what clever accountants were for.

He could hear a radio playing elsewhere, Bernadette, probably, for she loved her music. He recognised the hillbilly strains of 'Cotton-Eyed Joe' mixing with a dance beat. He wondered if she was dancing to it somewhere, then recalled she was pregnant again, so maybe she wouldn't. She looked good with it, a thought that had risen unbidden when she'd answered the door that morning. But then Bernadette always looked good. Her soft Irish lilt had invited him in, her dancing eyes, as usual, inviting other thoughts. She made him feel uncomfortable, right from the first time they'd met. He sensed there was an offer in the way she looked at him, in the way she smiled, in the way her hands would casually brush his. Davie was never sure of these things, but he couldn't shake off the feeling she was letting him know that she was attracted to him. He'd vowed never to act on it – Rab was his mate, and, along with Bobby Newman, his longest-standing ally. He'd managed to keep to that vow, too.

Until, the previous October, he broke it.

Davie felt the guilt stab at him as she opened the door. If she felt the same there was no sign. Her eyes were warm, sparkling as usual. Though she was as welcoming as ever, she drew the line at admitting the dog into her pristine home, though Davie had given him a bath first thing that morning and even blow-dried his hair with a dryer Vari had left behind, although he'd never tell anyone that. The dog had submitted to both indignities with good grace, perhaps understanding that they were necessary. He was now a handsome creature, completely transformed from the hungry and filthy animal of the previous night. He was thin and still had a haunted look in his eyes, but the soap and water had revealed traces of brown in his coat, and a white mark on his chest, shaped like an arrowhead. Davie had still not decided on a name, knowing that one would present itself sooner or later. He'd placed an old duvet and cushions on the floor beside his bed, which was where Abe used to sleep. But the dog, who had taken up a position on the rug before the gas fire, didn't move. Davie left him, wondering if he would make his way through during the night, but when he heard no movement he got up and crept back to the living room, to ensure the animal was comfortable. He was in a deep sleep where Davie had left him, his body jerking as if he was receiving tiny electric shocks. Davie carried the bedding from the bedroom and laid it beside dog, then went back to bed. And his own dream...

A windswept harbour.

The flash of a knife.

Blood-red streamers, caught in the wind.

Green eyes, accusing.

A voice he knew.

A voice he loved.

... *You could have saved me.*

... *You could have moved faster.*

... *Sooner...*

... *You could have saved me.*

And then Vari's voice, overlapping.

I can't compete with a ghost.

He woke up, shivering, thinking she was there in the room with him, hearing a voice, an echo, a memory that faded and vanished. But he didn't know whether it was Audrey or Vari and that confused him.

Davie led the dog to the rear of the Bothwell house, where he could run around and explore Rab's large garden in safety. It had high fences all around, and carefully positioned CCTV cameras covering the perimeter. The dog would not get out without being seen, although the cameras were there to detect anyone getting in. As Rab's stature in The Life grew, so had his paranoia. Davie doubted anyone would come after him in his own home, that wasn't the way things were done, but Rab wasn't so sure. Maybe he was right. The Life had changed over the years, drugs had seen to that. The old rules – Joe Klein's rules – had been swept away, many of them by Rab himself. In Joe's day, you did not involve civilians, particularly women or children. Family members were off limits. Not these days, though. Heroin had made The Life dirtier, meaner, just as Joe had predicted it would.

The snow had blown itself out overnight, though the forecast warned it wasn't away for long. It was a bright, clear, crisp morning and through the kitchen's wide picture window Davie could see the dog romping in the garden with Rab's daughter Lucia, named in deference to Luca Vizzini. Rab's son was named after Joseph Klein, which pleased Davie. He could see the boy now, standing on the sidelines watching his little sister shriek and laugh as the dog chased her through the snow. Davie had been concerned at first about the kids playing with the dog, but after a few minutes he saw that the animal had a kind and loving nature. Davie was uncomfortable around kids, but he found Lucia engaging and bright. The boy, though, was something different. He was around 13 now, nine years or so older than his sister, but there was more than just years separating them. It wasn't that he was introverted, it wasn't that he was shy, those traits Davie could understand. It was just that there was something… *off* about him. He was always polite, but there was something about the kid that rankled and Davie didn't know what it was.

Rab was eating breakfast when Bernadette showed him into the kitchen. She said she'd leave them alone, her hand caressing Davie's upper arm as she spoke. Rab didn't seem to notice. Rab looked tired, but then he'd been awake since he'd heard the news of Dickie's murder, making calls, gathering forces. Davie nodded when asked if he'd heard what had happened and Rab looked out the window at his children. He knew about Paddy's death, knew Davie had taken the dog. Davie felt he didn't want to discuss the situation just yet, so he remained silent. Then Rab said Michael Lassiter wanted to see him again.

Davie shook his head. 'Cokeheads can't be trusted.'

'Fuck, Davie, the man just wants to talk. And pay for the privilege.'

'Talk about what?'

Rab shrugged. 'Fuck knows. But did you hear me when he said he'd pay you just for a gab?'

Davie remained silent. Rab had become increasingly money-motivated over the years. Maybe it was something to do with having a family, not that Davie would ever know anything about that. Rab had changed, not just since fatherhood. He saw himself as a man apart from the rank and file and even though he would never presume to order Davie about, he still saw him as a subordinate. This idea of Davie trekking over to Bothwell regularly to drive back into the city, as if he was some sort of bodyguard, was an example. Rab had told him it was because he was the only person he could completely trust and Davie knew that was part of it. But there was more. One day the big fella would step over a line and the two old friends would have a conversation. When Davie saw Rab's brow furrow with irritation, he wondered if that moment had come.

'Fuck's sake, Davie, just do it, will you? Won't hurt to spend half an hour with the bloke, take his money and then that's it.'

'We've got more important things to deal with, Rab.'

'Aye, but half an hour, Davie. That's all, thirty fuckin minutes, have a coffee and a fancy biscuit, hear what he's got to say. Won't hurt you. He's a customer, Davie, he's gonnae be here for a coupla months. Think of it as public relations. And you can get Joe his autograph while you're at it.'

Davie sighed. Rab sighed. 'Come on, Davie – what harm would there be in talking to a Hollywood movie star for half an hour? Eh?'

Davie didn't know but he could not shake off the feeling that nothing good would come of it.

Maw Jarvis had been a head-turner as a young woman, and as she grew older, she remained strikingly attractive. Her hair was still dark, matching her eyes, complexion and, if truth be told, her temperament. She was never what anyone would call vivacious, having always had a mean temper and a tongue rough enough to strip the hide off a water buffalo. Her given name was Eunice, but no-one had called her that for years. Peter Jarvis had been a good husband to her and she had loved him in her way, but she had never been a one-man woman and had enjoyed a succession of lovers since the early days of their marriage. Peter hadn't minded – he was not the faithful type either. He often said that he thought monogamy was a property board game. Although they were each getting it regularly elsewhere, they still found time for each other, so when she started having kids he called her Maw and she called him Paw and the names stuck. It was the closest they ever came to showing affection, even though their sex life – both marital and extra – remained active right up until Paw Jarvis dropped of a heart attack at the breakfast table one morning. The night before had been particularly enthusiastic, involving some amyl nitrate that one of Maw's contacts down south had provided. The poppers had helped stimulate their libidos to such an extent that the friction they generated could've lit up the city. Maw often wondered if the drug had brought on Paw's death, but felt no guilt. He was a big boy – a *very* big boy, if truth be told – and no-one had forced him to snap the vial and inhale. The resultant head rush and increased blood flow did the rest – five times. It wasn't a record for them but, hey, they weren't spring chickens anymore.

On Paw's death a few of the players thought they could move

in on his patch, she being a burd and all, but Maw soon showed them what she was made of. Backed up by her four sons, she literally carved herself a slice of the city's drug trade, working at first from her council house in Possil. She and her boys ruled the streets of Milton and Saracen, even as far as Maryhill. If there was a drug being sold on those streets, she was behind it. The money was cleaned up through various legit enterprises, including Club Corvus. And it was that establishment which exercised her attention now.

'What did you do with your clothes?' She asked her youngest son. Scrapper sat at the kitchen table in their home, shovelling down a bowl of corn flakes. She was irritated, but she wasn't going to show it.

'Burned them,' he said. He appeared unconcerned about the events of the previous night. That pissed her off even more.

'Good,' she said. She had brought her boys up well. That kind of killing was a messy affair and Scrapper's clothes would be covered in the dead boy's blood. No amount of washing would cleanse the fabric, so the only thing to do was put a match to them. 'Anybody see you after?'

'Some junkie, but he'll no say nothin. A lassie in the lane, but she didn't get a good look at me.'

Maw Jarvis nodded, making him think she was satisfied with that. They might need to get the names of the junkie and the girl, have someone pay them a visit, but that could be dealt with later. Even if they named her boy, there would still be an ID Parade and they could be got at before then. She stood beside her son, watching him eat his breakfast, then glanced at her eldest, Jerry, who was eyeing her with interest. Stick-thin, with a scholar's face, a smile glinted behind his glasses and she knew why. He knew her well enough to know that her anger was rising and was waiting for it to explode.

'That all that saw you?' She asked.

Scrapper's hand paused as he raised his spoon to his mouth, his mother's tone signalling there was something he didn't know. 'Aye,' he said, but there was the hint of a question there.

'You sure?'

Scrapper looked at his brother across the table, saw there was no help coming from that direction. 'Aye, I'm sure, Maw.'

The slap across the back of Scrapper's head cracked through the air. Maw Jarvis was strong and she had felled many a big man with a punch. This was an open-palmed strike, but it was still enough to send her son flying from the table onto the floor.

Maw leaned over him and screamed, 'There was a fuckin dosser there, ya stupid wee bastard! Polis think he might've seen the whole thing. What the fuck were you thinking, doing that in my club? Killing a boy, Jesus! And with witnesses?'

Scrapper blinked at her, rubbing the back of his head with his hand. 'It just happened, Maw, honest. Him and his mate were puntin and we'd told them to quit it before, so it was just gonnae be a wee reminder of who's boss, you know? But then he cut Marty and...'

'Marty's cut?'

'Aye, boy had one of they flick knife things, opened his face.'

'Bad?'

'Aye, pretty bad.'

'What did you do wi' him?'

'Got Stewie to take him to the Royal and...'

'The fuckin hospital? What the fuck were you thinkin?' She raised her hand again, spittle flying from her lips as her anger rose further.

Scrapper cringed. 'S'okay, Maw – Stewie told them it happened in an alley up Sauchiehall Street, made a police report and everything. Gave a description of three guys. Made it all up. We even went up there, smeared some of Marty's blood on the snow. We thought that was best, throw them off the track. I mean, if Stewie and Marty was involved in the Club Corvus thing, why would they go to the hospital, make an official report, you know?'

Maw let her hand hover for a few moments while she thought it over. What Scrapper said made some sense, but it was still risky. Scrapper should have come to her first and they would've found a tame GP to stitch Marty up. It was done now, though. It would have to be dealt with.

She lowered her hand and said, 'Did you leave that boy's blade behind?'

'No, took it with us.'

Good, she thought, that was using the nut. 'What about his mate? You said him and a mate was punting gear. What about him?'

'Skooshie Thompson. We'll get him later.'

'Naw, you'll no. Don't you go anywhere near that boy, understand? You stay the fuck away from him.'

'Okay, Maw.'

'What did you do with the blades, yours and the boy's?'

'They're up in my room, wrapped up in a towel under my bed.'

Maw's hand was raised again and brought down with force but Scrapper wriggled away so all she connected with was a leg. 'You brought them here? Into my house? Ya stupid wee article, ye!' She stepped across him to gain better access in order to rain further slaps about his body as he curled up to avoid them, arms wrapped around his head. Finally Maw Jarvis straightened, panting. She wiped the back of one hand across her mouth and then said to her eldest, 'Jerry, find they blades and get rid of them.'

'Where, Maw?'

She turned her dark eyes on him and said, 'Do I need to think of everything? Just make sure they can never be found. Fuck's sake, if brains was dynamite, you boys wouldn't have enough to blow your nose.'

Jerry left the kitchen to collect the knives, leaving Maw with Scrapper still on the floor. The woman sighed, pulled a chair out from the table and sat down, her anger spent. Scrapper picked himself up, his movements sluggish, knowing there was something yet to tell her. And he was not looking forward to it.

'There's something else, Maw,' he began, edging towards the door, ready to flee if she got her dander up again.

'What?'

'The boy Himes that I did. Him and Skooshie work for McClymont.'

Maw Jarvis blinked once and stared at her son. Scrapper watched her, waiting for her fury to explode again. She sighed hard and looked away. 'Okay, so we can expect something in return. I don't want you going out unless you've got one of your brothers with you, understand? McClymont spent too long with that wee bastard Vizzini, so he's got this Sicilian thing going on. *Vendetta, Omerta,* all that shit. He might want payback. And they'll no be long working out it was you. You're never out of the Corvus.'

'We can handle them,' Scrapper said confidently.

'I don't want to handle them, y'understand? We've been doing all right, making some cash. We don't need a war with them getting in the way, clear? You stay around the house as much as you can and when you go out, take one of your brothers. At least one. And don't go back to that club.'

Scrapper looked crestfallen. 'Aye, Maw.'

She looked up at him and her expression softened. 'Come here, son,' she said, but Scrapper hesitated. 'Come here, I said. I'm no gonnae hurt you.' Scrapper moved forward slightly and she watched him, a welcoming smile on her lips. She held out her arms for him and he stepped closer. When she swung another powerful blow, this time with her right fist clenched, it connected with his jaw. He rocked back on his heels and she threw her left, snapping his head to one side. He spun round and landed on his hands and knees on the floor again. She rammed her foot against his backside and sent him sprawling onto his face.

'You ever go after anyone without my say-so again, Scrapper, I'll tear you apart, you get me? God knows what trouble your temper has got us in this time. You keep it under control in future, okay? And lay off the powder, too. That and your temper are gonnae get you killed one day. The only coke I hear of you takin better be out a bottle.'

'Okay,' Scrapper's voice was muffled and she could hear a sob cracking it.

'Now you stay there till I tell you to move, understand? And you think about what you've done.'

'Okay, Maw,' her son said and her lips stretched into a thin line as she stepped over him. Jerry came back down as she entered the hall, a towel bundled in his hands. He held it out to her as he reached the bottom stair. She took it, unwrapped the material and stared at the two knives, both smeared with blood.

'We're making a mistake here, Maw,' said Jerry.

Her eyes narrowed. Jerry had violence in him, a bit too much, she often thought, given his liking for inflicting pain, but he also had a brain. Her eldest was the smartest of the lot and if he said they were making a mistake, then they were. 'What?'

'Dumping the knife, the one the other lad used. You can use it.'

'How?'

'Deflect attention from Scrapper. The police will want this cleared up smartish. We can help them.'

She stared at him and his calm brown eyes smiled back at her. She thought about what he said and knew he was right. She looked back at the knives again. 'You touch them?'

He gave her a look to tell her he was no fool. 'Course not.'

'What you thinking?'

'I get rid of Scrapper's blade, no bother, but I plank the other one. Then I steer the info to the polis. Let them find it.'

'What about the other witnesses?'

Jerry smiled a thin smile and she knew what he was thinking. They'd deal with any blabbermouths easily. A word here, a threat there. They'd soon understand that silence is the best policy. Jerry would see to it. The priority here had to be to keep that dickhead Scrapper out of the jail.

'Do it,' she said as she wrapped the knives up again and handed the bundle back to him. 'And find Andy. We need to talk.'

Frank Donovan didn't see Bang Bang Maxwell until it was too late. It had been a long night and he was tired. One minute he was lost in his own worries, then he became aware of the large figure at his side, keeping pace with him. Instinctively, Donovan stepped to his left, hands coming out of his jacket, ready to fend off an attack. When he saw it was Maxwell, he put more distance between them and came to a halt, body tensed. You never knew which way Maxwell would jump. However, the big man drew his hands from the pockets of his thick wool coat and held them up in a placating gesture. The coat was very like the one Knight wore and Donovan wondered if they shopped in the same store.

'Easy, my man,' Maxwell said, his gravelly voice rumbling like a tipper truck, 'I come in peace.'

Donovan nodded, but remained on guard. Bang Bang Maxwell was a strong arm for Ray Neal, a money lender and all round piece of shit. However, he was the piece of shit Donovan owed money to. Maxwell was more to Ray than just a sidekick, though, for the dapper wee loan shark was the only openly gay ned in an underworld that was more than a little homophobic. It was ironic that two criminals could have a more stable relationship than a lot of cops Donovan knew. Including himself.

'Ray'll get his money, Maxwell,' said Donovan, mentally berating himself for being so stupid as to borrow cash from a Tally man in the first place. But a series of nags with wooden legs and some losses at card games had meant he'd been behind on the mortgage and the power bills. He'd kept the mortgage arrears from Marie, but when Scottish Power cut off the electricity, there had been some strong words. He'd told her it was a mix-up and he'd get it sorted. He'd borrowed some cash from his sister to get the lights back on, but that was like putting a sticking plaster on a shotgun wound. He'd bled himself dry. The bank would just laugh in his face and he couldn't bring himself to borrow from friends. Then he thought about Ray Neal. It had been a mistake that could cost him his job, if it got out.

'Shoulda got it three days ago, Frank,' said Maxwell, agreeably. He was always agreeable, was Maxwell. Until it was time to become disagreeable, and then he lived up to his nickname. Unlike The Beatles song, his hammer wasn't silver, just a plain old black one from B&Q, but it did the trick all the same. A finger here, a toe there, maybe an arm. And the hits kept coming until the debt was paid.

'He'll get it,' stressed Donovan.

'He'd better, my man,' said Maxwell, his tone matter-of-fact. 'Because you know what Ray's like when he doesn't get his callydosh. He gets grouchy. And when he gets grouchy, he takes it out on a person. That person's usually me, being the closest thing he's got to a wife. And that makes me grouchy. And when I get grouchy...' Maxwell smiled. 'Well, I expel my irritation with a bit of exercise.'

Donovan knew Maxwell was no jogger. 'I just need some time,' he said.

Maxwell drew in his breath. 'Ah, see – that means the debt'll just get larger. You know how it works. APR's a bitch.'

'Two weeks, I'll have it for you in two weeks.' Donovan's voice had taken on a pleading tone. He didn't like it much.

Maxwell stared at him. He was still being agreeable, but Donovan could see something beginning to harden there. 'Doesn't sound like good business, my man. You can't pay it now, what guarantee have I got you'll be able to pay two weeks down the line?' Donovan couldn't answer. Somehow, he didn't think Maxwell expected him to answer. Finally, the man tutted. 'But you know, I'm too soft-hearted for my own good. One week. This time next week. On this very spot. Seven days. And payment must be in full, otherwise... well, you know the rest.' Maxwell smiled. On anyone else and under any other circumstances, it would have been a pleasant smile. But not on him and not here in a deserted street, with a gentle snow beginning to fall and traffic sliding past on Cowcaddens. He gave Donovan a small shrug, then nodded. Donovan swore if he'd been wearing a hat, he'd have tipped it before he walked away in the direction of Port Dundas Street.

The flakes drifted down around Donovan as he wondered where the hell he was going to get one thousand pounds in the next few days.

Rab was silent as Davie drove him into the city. Davie knew he was still burning over his refusal to talk to the actor, so he let him fume. He'd come around, eventually. They had known one another too long to let something like that come between them. He was glad of the silence, for although the bulk of the snow had been cleared overnight from the main roads, and pushed into mounds lining the gutters on either side, there was still enough to demand that he focus all his attention on his driving. Radio 2's Sounds of the Sixties was playing softly on the radio, The Beatles and 'I Feel Fine'. Rab liked to hear the show when he could. Davie didn't mind, he had broad musical tastes. The dog was stretched out in the rear, half on his back, his legs extended and propped against the seat. They were queuing at traffic lights on Shettleston Road when Rab finally spoke.

'They Jarvises are really getting out of hand,' he said, his voice flat, as if he was forcing himself to speak. Davie did not reply. Rab went on. 'We need to send a message. A strong message. One they'll no forget.' Davie watched for the traffic moving ahead and waited for Rab to say more. Finally, Rab said, 'I need to know if you're on board, Davie.'

Davie was a hard man. He was the guy you wanted by your side when the fists flew and the bottles broke. But he was no killer. Joe Klein had always said that a killing had to be the final step and Davie had never yet taken it. That was why he didn't use a gun or a knife. It would be too easy to cross the line. There had been times, oh, there had been times, but so far he had never killed anyone. He had come close to it at least twice – once during a street fight with a young man years before and then with his father – but on each occasion someone else had taken the final, fatal step. Something told him that if he ever did kill a man, he'd be lost forever. But young Dickie Himes had been one of their own. Davie barely knew him but he recalled a young man with a quick smile. The primal part of him hissed that restitution had to be made, the more logical part of him urged caution. And it spoke in Joe Klein's voice.

'I'm going to do one of the brothers.' Rab's words came out suddenly and Davie glanced at him, knowing the shock had flashed on his face. Rab saw the look and said, 'A message has to be sent, Davie.'

'That's not a message, Rab, that's a declaration of war.'

'Then it's a declaration of war. Maybe it's time. You have to clean house now and then, Davie, you know that. The rubbish has to be taken out.'

Davie looked back at the traffic, saw it was beginning to move. He slipped the car into gear, took off the handbrake, edged forward. 'It's not a proportional response,' he said. Proportional response – it was a phrase often used by Joe the Tailor. It was a politician's way of saying an eye for an eye. Someone hits you, you hit back. It was expected. It was understood. And generally it ended there. Tit for tat. They had killed a low level player and by rights Rab should do the same, but he was intent on hitting back harder.

'Fuck proportional response,' said Rab, his voice harsh. 'I'm having one of they bastards dead in the fuckin street. They've gone too far this time. They've been like a fuckin flea nipping at my balls for too long and I've let them get away with it. It stops now.'

They were through the lights now and Davie could see the pub ahead. Davie's silence seemed to infuriate Rab even further. 'Fuck's sake, Davie, you no got nothing to say?'

Davie knew the Jarvis clan had to be taught a lesson, they had been getting out of hand recently and Dickie's death did merit some kind of payback. But what Rab was talking about was too much. 'What do you want me to say, Rab?'

'That you're with me.'

Davie turned right into the street alongside the pub and came to a halt. He switched off the engine and sat back in the driver's seat. He sat very still. Rab watched him. Rab waited. Finally, Davie said, 'You're going too far. Joe would never…'

'Joe's dead, Davie. Fifteen years, he's been dead. Luca killed him.'

Davie swivelled his eyes around to face his pal. 'And you killed Luca.'

Rab held Davie's gaze, but remained silent. A junkie had aimed the gun but Rab had pulled the trigger. It had remained unspoken between them for five years, but Davie knew. He had never mourned the death, for he had become convinced that the little Sicilian had killed Joe Klein. They'd originally thought it was a scroat who Joe had managed to gut before he died. But it had been Luca, Joe's old pal. There was no proof, of course, but Davie knew in his bones it was true. It had taken him over ten years to work it out. So, although Rab had never admitted he was behind Luca's assassination, Davie was glad he'd done it, for if he'd discovered hard evidence of the man's guilt, he might have been forced to break his own rules. Joe might have promoted the need for a proportional response but he also said that some men just needed killing.

'You'll put the city up like a balloon, Rab,' he warned.

'We'll see,' said Rab. 'But I need to know where you stand. You behind me or what?'

Behind me, Davie noted. He didn't pick him up on it, merely said, 'I'm beside you, Rab. Same as always. But I won't be part of a killing.'

Davie neither liked nor trusted Stringer. It wasn't because he didn't talk much, for McCall said very little himself, it was something similar to how he felt around young Joseph. Rab had found the man after a violent episode in Girvan, on the Ayrshire coast. Davie didn't know the full details, only that Stringer had come through in a pinch. He stood in the corner of the small office, his scalp, hair scraped clear, gleaming in the fluorescent light, his powerful arms folded across his chest. He worked out regularly. Davie had seen him at Bennie's Gym in Bridgeton, working the bag, lifting the weights. He said nothing during the brief meeting that morning, barely moving, just listening. Every now and then, his lips peeled back to reveal some startlingly white, very even teeth. Davie was the only one other than Rab to be seated, the chair against the wall, behind the other men in the room, the dog lying at his feet.

There were three others, giving the tiny room an even more claustrophobic feeling than usual. Wee Jinty, the cleaner, was working away in the bar, her bucket clanging as she joined in with 'Can You Feel the Love Tonight' on the radio. The cleaner wasn't so much singing along with Elton John as competing. And Jinty was winning. What she lacked in tone, she made up for in enthusiasm, and she screeched the words out like a cat in heat.

'Christ, Jinty's in good voice the day,' said Kid Snot, ending his observation with his customary snort.

'Kid, get out there and tell her to pipe down,' said Rab. 'Cannae hear myself fart here for her wailing.'

The Kid grinned and stepped out of the office. A few moments later the music was cut off, as was the off-key accompaniment. When the Kid returned he was still grinning. 'Wasnae best pleased, Rab.'

'Aye, but Elton sends his thanks,' said Jock Barr. Thanks to his love of chocolate, he was known to everyone in the room as Choccie Barr. He, like Kid Snot, had long ago decided the best way to deal with such a nickname was to go along with it.

'So,' said Rab, loudly, bringing them back to the matter in hand, 'we all keep on our toes, okay? We don't know whether last night was a one-off or the start of something, so until we do know, we stay alert.'

'Aye, Rab,' said Fat Boy McGuire, the reason for his nickname being evident in the bulge over his belt. 'Might be nothing, right enough, one of they things. But cannae be too careful, know what I'm sayin?'

'Aye,' said Kid Snot, the youngest voice in the room, 'but they bastarts are well out of order, so they are.'

'Skooshie and Dickie were punting gear there, though,' said Choccie, always the most level-headed of the crew. 'Let's no forget that. The Corvus is a Jarvis place, we all know that. They shouldn't have been punting gear there.'

'Davie and the Kid'll have a word with Skooshie the day about that,' said Rab. The Kid nodded. Davie remained still.

Fat Boy asked, 'Anybody know how Skooshie's taking it?'

'He'll be gutted,' said the Kid.

'So he should be,' said Choccie, his voice flat. 'He shoulda known better than to be workin a Jarvis place. Stupid wee bastard got his mate plunged.'

'Aye, well,' said Rab, knowing Choccie was right, 'Davie and the Kid'll make that clear to him. But what's done is done, right? Now we deal with it. You lot pass the message on – stay well away from any Jarvis sites, right? They see any of that crowd up ahead, they cross the street, right?'

He paused to allow comments, but Davie knew none was expected. They were followers, every one of them. Luca used to say that there were two types of guys – the sheep and the sheep dogs. Most people were sheep, running in flocks, waiting for the sheep dogs to herd them and point them in the right direction. Rab was a sheep dog. Davie wasn't a sheep, he never ran with the flock, but he wasn't a sheep dog either. He was aware that Rab was watching him carefully. However, it was Choccie who said, 'So, what we gonnae do about it?'

Rab paused, his eyes still fixed on Davie. Finally he said, 'We hit the bastards where it hurts most. In their fuckin pockets.'

Davie gave his pal a barely imperceptible nod. This was a wise course. Joe would have approved. But he wasn't fooled. Rab's blood was up.

Fat Boy asked, 'How we gonnae do that, Rab?'

'Leave that to me,' said Rab. 'It's all in hand. But when we do this, they're gonnae come back again. That's why we have to be on our toes, understand?'

There was a further silence as they took this in. Rab's face was tight as he kept his eyes on Davie, as if he was waiting for him to question matters, even though Davie would never do that in front of the others.

'Okay, that's us for now. But listen to what I'm sayin – keep your wits about you, okay?' Rab jerked his head to the door and the other three filed out. Davie sensed he was also surplus to requirements. Whatever that was to be discussed here did not involve him. He got up wordlessly, the dog did the same. Rab's voice stopped him as he was about to leave. 'Davie, make sure you phone that bloke, will you?'

Davie may have been wrong, but it sounded like an order. He didn't look back or reply as he closed the door behind him.

In the bar, where the aroma of the previous night's spirits lurked like a ghost, Choccie waited, breaking open a bar of Dairy Milk. 'The Kid said he'd get you outside, in the motor,' he said. The dog padded over to him, drawn by the smell of chocolate. Choccie said, 'Can he get a piece?'

Davie nodded. 'Not too much.' Chocolate was bad for dogs but he guessed a little piece wouldn't hurt him. Choccie snapped off a square and held it out. The dog barely sniffed it before he gently eased it from his fingers, chewed once, and then swallowed.

Choccie told him he was a good boy and patted his head. He slipped a portion of chocolate into his own mouth before he said, 'This is gonnae be bad, Davie.' Davie nodded. Choccie was always the clever one in the crew. He knew what was ahead. 'Can you no talk him out of it?'

'Not my concern.'

'You'll be part of it, no matter what.'

Davie snapped his fingers and the dog returned to his side. Davie clicked the lead onto his collar, then straightened. 'Then I'll deal with it.'

Choccie looked disappointed, as if he'd expected more from him. 'It's gonnae be bad,' he said again.

Davie pulled the pub door open and the bright winter sun burst through the gloom. 'Yes, it is,' he said then walked into the cold day.

Rab was silent for a few minutes, thinking about Davie. He was his mate, but sometimes he really pissed him off, recently more than ever. He'd been through a lot, but Rab had stood with him through most of it. It wasn't that Rab thought Davie wouldn't be there when pish came to shit, for Rab knew he would be. It was just that he wished Davie understood that things had changed. He was the boss now and Davie was just one of the boys, a valuable one, but when it came down to it, still just a soldier.

Stringer had carried the chair Davie had vacated to the front of the desk. He sat with one leg hooked over the other, waiting. He didn't move a muscle. Davie had a stillness about him, but Stringer was like a statue. Rab wondered how long he'd sit there without moving or speaking. Someday he'd find out. But not today. Today there was work to be done. 'Where is he?' he asked.

Stringer didn't need to ask who. 'Liverpool, still. But he's told the girl he'll see her tomorrow.'

Rab nodded. 'You ready?'

Stringer's head bobbed once. Rab picked up a pen from the desktop and twirled it in his fingers. He didn't even know he was doing it. His mind was on the matter in hand.

'What about the lassie? Will they know she's the one who fingered him?'

'What do we care?'

Rab shrugged. He took a deep breath, for he was about to give an order that never came easily. But it was an order that had to be given. The Jarvis clan had to be taught a lesson. A message had to be sent. Davie was right, it was a declaration of war, but Bernadette was right, too – it was necessary. He also knew that Maw Jarvis and her boy Jerry were not stupid. They would expect repercussions, but perhaps not the bold step Stringer was preparing. Rab had learned a great deal from Joe and Luca. *It's a magic act,* Luca once told him, *sleight of hand. Keep them watching one hand while the other one's up to all kinds of shit.* Luckily, Rab had already set something else up that may put them off the scent, make them think that there was nothing further coming. He'd strengthen that with another steer to Knight. All the while, the big slapdown was up ahead.

Stringer was still waiting patiently. Rab laid the pen down.

'Do it,' he said.

A cold wind whipped around Knight, snatching the smoke from his cigarillo and carrying it away. He pulled his thick coat tighter to his body and stared at the gravestone. MARY DAVIES. 1960–1993. Simple. To the point. He'd paid for it, so there was no sentiment. Jimmy Knight didn't do sentiment.

The flowers he'd laid at the base of the stone fell over in the breeze and he stooped to right them. He straightened again. She'd been a good tout, had steered some solid gen his way. She'd been a good shag, too, or had been, until she got the virus. He'd slapped her about a couple of times, always regretted it because he liked the girl. She hadn't always deserved it, but sometimes the mood just came upon him and when it did, there was no stopping it. She had no family, as far as he knew, or at least none that would claim her. So he'd had her buried, had the stone cut, came by every now and then with fresh flowers. He knew she'd have liked that. He didn't tell anyone, though. Might be a show of weakness. Or sentiment. And Jimmy Knight didn't do sentiment.

He saw Rab McClymont walking towards him up the hill, so he stepped away from the grave and moved to meet him.

'Just once, I'd like to meet somewhere it's warm,' said Rab.

'Quiet here. And in this weather we're unlikely to be seen,' said Knight. By necessity, they kept their partnership a secret. 'So, what's up?'

Rab handed him a slip of paper. 'Punt that address to your drug squad mates. They'll get a turn out of it.'

Knight glanced at the address. 'Up Saracen way? This another one of Maw Jarvis's operations? You getting her back for last night already?'

Rab shrugged. 'No time like the present. And they need a slap. They need to do it today or tomorrow, though. They'll be away after that.'

Knight kept looking at the slip of paper. 'They're geared up for that other thing you told me about.'

'I'm sure there's a few more bizzies they can pull in for this, eh? It'll be worth their while.'

Knight stared at Rab, trying to read his face. He knew this guy, knew that something else was brewing under that shock of black hair. Seeing nothing, he folded the paper up and slipped it into his coat pocket. 'Got a line on coupla names for doing your boy.'

'Scrapper Jarvis did for Dickie.'

Knight angled his head, conceding that. 'Maybe so, but the evidence is leading us to another two.'

Rab remained silent. Knight knew that whether the law liked it or not, Scrapper Jarvis would pay, one way or the other. Knight didn't care. He was focussed on the two names that had come his way. Didn't matter if they were guilty of killing that lad or not. They'd be guilty of something. All he wanted was a result.

Skooshie Thompson looked like death warmed over, but then, he'd hardly slept all night. The cops had seen to that, with their questions. He'd told them bugger all, nothing much he could tell them, really. He sure as shit wasn't going to tell them he'd been punting gear, and that he'd dumped what he had in his pockets before they arrived. He hadn't been in the alley when Dickie got done. He hadn't even seen Scrapper in the club, but he knew that was who'd done it. Some things you just know. Still, he didn't breathe a word to the cops. It just wasn't done.

'So, Skooshie, mate,' said the Kid, being pally. Sitting in the kitchen of Skooshie's house while his maw was away at the shops. Drinking tea and eating digestive biscuits at the formica-topped table. The other one, that bloke McCall, just sat and watched him, never said a word, his dog lying at his feet. Skooshie had never seen him with a dog before, wondered where it came from. He'd asked McCall its name, but he just got a shake of the head. Bastard hadn't even given his dog a name. That wasn't right. Every dog deserves a name.

The Kid said, 'You never saw what happened, like?' Skooshie wasn't taken in by the Kid's friendly tone, though. He knew this was good ned, bad ned. He knew he was in for it.

Skooshie shook his head. 'Dickie went for a pish, that was the last I saw of him.' Until he found him bleeding out in the snow, that was.

The Kid nodded sagely. 'Aye, poor Dickie was always a martyr to his bladder, so he was. So you never saw Scrapper or any of the Jarvis boys?'

Shooshie shook his head.

'Never knew they were there, right?'

Another shake of the head.

'But you were puntin, right?'

Skooshie sat very still, for the Kid's voice had turned a degree or two colder. The Kid came across as this chatty, matey bloke, but Skooshie had seen him operate. He could be a hard bastard when he took the notion. Maybe not as hard as McCall, but he didn't get into Rab's inner circle because he was a laugh. Christ, he'd even stopped sniffing, which was a bad sign. *Here it comes*, he thought.

'Skooshie – you were puntin, right?'

A nod then. He couldn't deny it.

'Did Rab no say to stay clear of the Corvus? Did he no say it was out of bounds?'

Another nod.

'But you did it anyway.' The Kid sighed. 'Skooshie, Skooshie, Skooshie... what did you do with the stuff? Before the cops came?'

Skooshie hesitated, but he knew he had to answer. There were many things he wasn't proud of, but what he was about to say made him ashamed. 'Planted it all on Dickie's body.'

The Kid's eyebrows shot up. 'Your dead pal?'

Skooshie's glaze dropped to the floor. He swallowed, trying to dislodge the bitter lump that had formed in his throat. 'Aye. I couldn't leave him there alone and I knew if I was caught with the gear I was gonnae be huckled, so I thought...' His voice trailed off, not wanting to say aloud what he thought.

The Kid said it for him. 'You thought it wouldn't hurt old Dickie any, that right? They couldn't charge a dead man for holding.'

Skooshie felt shame redden his face. Dickie had been his mate and he'd let him down. Sure, he hadn't forced him to go to the Corvus, but he'd promised him he wouldn't deal. Because they were mates, Dickie had believed him. But Skooshie had let him down. And got him killed. And then he'd unloaded his goods onto his body. Some mate he was.

'Rab's no happy, Skooshie, mate,' said the Kid. 'But I'm betting you know that, eh? He knows you're grieving, but he can't let it pass, you understand?'

Skooshie kept looking at the floor. He knew the score. He'd stepped out of line and he had to be punished. *That's the way it is*, he told himself, *for if Rab lets it pass, he'd be seen as weak and then others would take liberties.*

McCall moved before Skooshie even knew it. He pinned his left hand to the tabletop, seized the middle finger and jerked up and back, giving it a twist. The pain shot up Skooshie's arm and he cried out. He tried to pull away, but McCall already had the next finger and was giving it the same treatment. Skooshie thought he heard something click, even over his scream of agony. His pinkie was next and Skooshie thought he was going to pass out. He slumped over the tabletop, his head dangling over the side, a burning red heat sizzling along his arm. His eyes met the dog's as it watched him from the floor. The animal looked as if he was curious about his pain, then lowered his head again. A cold fucker, just like his owner.

'Hurts like a bastard, doesn't it?' the Kid said. 'Happened to me once, when I was boy. Slipped in the snow, landed wrong. Middle finger was bent back at the middle socket. Sore as fuck. But you're lucky, Skooshie, cos Rab didn't want you hurt too bad. Just a reminder, something visible, to let you know and let the rest know that when he says something, it's the law. Know what I'm sayin? When he says you don't go anywhere near a place, you don't go anywhere near that place, understand? And you sure as fuck do not punt gear there. What is it they say? That's just compounding the felony.'

Skooshie was whimpering as he straightened up, cradling his throbbing left hand with his right. McCall was on his feet now, the dog, too. The Kid was rising. 'Your mate's dead, Skooshie, and that's sad. But it's your fault, you know that. And the can you've opened has sent worms slithering all over the place. You're out of it, far as Big Rab's concerned. You're done. If I was you, I'd go get myself a job digging ditches or something. Once your hand's better, course.'

They left him in his mother's kitchen, nursing his pain, and mourning his friend. They left him alone.

The bookies was filled with men and smoke and smoking men puffing more smoke. There were a couple of women, older women, but the overall ambience was heavy with testosterone. The floor was strewn with discarded betting slips and fag butts, but Frank Donovan did not notice them. His attention was firmly on the excited voice coming from the speakers as it gave a hoofbeat by hoofbeat account of the 1.30 from Chepstow. Donovan held his slip in one hand, staring at the name of the horse as if that would make it run faster. Speckled Band was highly fancied and he had placed 50 quid on its nose. If it came home, he'd be 500 quid better off. And he badly needed to be 500 quid better off. It was a dead cert, he had been told by Nick the Bubble, a balding little Greek who would bet on anything that moved. Nick was at the counter, chatting to the black-haired girl who took the bets. The Bubble was seventy if he was a day, but he still fancied his chances with the ladies. He got lucky often, Donovan had been told, proving you can never underestimate the susceptibility of the west of Scotland female to the lure of exotic Mediterranean charms, even though the old Greek hadn't seen the land of his birth since he was ten. This girl, though, was having none of his patter, judging by her bored expression, forcing Donovan to wonder whether the stories of Nick's amorous adventures were closer to legend than fact.

The announcer's voice rose to such a level of excitement that Donovan feared he might burst something as Speckled Band went head-to-head with Kentucky Lady, battling for the finish line. Donovan unconsciously tightened his grip on the stubby brown pencil provided by the bookie as he listened. He'd forgotten he was still holding it. All that mattered was the race.

The other runners had been left behind, so it was just the two, Speckled Band leading slightly but then Kentucky Lady was closing the gap, just pushing ahead and Speckled Band was fighting back, a final stretch, getting a nose in front but Kentucky Lady wasn't done yet, she was edging forward again, getting out in front and Speckled Band had to really push to regain the pole position but the post was just ahead and it wasn't looking good and Kentucky Lady was drawing on reserves and widening the gap between them but Speckled Band was showing real pluck, wasn't letting go, but they were at the post now and it was Kentucky Lady first, Speckled Band second, what a magnificent effort from these two great horses, a real credit to their trainers....

Donovan crumpled his betting slip and let it fall from his fingers to join the detritus on the floor, his dreams of the 500 quid falling with it. He didn't really care what credit they brought to their trainers. He unfolded his other hand, saw the pencil nestling in his sweaty palm, then laid it down on the counter. He looked at Nick, who gave him an apologetic shrug of the shoulders. Win some, lose some, it said. Donovan had been losing too many these days. If only he had put it on each way, at least he would have come out with something. He sighed and walked towards the exit, pushing his way through the frosted glass onto Victoria Road. He would have to head home now, nothing else for it. Marie would be home, so he would have to argue with her before he would be able to catch a few hours' kip. Dropping another 50 down the drain would not make things better when she found out. And their daughter, Jess, would hide in her bedroom, no doubt waiting for the sound of the front door slamming shut behind him as he stormed out to start that night's shift.

A few flecks of snow drifted across his vision, but Donovan couldn't tell if they were latecomers to last night's fall or the advance guard of something far worse. The sky was dark and heavy and something was definitely up there waiting to drop. Donovan stopped on the pavement when he saw Knight grinning at him from a car parked at the kerb, one of those stinking little cigars clenched in his impossibly white teeth. Donovan groaned inwardly, because the sight of the Black Knight was just what he needed.

'How's it goin, Frankie boy?'

Donovan said, 'Christ, don't you ever sleep?'

Knight took the cigar out of his mouth. 'The pursuit of justice never sleeps, Frankie boy. Anyway, caught a few zeds this morning, after I left you. Right as rain now. You still look like shit, though.'

Donovan was not surprised he looked like shit. It had been a long night and he should have gone straight home at shift's end, but he kept putting it off, afraid of what the morning post might have brought. And the arguing, of course. Always the arguing. Finally, he made his pricey visit to the bookie. He frowned and said, 'How did you know I was here?'

'Know a lot about you, Frankie boy. It's my business to know things about people.'

Donovan stepped closer to the car, leaned on the roof and stooped into the window. 'You following me?'

Knight laughed and Donovan caught a faceful of cigar smoke. 'Don't flatter yourself, son. You know me, got eyes and ears everywhere. It's why I'm a DI and you're still a DS. And why I'll be a DCI and you'll *still* be a DS. Dedication, Frankie boy, dedication to the profession. Eyes, ears…' Knight placed the cigar back between his teeth and wiggled his fingers about in the air, 'conduits of intelligence everywhere. Tout of mine sees you in here a lot. You've been dropping quite a load this past wee while, I hear.'

'None of your business, that.'

Knight held his hand up like a shield. 'Easy, son, I'm no judging you. We've all got our recreational preferences. Whatever floats your boat.'

Donovan sighed. Knight made him feel even more tired. 'What do you want, Jimmy?'

'A tip, about your boy last night.'

'What sort of tip?'

'A good one. A weapon.'

'Why you coming to me, Jimmy? You usually want the glory all to yourself.'

Knight's face took on a wounded look. 'Frankie boy, you cut me to the quick. I thought, for old times' sake, I'd give you a helping hand. We made a good team in the old days.'

'Aye,' said Donovan, the single syllable heavy with sarcasm. 'So you got nothing better to do than spend time on a nightclub stabbing? Not enough work down there in Serious Crime?'

Knight smiled. 'Day off. So, you in or what?'

Donovan thought about it. Knight had more angles than a geometry lesson and he was trying to work out what it was this time. Then he thought, what the hell. He didn't want to go home anyway…

Once there had been a factory unit on the site, but no more. Now the patch of wasteground in Ruchill near the hospital was home to rats, broken glass and the casualties of modern consumerism dumped there by flytippers. Donovan saw an old cooker, a sink and a pile of worn tyres. The thick layer of snow gave the site a more pristine appearance than it deserved. An old settee lay in the centre of a ragged circle of bare, white ground and until a few minutes before, it had been surrounded by young men drinking cheap cider, smoking and, Donovan suspected, punting drugs. They had fled as soon as he and Knight had appeared at the edge of the waste-ground, the neds' uncanny nose for cops certainly not failing them. They scattered across the old site and vanished from view in the way that can only be achieved by those intimately acquainted with their surroundings. One minute they were haring across the ground, leaping over scrubby little bushes and skirting piles of concrete and rubbish, the next Knight and Donovan were alone, save for the impressions of feet in the snow. It was a trick that would make Paul Daniels proud.

'So, what did this tout of yours say, exactly?' Donovan said as they strode across the snow-covered ground, paying little or no attention to the bodies flitting in all directions.

'That a blade used in the Club Corvus incident had been dumped here,' said Knight.

Donovan stopped and looked around. 'That all? This is a lot of ground for two guys to cover, Jimmy.'

Knight simply grinned and wiggled his eyebrows like Groucho Marx. Donovan sighed, Jimmy Knight being enigmatic was a pain in the arse. Jimmy Knight being funny was a pain in the arse. Jimmy Knight being helpful was a pain in the arse. There was a pattern forming here and Donovan was beginning to wish he had never agreed to come along on this field trip. Let the Black Knight have all the glory, he was tired and wanted his bed. Knight walked on, but Donovan stood where he was, unwilling to move further until the other man came clean.

'Jimmy, what are you no telling me?'

Knight's pace didn't falter as he shouted over his shoulder, 'One helluva lot, Frankie boy. All you need to know is that I know what I'm doing. And all you need to do is watch me while I'm doing it.'

Donovan realised at that moment what this was all about. Corroboration was essential in Scots Law and Knight needed another officer with him when he made the find. Knight strode off towards a mound of concrete blocks and twisted metal, remnants

of the factory building, but Donovan stood still and seethed. This
was typical of Knight, to follow his own agenda and use whoever
he liked to achieve it, but eventually Donovan decided he was
better in than out, so he began to move again. Knight was walking
around the pile of masonry by the time he caught up with him.
The big cop's eyes crawled over the dirty bricks and scabby cinder
blocks like a lizard searching for a cranny in which to hide. He
stopped and took a step backwards, his upper body tilting to the
side for a better look. Then he nodded and motioned Donovan to
come closer. Donovan sighed and stepped round the mound as
Knight pointed at a cleft between two large concrete slabs.

'My tout said the blade's in there,' said Knight.

'Pretty precise tip. You sure your guy didn't plant it here, too?'

Knight gave him a smile that told Donovan not to probe too
far into the source of the tip, then he gestured at the hole. 'On you
go, then,' said Knight.

Donovan frowned. 'On you go what?'

'Haul it out.'

'Why me? It's your tip.'

'Cos I'm wearing fuckin cashmere and you're in your BHS best
anorak.'

Donovan looked down at his jacket. It was not an anorak, it
was a thick, padded jacket, and he was offended at Knight's dig at
his sartorial elegance. 'That's another reason you've not got on in
life, Frankie boy,' Knight said. 'You've got to look the part. Christ,
did you not learn anything from Gentleman Jack?'

Jack Bannatyne was the snappiest dresser this side of Beau
Brummel and Knight, who always had his lips plastered so close
to their old boss's backside that he could tell what the man had
eaten the night before, liked his style. Donovan, though, always
looked like he had been let loose at a jumble sale clothes counter
with a handful of coins and a time limit. He could not help it, he
never looked tidy.

Donovan sighed and stooped to peer into the hole. He didn't
fancy sticking his hand in there one bit.

'What you waiting for?' Knight asked.

'Gimme a minute, will you!' Donovan snapped. 'I'm just checking it out.'

'It's a hole, what is there to check out? You frightened something will bite you?'

'No, I'm not frightened something will bite me,' Donovan said, irritably, even though he had, in fact, been frightened something would bite him.

'Don't worry, Frankie boy,' Knight said reassuringly. 'I've not seen a crocodile in Ruchill for many a year. Go on, ya big jessie, stick in your thumb and pull out a plum.'

Knight edged closer, wiped some snow from the hole to make it a bit wider and then slowly inserted his hand into the hole.

Knight said, 'Mind you, there could be a rat in there...'

Donovan jerked his hand back instinctively, but immediately regretted it when he heard Knight laughing behind him. 'Man up, for God's sake. I'm ashamed to be seen with you.'

Donovan took a deep breath and, wondering how fast rabies can take hold, thrust his hand back inside. There was quite a deep cavern there and he felt around for a good few seconds before Knight's impatience got the better of him and he said, 'Fuck me, Frankie, you pretending you've got your hand up some tart's fanny? What's keeping you?'

'Gimme a second, Jimmy, I don't know how far back this hole goes.'

'As the Bishop said to the actress.'

Donovan shot Knight a dirty look over his shoulder, but the big detective simply gave him a sweet smile in return. Or as sweet as Knight could make it. Donovan was delving in the fissure up to his shoulder, but all he could feel was bricks, metal and something soft and oozy, which he hoped to God was mud. Then, just as he was about to pull free, his fingers brushed against fabric.

'Hang on,' he said, 'got something...'

Knight craned closer as Donovan flexed his arm as straight as it could to allow his fingers to hook the cloth and drag it closer to the opening. He grasped it firmly and carefully withdrew it from its hiding place. It was a tea towel bearing scenes from across

Scotland, the sort of thing Donovan's granny used to have in her kitchen. It was old and threadbare and it was wrapped round something solid.

'Let's see it, then,' said Knight, and Donovan handed the bundle over to him. Knight carefully unfolded the ends of the towel to reveal a bloodstained flick knife.

'Nasty bit of kit, that,' said Knight.

'Aye, but it's not the blade that stuck that boy Himes. Wrong shape.'

Knight gave him a grim little smile. 'You're a betting man, Frankie, how much would you bet that, when we check that blade, we'll find Dickie Himes' prints all over it.'

Donovan knew from Knight's grin that he was staring at that most elusive of punter's dreams, the sure thing. 'So the blood's not Dickie's?'

'No. I'll give you double or nothing that Dickie cut someone last night, one of his attackers. And that means we'll get a blood type and DN-fuckin-A. This is your case, Frankie boy, right here. All we need to do is find a boy who got cut last night and we've got our killer. And find that homeless guy, hope he's compos mentis enough to make an ID and Bob's your proverbial.'

Donovan could feel the excitement building in his chest, but something Knight had said gave him pause. 'All "we" need to do, Jimmy? Thought you were just giving a helping hand here?'

Knight looked hurt. 'Frankie, you want to cut me out now? After me leading you to this? That's cold.'

Donovan looked from Knight's feigned hurt feelings to the knife. He could not shake off the feeling that this was all far too easy and that Jimmy Knight was leading him by the nose for reasons best known to himself. On the other hand, a quick result would not do him any harm. He could do with a win.

'Okay, so we take it back to Stewart Street.' Donovan said. 'Get it dusted to confirm it's Dickie's, get the blood tested, check the hospitals and clinics for reports of knife wounds.' *And while all that is happening,* Donovan told himself, *I'll find a nice cosy cell in the custody suite and get my head down for a few hours.* He had a clean shirt in a drawer at the station, he'd be fine. It would also mean he didn't need to go home and face Marie.

'We could do that, Frankie boy,' said Knight, nodding sagely. 'We could do all of that, and we will, believe me. Take a coupla days, right enough. But see just to save a wee bit of time,' he held his free hand up, finger and thumb barely apart to show just how much time they would save, 'just a wee bit, we could go see this boy I heard got his face opened last night. You know, just to eliminate him from inquiries.'

Donovan's eyes narrowed. 'You've got a name?'

'I've got two names. But no the now, son – you look done in. He'll keep till tonight, after you come on shift. You can tell old by-the-book Bolton, if you like, earn some brownie points.'

Knight gave Donovan a broad smile. Donovan nodded. 'And when were you going to tell me about this boy?'

Knight's face would have been an open book if Donovan did not know him so well. 'Frankie, I kinda thought I just did.'

Davie was happy in his own company, but as he sat in the gathering gloom of the living room, alone, listening to the muted rumble of the traffic drifting down from Duke Street, he couldn't help but feel a sense of loss. The dog lay on the floor in front of the gas fire. Abe used to lie there, Davie recalled, and in the same way, head on his front paws, watching Davie carefully, waiting for him to either feed him or take him for a walk. Or just to move. For wherever Davie went, so did Abe. Dave flashed back to one night, years before, when he and Audrey had been together in this room, on the couch, hands exploring bodies, touching, caressing, stroking. And Abe had watched them, eyebrows beetling. That was the night Joe had died. That was the night everything changed.

You can never love me, Vari had said.

You can't let go...

He knew what she meant. He was unsure what love actually was. He'd loved his mother, sure, he'd loved Abe. He even loved this dog, even though he'd only had it for a day and the animal didn't yet trust him fully. But the kind of love Vari wanted? He was fairly certain he'd experienced that only once. And that had been taken away from him on a windy afternoon down the coast. That seemed to be the way it was for him – anything he loved was taken away. His mother, his dog and Audrey. Two of them murdered by a madman while Davie watched and did nothing. The madman who was his father.

He closed his eyes to block the memories and took a deep, cleansing breath, but nothing worked. He did not make a habit of looking back, for he knew the memories were there, over his shoulder. The recriminations. The pain. The accusing look in Audrey's eyes as she died. But he couldn't block out the voices, echoes, whispers.

You could have done something.

You could have saved me.

He had been unable to move. Years of fear, of dread, regarding his father had rooted him to the spot until it was too late.

You could have saved me.

The green eyes being bled of life, staring at him, a single tear trickling down her cheek.

You could have done something...

His eyes snapped open again when he heard the rapping at the door. The dog's head raised. Davie thought about ignoring whoever it was, but then realised it would be a means of banishing the ghosts that haunted him, if only briefly. Vari had done that, more often than she realised.

Bobby Newman was leaning against the doorjamb when Davie opened it. His face was unusually serious. 'You okay?'

'Why wouldn't I be?'

Bobby rolled his eyes and stepped past Davie without an invitation, because he knew he didn't need one. Along with Rab, he was Davie's oldest friend. He stopped when he saw the dog standing in the hallway, his tail wagging, but only slightly. Bobby turned and jerked his head in the animal's direction. 'New arrival?'

'Yeah.'

Bobby knelt to give the dog a two-handed rub around his head. 'What's his name?'

'Haven't thought of one yet,' said Davie.

Bobby straightened then said, 'Okay. Needs a name, though.'
'Yeah.'

Davie followed him into the living room. Bobby took in the darkness and said, 'Jesus, Davie – you no paid your leccy bill?' He clicked on a lamp sitting on a table beside the phone close to the door, then moved to an alcove near the window to click on another. When he turned, his face was still serious, and he said again, 'You okay?'

Davie gave him a thin smile. 'You've heard, then?'

Bobby nodded. 'Vari phoned Connie.' Bobby's wife, school-teacher, at home on Edinburgh Road with their newborn kid, a girl they'd called Susan. 'Thought I'd come over, see if you're okay. So, you okay?'

'I'm fine, Bobby. Honest.'

'For the best, right?'

'Yeah.'

'Better for her, right?'

'Yeah.'

'Bollocks, Davie.' Bobby took off his coat and settled in the armchair nearest to him. 'You liked that lassie.'

'I did,' Davie conceded.

'And you've been sitting here in the dark convincing yourself that it's best for her, that you're happier on your tod, right?'

Davie didn't answer. Bobby knew him too well.

'Utter bollocks, Davie,' said Bobby again. 'You need her. That lassie kept you human, son.'

Davie perched on the edge of the settee, as if he was ready to take flight. Bobby was his mate. Bobby knew him better than he knew himself, but he was uncomfortable with someone being so prescient.

'And see, the thing is, Davie,' Bobby went on, 'you know that, too. She told Connie she left cos you can't open up. What's the phrase they women's mags use? You're emotionally unavailable. And that's true enough, you're emotionally unavailable. You've got a dark side, Davie McCall. Christ, you've got a dark side that would have Darth Vader reaching for a torch. I've known that for years, since we were boys. But you control it. You use it, too. To keep people away. Vari's one of them.'

'I'm no good for her, Bobby.'

Bobby's face creased as he dismissed Davie's words with a wave
of his hand. 'You were the best thing that happened to that lassie.
She was a wreck when you met her. Okay, she was working and she
was existing, but she was getting used by... well, people like me.
She was a bike, Davie. Christ, that's why I had her at your coming
out party.'

Five years before, when Davie got out of jail, that's when he'd
met Vari. Bobby had always been a bit of a lad, until he met
Connie, and he knew the girls who were free with their favours,
the bikes as he called them. Always there for a ride. He'd invited
Vari to the party and the rest was history.

'She was broken, you know that, but being with you fixed it all.
Davie, you healed her.'

Davie sent a short, sharp breath down his nose. 'Some healing.
You remember what happened to her?'

'Wasn't your fault.'

'He was my father. He'd never have gone after her if it wasn't
for me.'

'Not your fault, Davie. His. Not yours.'

Davie shook his head slowly. He knew Bobby was trying to
make things better, but there were some things that would never
heal. And once again, he flashed to Audrey sliding to the ground,
her throat sliced open, the life leaving her in gouts of blood that
stretched in the wind like red ribbons. Her green eyes on Davie.

You could have saved me...

Davie forced the image from his mind and said, 'It was time,
Bobby. I couldn't give her what she wanted. She wanted what the
straight arrows want – a home, a family, a life. I can't give her
those things.'

'Why not?'

Davie didn't answer. He wanted to say *because I'm Davie McCall.*

He wanted to say *because those things are not for me, never
will be.*

He wanted to say *because I'll never see my 40th birthday...*

He had long known he would never see old age. After Audrey's death, he had given the violence, the dark thing that nestled within him, free rein. He had cast off his initial reluctance to become involved in Rab's drug business and had profited from it. He had beaten and he had battered and he had felt nothing when doing it. Earlier that day, he had broken a boy's fingers as if it was the most natural thing in the world. For him, it *was* natural. It was his nature. The dark had almost consumed him and it had cast its shadow over his life with Vari. That's what she meant when she said that he wasn't really there. The Davie McCall that Audrey loved had also died on that wind-swept harbour. For a life with Vari to work, that Davie McCall would have to be resurrected.

But he didn't think that was possible.

Marty Bonner's face looked like a character in *The Broons* with the mumps. He had a bandage wrapped around his head, holding a thick piece of gauze in place over the wound left by Dickie Himes. It stung like buggery, the painkillers weren't worth a damn, and he wanted to rub it but he was frightened to touch it, even through the dressing. His girlfriend, Sonya, sat across the living room from him, a women's magazine on her lap, but she wasn't looking at it, she was looking at him, her face still worried. He had told her the story of how he and Stewie Moore had been caught by three lads up Sauchiehall Street and she had bought it. There was no way he would tell her where he'd really got the sore face. Sonya was brand new about stuff, but she would not accept him being involved in a murder, no way. Even though he'd really had bugger all to do with it, apart from being there. That was enough, though.

Marty froze when the doorbell rang, Sonya too. They both looked towards the square-shaped hallway beyond the living room as if they could see through the wooden front door. It rang again and Sonya rose without a word to answer it. Marty felt his muscles relax when he heard Stewie's voice and then his mate appeared. He looked pale, nervous, as if he hadn't slept. Join the club, Marty thought.

'Cuppa tea, Stewie?' Sonya asked, always the first words out of her mouth when they had company.

'Just the job, Sonya, hen,' said Stewie, his voice light, breezy even, but he didn't fool Marty. They'd been pals for too long. He knew Stewie was worried shitless. Sonya gave him a small smile and stepped into the kitchenette, which was little more than a cupboard off the living room. Marty heard the transistor radio being switched on and the sound of Bruce Springsteen walking through 'The Streets of Philadelphia' rumbled out. Sonya knew they wanted to talk and she knew she didn't want to hear what was being said. She was a good girl.

'They're deid, Marty,' said Stewie, his voice low, hoarse. 'Both of them.'

Marty nodded. He'd heard it on the news. Dickie Himes and that lad who just happened to get in the way. A double murder.

'Fuckin Scrapper,' said Stewie, for what was perhaps the thousandth time since the night before. *Fuckin Scrapper.* 'It was all down to him. We was only there for back-up while he gave Dickie a slap or two.'

'Aye,' said Marty, 'but we were there, that's the point. We're just as guilty as him.' Marty felt his own self-denial evaporate as soon as the words were spoken. We were there. Just as guilty. That's all there was to it.

Stewie fell silent and Marty saw his eyes begin to water. He was always the weak one, never a hard lad. Marty had protected him more than once, but he couldn't protect him from this. 'Scrapper's nuts, so he is,' Stewie said, the words trembling. 'Total fuckin bananas. He had no call to plunge the boy like that, cut him a bit, aye, because he had to be punished for what he'd done, especially after he opened your face, but he didnae need to go and slice the poor bastard to pieces.'

'That's Scrapper,' said Marty, as if that was all the explanation that was needed. They'd both heard him say it often, *never leave a job half done.*

Stewie nodded and said softly, 'And that other bloke...'

Marty closed his eyes, as if against the pain from his jaw, but really it was to try and block the memory of what happened. But closing his eyes didn't do the trick, because he saw once again the guy stepping in their way and Scrapper swinging his blade, automatic-like, because his blood was up, and then the boy's hands were at his neck and there was blood spurting everywhere, Marty and Stewie had to dodge away to avoid being splashed with it. There was a lassie screaming and they saw her in the shadows behind some big wheelie bins, her face lit up by the flickering light. Scrapper would have done her too if Stewie hadn't grabbed him and pulled him away. For a minute Marty really thought Scrapper was going to plunge Stewie, too, but he came to his senses and the three of them legged it along Buchanan Street.

It was a mess. A right royal mess.

Fuckin Scrapper.

Marty opened his eyes and saw Sonya standing in the doorway to the kitchenette, two mugs of tea on a tray with some biscuits. Chocolate digestive. Always chocolate digestive. He saw the concern on her face and that made him feel good, despite everything. He looked around their neat wee living room. She had moved into his one-bedroom flat near Saracen Cross six months before and had done wonders with the place. Before she came, it was pretty much a shithole, but she had redecorated and replaced his old scabby three-piece suite with a new one, second-hand, sure, but it was far nicer than the old one. It was a home now, thanks to her. She wanted to get married, which he wasn't sure of, he didn't know why. After all, she was living with him, what harm would a slip of paper do? He already had responsibilities, so getting hitched was only a formality. He'd have to get a job, too. Couldn't work for Scrapper and his family for the rest of his life, no future in that. He didn't have a scooby what he would do, but he knew for certain that he'd have to put distance between him and the Jarvis clan, especially after last night. That'd please his granddad, who didn't like him mixed up in The Life, not that he had much say in it, though. Course, if he did give it a chuck, it would mean he wouldn't see much of Stewie, who he'd known since school, but there's a price for everything. Yeah – it was time, Marty decided. What happened in the club was a wake-up call. Pity the two boys died, but maybe some good would come out of it after all. Last thing he wanted now was to end up in the jail. His granddad had done thirty years for something he didn't do, Marty didn't want to follow in his footsteps.

But when the doorbell rang again, he knew in his heart that nothing good was going to be standing on the other side. Stewie's face blanched even further, too. And when Sonya showed in the two men, they both knew instantly they were cops. One of them, big dark-haired bastard dressed like he'd just fallen out of Burton's the Tailors, smiled at him. Marty knew his face, was certain he'd worked Saracen police office at some time.

'That looks like a right sore face you've got there, son,' said the cop. 'Cut yourself shaving?'

The other cop, the one not dressed so niftily and looking like he'd done an overnighter, cleared his throat and asked, 'Martin Bonner?'

'Aye.' What was he going to do, deny it in his own flat? Sonya stood there looking from the cops to him, her eyes strained, red-rimmed, like she was about to cry. He wanted to get up, cross the room and give her a cuddle, tell her everything was alright. But he would've been lying.

'DS Frank Donovan, Stewart Street.' He held up a leather wallet, showing them his card. He didn't bother introducing his mate. 'Need you to come with us, son.'

'What for?'

'A few questions.'

Sonya said, 'Is this about Marty and Stewie getting jumped? You got the guys that did it?'

The big, dark-haired cop smiled at her, looking her up and down like she was a piece of meat. Marty felt heat growing in his cheeks and he shot a protesting glance at Donovan. He'd seen his mate giving Sonya the once-over and he didn't like it, but didn't say anything. *Cops*, thought Marty, *always sticking together*.

'Aye, hen,' said the dark one, 'it's about last night.'

Marty sensed danger from this cop but he still said, 'You frae Stewart Street, too?'

'I'm just here to observe.'

'Oh, aye?' Marty felt his anger rise. The look the guy had given

Sonya had really pissed him off. He raised two fingers. 'Want to observe this, then?'

The big cop lowered his head and glared at him from under dark brows. His smile was still in place, but Marty felt it was more a show of teeth than anything else. The other cop, Donovan, cleared his throat again. 'Don't make things worse, son. Go get your coat.' He swivelled his head in Stewie's direction. 'Who you, son?'

'Who's askin?' Marty almost smiled. Stewie always picked the wrong time to try to get tough.

The cop studied Stewie. He wasn't as dangerous as his mate, but his brown eyes didn't miss much. 'We're the polis, son. And here's how it works, we ask, you answer. Now, let's try again – who are you?'

Stewie swallowed, all pretence of bravado gone. 'Stewart Moore.'

Marty saw the big cop's eyebrows shoot up. 'Saved us a trip then. We need a wee chat with you, too.'

Stewie swallowed hard and Marty could tell he was close to breaking down. Stewie was no tough guy, no matter how hard he tried. He was okay in a crowd, but get him on his own and he would greet like a kiddie. Marty hauled himself to his feet, keeping his eyes on his mate, waiting for him to look in his direction. When he did, Marty saw the terror in his eyes. 'Don't worry, Stewie,' he said, trying to sound reassuring. 'We've no done nothin. Just keep the heid, we'll be fine.' Marty hoped Stewie understood what he was saying – *say nothing*. The big cop certainly cracked the code, because he laughed.

Marty reached for a jacket draped over the back of an old wooden kitchen chair by the window. Sonya had found the chair on a skip and had stripped it of its decades of varnish and buffed it up to a polished light wood. She'd done a good job, so she had. He'd hoped she'd be able to strip away the shit that had built up on him over the years, too, but there was always another layer.

'He's no well,' Sonya protested. 'Can you no talk to him here?'

'No, hen,' said Donovan, 'best down at the station.'

Sonya was going to argue the toss, but the big cop gave her another of his looks, up and down, taking in every part of her. She took an involuntary step back and crossed her arms protectively over her breasts. Tears flooded her eyes and she looked at Marty.

'It's okay, love,' he said. 'I'll no be long.'

He gave her a hug and she clung to him like it was the last time they would be together.

Scratchy felt safer here. Tucked up in the old shed. Scratchy would be safe here for a night, no longer than that. They'd be there the next day, the people who worked the allotment, they'd chase him out. They'd come back, snow or not. He'd seen them, the weekend gardeners, sitting in their sheds, drinking tea. They'd be back on Sunday, no doubt about it. Snow or no snow. Then they'd chase Scratchy out.

Scratchy wanted to stay away from the usual places. The hostels. The well-known skippers. The bothies. Scratchy knew they'd find him there. Scratchy didn't want to be found. He couldn't be found.

Outside he heard the wind making the trees of the park creak and sigh. He pulled the fabric of his coat tighter to ward off the chill. Scratchy was cold but he was safe. They'd never find Scratchy here.

Scratchy slept.

SUNDAY

Detective Sergeant Colin Malone popped an extra strong mint in his mouth, his eyes never leaving the opening to the tenement block. He sat in the passenger seat of the white transit, heater going full blast. Behind him, another five plainclothes officers waited with varying degrees of patience. The operation had been hastily thrown together, but it would be a relatively simple swoop and lift job. He didn't know these guys, the bulk of his Drug Squad mates being involved in a larger operation between Liverpool and Glasgow, also set to go down that day, so they'd drafted in some assistance from C Division. The van was parked a good 100 yards from the target tenement, in a street not far from Saracen cop shop in Barloch Street, which the drug squad officers thought was a bit cheeky. They'd been given names and they'd been given the address and they'd been told there was a mini factory in there. All they had to do was wait.

Around them, locals went about their lives, some clearing away the last vestige of snow from the pavement outside their homes, women heading out to the shops, all unaware that their street was being used by scroats up to no good. This time tomorrow, it'd be the talk of the steamie, DS Malone thought as he sucked on his mint. He wished he'd brought a flask of coffee, too.

He straightened in his seat when a flash BMW slowed to a halt at the close and a face he recognised got out. Here we go, he thought.

'That him?' DC Crowther was in the driver's seat. Young cop, one of the lads from the Maryhill office.

'Aye, but let's give it a minute or two, we're waiting for two more. No point in going off half-cocked.'

Two extra strong mints later, a second high-end vehicle cruised up and two other faces climbed out, each carrying bulging black bin bags. DS Malone knew his men were waiting for the word, but he wanted to give the targets time to get in and get started. Finally, he said, 'Okay,' and climbed out.

They charged along the pavement, reaching the close just as an unmarked car came to a halt and a further four plainclothes officers piled out, one carrying an enforcer, a battering ram that could be wielded with ease by a single officer. They pounded up the stairs to the second-floor flat and halted at the door on the left of the stairs, but didn't bother to knock. The enforcer was swung with precision at the lock and the door burst like kindling. The police officers surged through the gap, identifying themselves, issuing orders, all at a shout, a bellow, for intimidation was as vital here as surprise.

Andy Jarvis was in the kitchen doorway, his hands encased in a pair of Marigolds as if he was doing the dishes. But the rubber gloves were stained with brown powder. He was standing stock still, the speed of the raid freezing him to the spot. DS Malone gave him a cheeky grin and stepped past, leaving Crowther to cuff him. In the kitchen, the other two men sat at a Formica kitchen table, blocks of brown in front of them, each wearing rubber gloves, each with a set of kitchen scales in front of them.

'Hey, lads,' said Malone, 'it's not Pancake Tuesday already, is it?'

He picked up a bag filled with a white, crystalline substance. Mannitol, a baby laxative. They called it 'Bash', because you simply bashed it into a basin of smack. The men had been in the process of cutting the heroin into smaller quantities for dealing on the street, diluting the narcotic with the diuretic. What Malone was looking at here was a batch of brown that would have netted hundreds of thousands, maybe more, if it had reached the streets.

He wondered how his colleagues were faring on the motorway.

They had no idea they'd been tailed from Glasgow to Liverpool and back again. There were four cars in the convoy, all hired, but only two would carry the gear back. The other two, filled with some of Maw's hardest lads, were back-up should things go tits-up with the Scousers. She did not expect any trouble back in Glasgow, but that was exactly where the trouble lay in wait.

As Detective Inspector Russell Flannery of the Drug Squad would later tell a courtroom, they were acting on information received that a consignment of Class A drugs, namely uncut heroin, was being transported from Liverpool into Glasgow. Their informant had told them when the cars would leave and when they were due back, but they tailed them anyway, two teams of officers in two separate vehicles trailing the hired cars to the city in the south, where they promptly lost them. What they should have done was liaise with their Merseyside colleagues, but they didn't, and their unfamiliarity with the city meant their quarry, who had made this run before, slipped through their fingers. They picked them up again, though, as they made their way back to the M6 to head for the M74.

But only three cars were making the return trip to the city. Somewhere, somehow, they'd lost the fourth.

Said information duly relayed back to base, the officers were told to stay with the three, which they did, all the way back to Glasgow. The convoy joined the M8 in the east and followed it through the city and on to Port Dundas, where the gear was due to offload in a factory unit.

DI Flannery gave the order to hit them at Speirs Wharf, where the road widened beside the Forth and Clyde Canal. It was Sunday, it was quiet, and if there was any unpleasantness, there would be no bystanders. It was a hard stop – one car jutting in front of them, another screeching behind, while two more skidded to a halt beside them, jamming them in. They had been told these men might be armed, so the plainclothes officers were tooled up themselves and protected by body armour. They swarmed from their cars, screaming 'Armed Police' as loud as they could, making sure the guys in the motors could see their short-barrel Heckler and Koch assault rifles and .38 Smith and Wesson revolvers, the police believing that with this crew, there was no such thing as being under-prepared. An extendable baton was swung at the driver's window of the lead car and the glass smashed.

Detective Constable Rebecca Stephenson, her cut-glass tones betraying her Bearsden background, peered in and smiled. 'Hello, gents. Someone order a jail term?'

The driver saw her long red hair tied back in a ponytail, heard her voice, saw she was attractive and thought she was a pushover. He reached for the glove box, where he had an automatic pistol, but she rammed the baton into his neck and swung her .38 into his face. 'Don't test me, pal.'

She spoke very quietly and the driver knew with certainty that she would not hesitate to follow through. He pulled his arm back slowly. She smiled at him and it might've been sweet if it wasn't for the gun in her hand. 'Good boy,' she said. She reached through the window and retrieved the weapon, then jerked her own weapon twice to the side. 'Now, out you come.' The driver climbed out, followed by the two men who had been catching some sleep in the back seat. They were still bleary-eyed, but waking up fast.

Weapons trained, they hauled a total of eight men out of the three cars. The bonnet of the middle car was popped and there they found black plastic bags filled with bars of brown heroin. The street value of this haul was somewhere north of five million. DI Flannery smiled at the sight and looked back at the men they'd arrested.

'No sign of Marko Jarvis?' He asked DC Stephenson.

She shook her head, her weapon still at the ready in case one of the jokers decided to leg it. 'Must've been in the car we lost, boss.'

His nose wrinkled in disappointment and he lifted one of the bars of brown. Never mind, he thought, it was still a result.

As they were told to lie down and clasp their hands on the back of their heads, each of the eight men had one single thought.

Maw would be spitting blood.

'It was that bastard McClymont, I fuckin know it!'

Maw Jarvis was raging at Jerry and Scrapper. 'Near six million quid's worth of gear gone and your brother banged up.'

Neither brother ventured a word. They'd seen their mother in this mood before. No matter what they said, she'd jump down their throat, or worse. They waited until she asked them a direct question. They didn't wait long.

'McClymont grassed us up, the bastard. So, what are we going to do about it?'

Jerry cleared his throat. 'No much we can do, Maw. We've no got his contacts yet, neither we have. I'm workin on it but we cannae fire him in for anything cos we don't know what he's got going.'

Maw glared at her eldest. 'Work on it harder.'

Jerry gave her a thin smile. She knew she was giving him permission to get tough and with her eldest, God knew where that would lead, given his nature, but she didn't care. She wanted McClymont hobbled, somehow. The big bastard had cost her money.

Scrapper leaned forward eagerly. 'Right, Maw, I'll get the boys out and...'

'You'll dae fuck all, Scrapper. This is payback for what you did to that boy the other night, I know it.'

'Ach, Maw...'

Her dark eyes flashed danger signals and he clammed up. 'Don't "ach, Maw" me. Your temper and fondness for sticking shite up your nose has just cost me a fortune – and your brother in the jail. So I think you'll be keepin your "Ach, Maws" to yourself.' Her face was like granite as she glared at her youngest and he shrivelled in his chair. She turned to Jerry again. 'Find me something, Jerry. I want to squeeze that big bastard's pockets till his balls burst.' Jerry nodded and stood. 'And find Marko, for fuck's sake!'

Another night, another visit from Bobby Newman. Davie was beginning to think he was using him as an excuse to get out of the house and get some peace from the baby. Or maybe Connie just wanted him out from under her feet. Whatever, Davie knew they were both genuinely concerned about him and, even though he'd never admit it, he was grateful for the company. Bobby had arrived breathless with the news of the two drug raids earlier that day. Davie immediately guessed that Rab had steered the info to some friendly copper. The discussion naturally moved to the murder of Dickie Himes. Bobby knew him a little – sometimes Davie wondered if Bobby knew everyone in Glasgow – and said he didn't deserve to go that way. Davie trusted Bobby implicitly, he was perhaps the only other human being he had absolute faith in, so he told him about Rab's desire to hit back hard.

'It's going to get out of control really fast,' said Bobby.

'Tried telling Rab that, but you know what he's like,' said Davie, taking a sip of his coffee. It was good. When he made it for himself he either made it too strong or too weak, but Bobby had got it just right. Vari could do that, too.

Bobby said, 'Maw Jarvis is a brammer. But her boy – Jerry?' He blew out his cheeks and raised his eyebrows. 'He's a piece of work, so he is. They call him The Butcher, you know that? And it's no cos he punts sausages.' Davie nodded. He'd heard of Jerry Jarvis, but had never met him. 'He's a vicious sod when he gets going. He's a speccy, skinny-arsed wee bastard, but he's no to be taken lightly. Rab takes them on, he'd better have a bucket of Germoline in his first aid box.'

The doorbell rang and they sat in silence for a moment, both knowing that the only regular visitors to the flat were sitting in the room. Davie would have ignored it, but Bobby got up to answer it, eager to see who was visiting his pal other than him. The dog, lying in what was becoming his accustomed place in front of the gas fire, looked up, ears cocked, eyes alert. Davie heard voices then Bobby came in, his expression one of bemusement and excitement. A figure loomed behind him in a long, waterproof coat flecked with snow and a hat pulled down low over his face. Davie knew who the newcomer was even before he took the hat off and flattened the collar of the coat. Bobby was grinning like a schoolboy now. Starstruck, thought Davie, with some disappointment. He expected his boyhood pal to be cooler. The dog rose and moved to greet the newcomer, whose face lit up when he saw the animal.

'Hey, boy,' said Michael Lassiter as he held one hand out for the dog to sniff before getting down on one knee and giving his head a rough rub with both hands. The dog loved it. Lassiter looked up at Davie. 'What's his name?'

When Davie didn't answer, Bobby said, 'Not got one yet.'

Lassiter was still rubbing the dog's head. 'Dog needs a name. I love dogs, got three back home. I miss them.'

'Davie says one will present itself when it's ready.'

Lassiter looked surprised. 'That right? Never pegged you for that kind of guy.'

Davie asked, 'What kind of guy?'

'A fatalist. Leaving things to destiny.'

Davie said nothing while he waited for the actor to explain his presence. Lassiter gave the dog a final pat then held out a hand to Bobby. 'Hi, I'm Michael Lassiter.'

Bobby shook his hand. 'Thought you looked familiar,' he said making a belated attempt at Glasgow nonchalance. He said, 'Davie, it's Michael Lassiter.'

Davie nodded.

'You never told me you knew Michael Lassiter.'

'I don't,' said Davie, flatly.

Bobby faced the visitor. 'Mister Lassiter, you make a point of knocking on random doors in Glasgow's east end?'

Lassiter smiled. 'Davie and I met the other day. He's being discreet.'

Davie asked, 'What you doing here?'

Lassiter had moved into the room and stood in front of the gas fire. He was suddenly nervous, like a student at his first audition. 'That fella you were with, the one with the permanent sniffle?'

'Kid Snot?' Bobby asked.

'That's the guy – he really should see a specialist about that. Good man would clear that problem right up. Anyway – I told him I wanted to speak to you, he brought me here.'

Davie made a mental note to have a conversation with the Kid, then realised that Rab probably put him up to it, because he smelled a quick buck and didn't trust Davie to contact Lassiter. He'd been right, too – Davie'd had no intentions of meeting up with the actor.

'So here I am,' said Lassiter. It was followed by an uneasy silence during which Davie saw it dawn on Lassiter that he may have stepped over a line. He came from a world where he was given anything he wanted and it never occurred to him that someone might not want to see him.

'You want a cup of coffee or anything?' Bobby asked, knowing Davie would never think of being a host. 'We don't have anything stronger, Davie not being a drinker.' It sounded like an apology.

'Coffee's good,' said Lassiter. 'It's kinda nippy out there.'

'Ah, that's nothing,' said Bobby, 'when this snow clears we're in for a freeze, I hear. Temperature's gonnae drop well into the minuses. Brass monkeys'll no be doing much shagging, I'm afraid.' Lassiter smiled. 'I'll get you a coffee – milk? Sugar?'

'You got cream?'

'Sorry, even the milk's semi-skimmed.'

'Black'll be fine.'

'One black coffee coming up. Take a seat, make yourself comfortable. He'll never offer, so don't wait. You two can talk among yourselves.' Bobby gave Davie a reproving glare and crossed the hallway to the kitchen.

'Nice guy,' said Lassiter. Davie didn't reply. 'Reminds me of Bob Redford.' Davie remained silent, but it had been said before about Bobby. Lassiter asked, 'You mind if I take my coat off?'

Davie nodded and the actor peeled off the high quality waterproof, then sat down in the nearest armchair, the coat laid over his lap. Davie had meant he did mind but Lassiter had taken it as permission. Davie let it go. He heard Bobby rattling about in the kitchen, opening cupboard doors, no doubt looking for biscuits. He knew Vari would have them in there somewhere.

'I need your help, Mister McCall,' said Lassiter.

'I don't store the medicine, I just deliver it sometimes.'

'No, not that. Look...' Lassiter leaned forward. 'I'm here to make a movie. It doesn't begin shooting for a month or so but I'm here early, under the radar.' He paused, waiting for Davie to speak. Davie looked at him, his face blank. Lassiter swallowed. 'I play this American hood who was born in Glasgow who comes back to find his long-lost brother. Kinda like *Get Carter* in a way. You seen *Get Carter*?' Davie nodded. Encouraged, Lassiter became more animated. 'So, I've got time before shooting starts and I wanted to get a feel for the city, that's why I'm here early. I thought maybe you could show me around.'

'There are tour buses.'

'I don't want to see the tourist traps. And I also thought you'd show me a few things about the city's underworld. I'd pay you.'

'What makes you think I know about the city's underworld?'

Lassiter smiled. 'You delivered my medicine. You're no pharma-

cist. And I asked about you. You're like a legend here. Something
to do with a fight on Duke's Road?'

'It was Duke Street,' said Bobby, bustling in with a tray carrying three more coffees and a plate with a handful of tea biscuits.
'Sorry about the biscuit selection, Davie may be a legend but he's
no much of a shopper.'

'So the fight was real, it's not just a story?'

'It was real. Just up the road there.'

'The guy had shot a cop, right?'

'Aye, just downstairs. Davie went after him, caught him, battered
fuck out of him. Then the cops came and put a bullet in the boy.'

Lassiter spoke to Bobby but his eyes were on Davie. Davie kept
his face immobile, even though Bobby's words had brought back
memories of that night. He felt the heat in the air, heard the thunder
as it crackled and rumbled above the city, saw Clem Boyle's face,
hate cutting deep lines around his eyes and mouth as he raised a
gun in Davie's direction.

'That's what I heard,' said Lassiter. 'Also, I don't know if you've
noticed this, but we're kinda similar. Same build, same colouring,
same blue eyes. I thought I could maybe pick your brains, find out
what makes a Glasgow guy like you tick? What do you say?'

'No,' said Davie without hesitation.

'Can I ask why not?'

'I don't want to be studied.'

'I don't want to psychoanalyse you! I just want to soak up a bit
of your reality and maybe transfer it to the picture. And I'll pay.'

'No,' said Davie. Lassiter gave Bobby a look, as if he was a
court of appeal. Bobby shrugged, telling him he couldn't help.

Lassiter reached for his coffee, sat back and stared at it for a
moment. 'I was told you'd co-operate.'

Rab, thought Davie. 'You were told wrong.'

Lassiter stared at the liquid as if it could tell him what to say
next. Davie saw in his face that he was unused to people saying no
to him. Davie knew something about him – father a star from the
1960s, now big on TV, his brother a top director, Lassiter himself
one of Hollywood's most bankable stars. All his life he'd probably

pointed at what he wanted and everyone had bent over backwards to get it for him. Disappointment was not something he often experienced. *Be a new experience for him, then,* Davie thought. *Character building.*

'Okay,' Lassiter said, laying the mug down on the coffee table and standing up. 'If you change your mind, you know where to reach me.' He began to pull on the coat again. 'Thanks for the coffee, Bobby, is it?'

Bobby glanced at the mug, saw Lassiter hadn't touched a drop, but said, 'My pleasure. How will you get back?'

'I'll grab a cab.'

'You can do that?'

Lassiter smiled. 'Sure, even movie stars can use cabs.'

'I mean, won't you be recognised?'

Lassiter held his hat up in one hand. 'That's what the disguise is for.'

With a final nod towards Davie, Lassiter followed Bobby out. Davie heard the door open, more words being exchanged and then closing again. When Bobby returned he was grinning from ear to ear. 'Michael Lassiter,' he said, 'I mean, what the fuck? Wait till I tell Connie, she'll wet herself.'

MONDAY

They called him Marko, a childhood nickname that stuck, but Mark Jarvis didn't mind because he thought it gave him a taste of the exotic. His dark skin, dark eyes and handsome face did not yet bear the signs of abuse to which he had already subjected his body, so that meant he could pass himself off as anything but a Glasgow ned. Until he opened his mouth, and then there was no mistaking his background.

His voice was the loudest thing in the café on Maryhill Road, which was the way it usually was when he was holding court. He had two mates with him and they were listening with rapt attention as he talked of his adventures that morning. They knew better than not to listen when Marko held the floor. He wasn't as unpredictable as Scrapper, but he did have Maw Jarvis's temper. There was no-one else in the place now, the two boys who had been in earlier had swiftly knocked back what was left of their coffee, picked up their rolls and sausage and left as soon as they saw Marko and his lads enter. The owner retreated to the small kitchen, trying hard not to listen to what was being said at the table by the wall. He would never breathe a word of what he overheard, he knew the score, but he still preferred not to hear it. So he'd turned the transistor radio up a bit and let Radio 2 drown the words out.

Marko was telling his mates he'd never had any intention of coming back to the city after the Liverpool run. There was a lassie in East Kilbride he'd been shagging for two months and he'd told her he'd call in on the way back that Sunday. She was, he said, always up for it. It was just as well he'd felt the need, because he would've been hoovered up with the rest of the lads when the drug squad hit them. Anyway, he'd spent the night with her and was heading out of the town, working his way round the various roundabouts that dotted the routes back to Glasgow when he was stopped.

'So fuckin Polo Mint City, right?' he said. 'You know what it's like, you get round one of they bastards and there's another one up ahead. So I'm toodlin along there, feelin well satisfied, know what I'm sayin? Listenin to Todd Rundgren on the CD player, no having a fuckin scooby what's happened back home, when I looks in the rear-view and there's this fuckin jam sandwich bombin up my backside wi the disco lights goin. I'm tellin you, nearly crapped my load right there, but what was I gonnae do? Make a break for it? They fuckers can drive, you know? And I'm in some shit piece of tin cos Maw doesn't want me to draw any attention.'

He paused to take a final sip of his coffee and a draw at his fag before he stood up. One of his mates rose with him and said, 'So what did you do, Marko?'

'What the fuck could I do? I pulled over. These two cops came up to the side window and one of them asked me to get into the back of their motor. I says, "What's the trouble, Constable?" – innocent as fuck, you know? He says, "You were clocked doing 60mph back there. Did you know it's a 50mph limit on the Kingsway?" So, I gives him a wide-eyed look and says, "No, Constable, I'm not from East Kilbride and I really was not aware."'

Marko was at the counter now, cash in hand, his pals at his heels. 'Anyway, I goes into their motor and he's talking to me but I'm watching his mate, walking round my motor, checking the tyres and stuff. So, there I am with my, "yes, constable, no, constable, three bags full, constable," and all the while my arse is poppin buttons cos I've got a fuckin sawn-off and a Beretta in the boot and this bloke's sniffin around like one of they drug mutts. Luckily I'd made sure there was new tyres on that motor before I went down south, so he didnae find nothing and he didnae ask to see the spare, which was a thought that hit me like a super-strength laxative, know what I'm sayin? They let me go with a ticket and I was drivin out of there – under the speed limit, cos they was behind me all the way practically to Busby – and I was thinkin that, see if they'd just asked to open the boot, they'd've been fuckin promoted! I mean, they'd've been made, man.'

He passed a fiver to the café owner, who was still looking nervous. Far as Marko was concerned, he should've got the rolls and coffees for free, but Maw insisted they paid up. Jarvises always pay their way, she said. Marko told him to keep the change.

'This gink on a motorbike roared past while they were dealing wi me,' he said, turning away from the counter. 'Shoulda seen their faces, cos he musta been goin a hunner miles an hour. But they were busy wi me.'

One of his pals asked, 'You told your maw you got pulled over?'

Marko shook his head. 'No yet, man – she'll have me flayed. I was supposed to come straight back to Glasgow wi the rest of the boys, no go a wee detour to Polo Mint City for some afternoon delight. You know Maw – you follow her instructions to the letter.'

'She'll be glad you wurnae lifted, though, right?'

'Aye, but still.'

They were outside now, on the street. A motorbike was parked in front of Marko's own car and something sparked in his mind. 'I'm no lookin forward to tellin her I was away getting wee Marko a seeing to and left the gear wi the others, you know? There'll be questions asked.'

They each murmured their assent, knowing the kind of questions Maw Jarvis would pose and the way they would be posed. Marko stared at the bike, remembering the one that had roared past him in East Kilbride. He recalled the echo of the high-powered engine staying with him as he was dismissed by the police. The spark in his mind caught alight and he knew he was in trouble.

The thought was shattered by the bullet that ploughed through his brain from behind.

Frozen by the explosion of the gunshot, his pals could only watch as Marko folded to the ground and the stocky figure in biker leathers and dark helmet emerged from the shadows of the tenement door beside the café. He stepped over the body quickly, straddled his bike, revved up and zoomed into the traffic.

There was a time when Detective Superintendent Jack Bannatyne thought Jimmy Knight was the best cop he'd ever met, bar none. He had believed he was a dedicated thief taker, a copper's cop who did the groundwork and brought in the bodies. Certainly he cut a few corners here and there, but so had Bannatyne, over the years. No decent cop could exist by sticking rigidly to the letter of the law.

Now, though, he wasn't so sure.

Bannatyne knew that cops and crooks alike called the man in front of him the Black Knight. It suited him, for he was a big fellow – dark hair, dark shadow on his chin. He had dark moods too, or so he'd heard, for Bannatyne was never a boss who grew too chummy with his officers. There had been stories of Knight stepping over a line or two here and there – a slap, a punch, sometimes worse. The manipulation of evidence when needed, a verbal – putting words into the mouths of suspects – when necessary. Nothing major and always merited in the interests of banging up the right person. Justice was blind and sometimes it needed a helping hand to get where it needed to be. Occasionally a complaint was levelled, but none ever went anywhere. Knight was always clever enough to leave himself with wiggle room. So it was overlooked because he dug up the evidence and he made the arrests.

For Bannatyne, that was no longer enough.

The gilt had begun to wear off the gingerbread when Knight told a young cop his wife was having an affair with a known criminal. It turned out not to be true, the woman had merely pissed Knight off, but it resulted in her death and the cop losing his job after gunning a man down. That the man needed to be put down was not in dispute, but the young cop used an unauthorised weapon and should never have been there in the first place. Bannatyne had been unhappy with Knight's part in the tragedy. After that, he trusted him less.

But the Black Knight continued to get results. He was promoted to Detective Inspector and sent to 'C' Division on the city's North West for a couple of years. Now he was back in Serious Crime and again under Bannatyne's command. Knight's promotion had made him even more arrogant, even more of a maverick than before, something that Bannatyne had pulled him up for on more than one occasion, but it never seemed to take. The problem was, Knight digging away on his own, and often on his own time, seemed to unearth more intelligence and arrests than the rest of the squad on a full shift.

'I hear you've been unofficially assisting 'A' Division with a murder inquiry,' said Bannatyne. He was behind his desk in Pitt

Street headquarters, the strip lights in the suspended ceiling burning for the grey sunlight beyond the large window looking towards Charing Cross barely illuminated the office. The weather girl on the BBC news that morning could not rule out the possibility of further snow, maybe even a blizzard, in the following few days.

Knight sat in a chair opposite, perfectly relaxed. 'On my own time, boss. Just giving them a wee hand.'

'Why?'

'You know me, boss – always willing to help out. And I get kinda fidgety when I've nothing to do. Plus it involved the Jarvises.'

Bannatyne nodded. He knew what the case was and who it involved. 'DCI Bolton is peeved.'

Knight dismissed any consideration of DCI Bolton's happiness with a shrug. 'I brought him his only lead.'

'I understand it was Frank Donovan who brought those boys in.'

'After I took him by the hand.'

Bannatyne looked down at the notes he'd scribbled on a pad earlier that morning. 'Anonymous tip, right?'

'Through a tout of mine.'

'Must be a good tout.'

'Never let me down in the past, boss.'

Bannatyne pursed his lips and leaned back in his chair, idly tapping his pen on the pad. He wanted to know who this tout was, but knew Knight would not tell him. He guarded his army of informants like a father protecting his daughter's virtue. 'This victim, Himes, he work for Rab McClymont?'

'Dunno, boss, but his mate, Skooshie, does. Reasonable to assume Himes did, too.'

Bannatyne agreed it seemed reasonable. 'And now we've got Marko Jarvis down.' The news had come in an hour ago.

'No great loss to the world there.'

'No, but it also seems reasonable to assume that the two deaths are connected. Tit for tat. And I don't like a bunch of tits tatting about with firearms, not in my streets. With that in mind, we're now officially taking an interest in these matters. Fingerprints on the knife match the victim, two blood types found – one the victim, the other matches this Martin Bonner. DNA will take a bit longer, but I'm betting it'll match, too.'

'That's good news, boss.'

'You're already up to speed, so I'm leaving you on it. For now.' Bannatyne knew that Scott Bolton would be furious, but it made sense. And if anyone could guide him and Frank Donovan through the labyrinth of criminal families in Glasgow, it was Knight. He may not be the blue-eyed boy he once was, but he knew his way around the city's pond scum like no other.

'Glad to hear it, boss.' Knight was smiling.

'I don't want this turning into a full-scale war, understand? It's been nice and quiet for years. I don't want a repeat of 1980.' There had been a lot of killing in the city that year, most of it unsolved. 'Get this wrapped up, nice and neat.'

Knight stood up.

'Oh, and as for DCI Bolton? You're working with him, he's not working for you. And don't forget he's a DCI. Find a way to play nice.'

Marty and Stewie appeared in the Sheriff Court that morning and were charged with Dickie Himes' murder. The blood on the knife matched Marty's type. He had an obvious wound that had been left by a similar blade, Dickie's prints were found on it, Stewie had admitted he'd been with Marty all night – it was enough to bang them up on remand while the cops dug out more. It was a simple, quick procedure. Neither of them said anything as they stood side-by-side in the small courtroom. They each had a solicitor, no plea was made. It was little more than a means of completing paperwork.

Marty was aware of Stewie trembling beside him, though. He'd never been in trouble before, but he'd promised Marty he'd told the cops nothing during his interview. Marty believed him. But he didn't know how long he could go without cracking. 'Take it easy, Stewie,' he whispered.

'Quiet, you,' said the cop at his side. The Sheriff looked up. He was a stern-faced guy with thin grey hair and tiny rectangular glasses.

'You have something to say, Mister...' he glanced down at the sheet before him, 'Mister Bonner?'

Marty glanced at his solicitor, who shook his head. 'No, sir.'

'Very well. Then please remain silent.' The Sheriff gave Marty a look that warned him to behave, then went back to his form-filling.

Marty could feel his granddad's eyes on him. He was behind them, in the tiered benches that made up the small public gallery. His brother Jimsy was there, too. Marty didn't turn round, for he knew there would be another rebuke coming his way if he did. But he didn't want to meet the old man's gaze, either. He couldn't take the disappointment he knew would be swimming there.

They were taken down to the cells below the court complex on the southern bank of the River Clyde, from where they would be placed on the first available van to carry them through the city to Barlinnie in the east. After a brief word with their solicitors, they were led to a large lock-up, crammed with other guys waiting to either go with them or for their appearance in the courts above. It was a soulless area, filled with smoke and swearing and tension. Marty and Stewie found an empty space on a bench and sat together. Marty could feel the terror seeping out of his pal's pores.

'We're gonnae be okay, Stewie,' he said, his tone soothing, even though the stress was also building within him.

'Fuck's sake, Marty, we're up for murder.'

'I know.'

'But we didnae do it. We didnae plunge that boy.'

'I know.'

'They cannae do us for murder. No when we didnae dae it, surely?'

'They have.'

Stewie shook his head. 'It's no right, Marty. We never did that boy, it was Scr–'

Marty nudged his pal sharply in the ribs. 'Shut it, Stewie!' He looked around, but no-one seemed to be paying attention. However, Marty was wise enough to know that there were grasses everywhere and all it took was one boy to overhear them and tell tales to help reduce his own sentence. Stewie fell silent. He'd been dry-washing his hands in his lap and he looked at them as if inspecting them for dirt. Or blood.

There was nothing Marty could say that would ease Stewie's stress. No, they hadn't killed Dickie, but they'd been there, it was as simple as that. They were just as guilty. It had happened to his granddad, the very same thing. He'd been on a job that went pear-shaped and an old boy ended up dead. His granddad didn't pull the trigger, but he'd been there. He'd tried to get Marty to leave The Life behind, had hoped Sonya would lead him out of it. He wished he'd listened to the old man. He wished a lot of things. But here he was, sitting in a scabby holding area in the Sheriff Court, waiting to be taken to the Bar-L.

It was a reasonably short ride to the jail. Marty didn't know what route the van took because the windows were opaque. They and half a dozen other boys were led into the reception area of the Victorian jail and processed.

And then they were placed in the dog boxes.

Officially they were 'holding cubicles', a way-station where prisoners were stored until their documentation was processed and they could be taken to one of the Halls. They could be an ordeal for experienced lags, but for Marty and Stewie, the experience was terrifying. They were jammed into what was little more than a cupboard with a bench at the far end, where an older man already sat. Stewie's face was ashen and his eyes swam with terror. Marty wondered if that was how he looked, too.

The older man sat on the bench smoking a roll-up as if he was waiting for a bus. The dog boxes were clearly not a new experience for him. His dirty grey hair was swept back from his face into a sharp widow's peak and a deep scar ploughed a furrow down his left cheek. He appeared relaxed as he drew deeply on his cigarette and regarded them with an amused expression.

'You new meat, eh?' He asked, his voice as scarred as his face.

Marty nodded and the man flicked a tube of ash onto a floor strewn with fag butts and bits of discarded food. 'You'll get used to it,' said the man. 'It's no all as bad as the dog boxes, believe me.' He took another drag on his cigarette, then added. 'Bad enough, though.'

Marty turned round in the confined space and pressed his face against the toughened glass of the observation window in the door. It felt cool and helped soothe him a little. He saw the rest of the new intake being guided and prodded through the process, the yelling penetrating even the thick glass. Many of the prisoners knew what to do before they were told, others – obviously 'new meat' – moved dully and leadenly. One or two young men were crying, but no-one cared much. Maybe they would be weeded out at the medical as suicide risks, Marty did not know.

He heard the man croak behind him, 'You both on remand?'

Marty turned back and nodded. Stewie had seated himself on the bench beside the man and was cramming himself tightly in the corner against the wall. He'd wrapped his arms tightly around his body, as if he had a stomach ache.

'What you charged with?'

Marty paused. He was not inclined to say too much to a complete stranger but he saw no reason not to reply. 'Murder.'

The man's eyebrows shot up then bobbed his head, as if impressed. He looked at Stewie. 'What about you, son?'

Stewie gave him a scared look but did not answer. He unwrapped his arms and shoved his hands under his buttocks to keep them from shaking, but there was nothing he could do about his arms, which trembled as if someone was running an electrical current through them. 'We're together,' Marty said.

'Pair of desperados I've got here.'

'We're innocent,' said Stewie, his voice as scared as he looked.

The man smiled and took a final draw on his roll-up before dropping the butt on the floor and pressing a foot on it. 'We're all innocent, pal. Jail's full of innocent men.'

The boy asked, 'What about you? What you in for?'

The man smiled, his teeth showing the result of years of smoking unfiltered tobacco. 'The way the PF has it, I banjoed a guy for taking liberties.'

'What sort of liberties?'

The smile broadened. 'They say that he didn't want to give me the bag of cash he was carrying into the bookies. If it was true –

which it's no – that woulda been a fuckin liberty. So who'd you kill?'

'We didn't kill anyone,' said Marty.

'Aye, right – sorry. Forgot. You're both innocent.'

'Like you.'

He smiled again. 'Aye, like me. So, who was it you didnae kill?'

'Just a guy.'

'Just a guy,' the man repeated. He looked at Stewie again. 'And you didnae do it, right? But you were there, eh? I'll bet you were there.'

Marty began to grow suspicious and he manoeuvred himself around again to watch the activity outside. Behind him he heard Stewie sobbing and the older man tutting in disgust. Marty turned back to find Stewie hiding his face in his hands, his shoulders heaving as he wept. A dark stain spread through his crotch and a trickle of urine seeped from the hem of his jeans to form a puddle on the floor. The man pressed himself harder against the wall and jerked his feet away before they could be contaminated by the spreading piss. Marty looked at his friend, but did not move to comfort him. There was nothing he could do or say to make him feel better. The truth was, he felt like crying himself.

Marty said nothing more to the older man, though he continued to prod. Eventually he gave up, rolled himself another fag and sat back to enjoy it. Stewie didn't say anything either. He cried some more. He shook some more. Every now and then, Marty gave him a worried look. He knew Stewie couldn't take to life inside, even on remand. He knew Stewie could crack.

And there was nothing he could do about it.

Maw Jarvis took the news of her son's death silently, which was unnerving, even for Jerry. She had simply turned, disappeared into her bedroom and didn't emerge for two hours. And when she did come back downstairs, she was dressed from head to toe in black. The last time Jerry had seen that outfit was when his dad died.

Jerry felt the loss of his brother, but he couldn't help but condemn Marko's stupidity. What the hell was he thinking, vanishing after a run? He should've come straight home after Liverpool. He'd gone to East Kilbride after some burd, that was all his mates knew. Jerry would sniff around, but he didn't think he'd find her – Marko had women tucked away all over the place. It was something he'd always envied in his younger brother, his skill with women. It seemed so easy for him, whereas Jerry never had much luck there. Where Marko had inherited his mother's dark looks and had a powerful frame, Jerry was pale and slim, his weak eyes needing thick glasses. He made up for it in other ways, though – ways that were more helpful to the business, which Marko's shagging around never was.

'They've gone too far,' she said. 'We need to hit back.'

He gave her a thin smile. He hadn't been idle while she was upstairs. A call had been made. 'I've spoken to my man over there. I've got a name for you.'

Bernadette was grateful Rab did not invite Stringer into their home. She was not a fan, something she shared with Davie, although she didn't know that. He stood at the front door, talking with Rab in hushed tones, and she wondered if she should put her husband's dinner under the grill to keep warm. The children barely noticed, kept eating, because their dad often had to go and do something at meal times – answer the door, talk on the phone, see some men in the kitchen. Bernadette laid her own knife and fork beside her plate and waited.

She knew why Stringer was there. She knew things had gone according to plan. But she waited at the table because no-one apart from Rab knew how involved she was in the business. Not even Davie McCall knew that Bernadette was privy to every move, every plan, every step Rab took.

Rab came back to the dining room table and took his place. He gave her a quick nod to tell her everything had gone to plan.

She smiled and resumed eating. It would all kick off now. She looked at young Joseph and little Lucia and then thought of her unborn child. What was about to happen would not be pleasant, but it was necessary. What Rab was doing – what they were both doing – was for their children. Family was important. Her father back in Belfast always said it – keep the family close, keep it tight, for when it came down to it, family was all you had. You could trust family. And her father had survived sixty years of hard-nosed crime in a city riven by criminal and sectarian rivalries simply by putting his faith in family – her brothers, her uncles, her cousins. Close-knit, faithful. Loyal.

Stringer wasn't family, but he was useful. If not fully trusted.

Davie was the closest thing Rab had to family, but Bernadette had no trust for him either. She didn't believe Davie would ever turn grass, but she knew that Rab had held a secret from him for fifteen years. For it had been Rab who had turned Davie in for robbery, had to do it to keep the peace. He'd feared Davie would go on a revenge-fueled rampage for the murder of Joe the Tailor, the man who was mentor to both of them. Rab had agonised over it, for Davie was his best friend, but in the end it had been necessary, for the good of the business. Davie had ultimately spent ten years inside, six years more than he should have. He'd had some trouble in prison, had been attacked by another inmate, and Davie McCall did what Davie McCall did. He'd hurt the man badly and was given extra time. He never really knew why he'd gone for him.

But Bernadette did.

She'd set the whole thing up – and other, subsequent attacks, which also failed – through contacts of her father. Rab knew nothing of this, but it had to be done. Of all the men Rab had dealt with over the years, Davie McCall was the one she feared most. There was no saying what he would do if he ever found out that Rab had betrayed him all those years ago. Bernadette had wanted him taken out of the game, but he had proved too much for every man she sent. So when he got out, she took another approach. She knew he was susceptible to female charms, so she paid him special attention, a smile here, a gentle touch there. It was easy, for she did find him attractive – those sad blue eyes would make any woman's resolve wilt. For the first few years that was all it was – a smile, a touch, a glance – while she told herself that she would not take that final step because she loved Rab deeply. What she did, she did to protect her family. She would never take it that far.

But when her old mammy coached her in the ways of men, she

warned her never to under-estimate lust in man or woman. 'We've all got it in us,' she said in her County Cork accent. 'Call it what you will – chemistry, hormones – it's powerful stuff. Sure, the church tells us never to give into it, but that's like the little boy with his finger in that Dutch wall. No matter how much you hold it back, lust, like emotion, will always seep through and sometimes that wall will come down.'

Bernadette knew she was playing a dangerous game, but she thought she could control it. Until, one wet afternoon the previous October, the wall began to crumble. She and Rab had been fighting. They had periods when they each annoyed the other so much that the only way to ease the pressure was to argue over inconsequential matters, and she'd hit the wine at midday. She didn't do that often, not having a head for drink, but this day she had. She blamed the alcohol, of course, but deep down she knew what happened was something she wanted, if only at that particular moment. That it didn't go further than it did was not down to her.

But Rab would need Davie in the coming weeks, so it was time she brought more pressure on Davie. It was a risk, given what had happened back then, but it was one she believed was worth taking.

When Davie heard the doorbell, he thought it was Bobby back again. As he walked the length of the hallway, he wondered if he should give his old pal a key so that he could let himself in. He was smiling as he pulled the door open, an insult dying stillborn on his lips when he saw Bernadette. He looked beyond her for Rab, but she was alone. Guilt pulsed through him like a surge of electricity and he froze in the doorway, unsure of what to do or say.

Bernadette smiled. 'You going to ask me in, Davie?'

Davie hesitated then stepped back. He didn't know why she was here, but he knew it was a bad idea. He'd resolved never to be alone with her again. Not after last time. He followed her down the hall and into the living room. This was all kinds of wrong, he told himself, he should never have let her in. When she peeled off her coat and gloves, she wasn't dressed provocatively – a pair of black jeans, boots and a loose fitting red sweater – but Davie couldn't help himself from admiring her. As Bobby had once observed, Rab was punching above his weight with regards to his wife. She shook her long, dark hair loose and turned to face him.

And in that moment he recalled the last time they'd been alone. It had been in the Bothwell house and Davie was supposed to meet Rab there, but he'd phoned just before he arrived to say he would be two hours late. Young Joe was at school, Lucia having a nap, so they had the house more or less to themselves. Bernadette seemed unusually buoyant, her eyes danced more than usual, she touched him more than ever. He should have left, said he'd come back, but he didn't. He should've been stronger, but he hadn't been. And when she leaned in to kiss him, he should've pulled away. But he didn't.

Within seconds, they were all over each other. She was wearing a white blouse and he clawed at the buttons while she did the same with his shirt. And as they kissed and caressed and fondled, a little voice in the back of his head told him to stop, to get up and leave. Rab was his mate, this was his wife. This was wrong. He tried to ignore it. He was only human. Bernadette was an attractive woman and she'd been flirting since they'd met. Right then, he wanted this.

But then, just as Bernadette was working at his trouser belt, he heard a voice, far away, carried on a wind and he caught her hands. She raised her head, gave him a quizzical look, but all he did was shake his head. For a moment he thought she was going to argue, saw a flame blaze in her eyes, but it was doused with a sigh as she snatched her hands from him. She turned away, clutching her blouse across her nakedness.

Nothing was said as he buttoned his shirt and left the house. There was nothing to say. And it was never mentioned again.

Now, as she stood in his living room, he said, 'You shouldn't be here.' It was the logical, loyal part of him talking, but another part was already aching with excitement. God, he was weak. He reminded himself she was pregnant, even though she was barely showing.

She inclined her head a touch to tell him she knew she shouldn't be there. 'I need to talk to you. Rab's told me about the Jarvis situation.'

The Jarvis situation – a delicate way of putting it, Davie thought. His discomfort deepened at the prospect of discussing business with Bernadette. 'What's he told you?'

'Enough to know that this is critical – and that you're hesitant about what needs to be done.' She moved closer to him and he caught the aroma of her perfume. It was the same one she'd worn the first day they'd met, right here in this room, just after he'd got out of jail. He wondered if she'd worn it specially. He wanted to step away, but he didn't want to hurt her feelings. That's what he told himself, at least. There was caution in his voice when he said, 'Bernadette...'

'Rab needs you in this, Davie.' She took his hand and held it between them, allowing it to brush against the fabric of her sweater and he felt the merest suggestion of her body under the material. Her hands were cool and soft, her voice low and pleasant. 'But more than that, I need you.'

Davie forced himself to draw his hand back and pull away. 'Bernadette...'

'Not that way. Yes, there's an attraction there, there's no denying it. But that's something I have to deal with – something we both have to deal with, because I know you feel it, too. But I need to know that you've got Rab's back. I need you to support him. Of all the boys, you're the one he trusts the most – the one I trust the most to keep him safe. Can you do that? Can you do that for me?'

She had stepped closer again, as close as she could without actually touching him. Her scent caressed him, her eyes stroked his face. He thought about that day in October and he wanted to reach out and touch her, wanted to feel her hands on him. God help him, he felt himself harden at the thought of it. He was supposed to be the ice man, the thug with no heart and yet all it took was a pretty woman to smile at him and he lost the place entirely. Come on, McCall, show how tough you are. You've beaten men, you've damaged them, let's see what you're really made of – let's see you push her away. You let Vari walk away, surely she meant more to you than your mate's wife? You let Audrey die...

He didn't push her away. He didn't dare touch her. Instead, with an effort, he stepped back and sat down on the settee. 'I'd never let anything happen to Rab,' he said, impressing the hell out of himself by keeping his voice steady. 'But he's talking about extreme measures.'

Extreme measures. The Jarvis situation. Why were they talking like CIA agents in a spy movie?

She nodded. He was slightly surprised at how unsurprised she was. Exactly how much did Rab discuss with her? 'Extreme situations require extreme measures,' she said.

'I won't be part of killing.' Again, she appeared unfazed. Something between them had changed and he began to see Bernadette with fresh eyes. She was no stay-at-home wife. She knew more about Rab's business than he'd ever suspected. He remembered Bobby telling him her family were heavy back in Belfast, so she was no stranger to 'extreme measures'.

Her gaze was steady as she looked down at him and he held it, his earlier discomfort evaporating. The pressure on his groin had eased. Finally she shrugged. 'Fair enough. We'll keep you out of anything heavy.' Davie couldn't help but notice the 'we'. Interesting, he thought, and disappointing. She retrieved her coat from the armchair, pulled it on as she walked into the hallway. Davie followed her, opened the door for her. She stopped before stepping out, faced him again. 'The Jarvis clan won't be so squeamish, Davie. They know you're part of Rab's crew and they'll see you as a danger. You watch your back.'

Then she turned and walked down the stairs. He remained in the doorway as she vanished from view, her perfume lingering like the echo of a sad song.

The night brought with it a real tumble in the mercury and Davie's footsteps crunched as he stepped on the frozen surface. The moon was full, but every now and then a heavy cloud passed across it. He hunched deeper into his coat and pulled the collar up around his neck with one hand, the other holding the dog's lead. He loved the city streets at night, especially when he felt he had them all to himself. He liked the solitude, the emptiness. And it would help clear his mind completely of Bernadette.

Except he wasn't alone.

He'd spotted the figure as soon as he turned out of Sword Street and into Duke Street. The guy had stepped out of a closemouth on the other side of the road and began to shadow him. Same height as Davie, long coat, something in his hand. Davie knew who he was, but didn't let him know he'd seen him, just kept walking, as was his habit, both hands now deep in his pockets even though one still held the lead, boots leaving a trail in the deep and crisp and even.

That man didn't bother him.

It was the other two who picked him up in Sword Street that he had to keep an eye on.

Davie kept his usual pace along Duke Street until he reached the point where Millerston Street joined from the right and Cumbernauld Road jutted off left. He crossed the road and walked over the bridge, crossing the railway line, and turned left into Paton Street. He knew something was going to happen and he didn't want to run the risk of anyone seeing. The railway line ran to the left and no tenements overlooked the street, just the edge of a large bakery. The site was illuminated, but there was no-one in view. He picked up his pace, keeping to the shadows created by bushes to the right, heading for the waste ground he knew lay at the upper end of the street. Beyond that was a factory unit and more open space, but there was a locked gate, too. If he had to, he could get over it, but he didn't plan on needing to. The stretch of open ground was pitted by scrubby little bushes already cloaked in frost. The moon shone brightly, brighter than any street light, and the hard snow glistened with tiny dots of light. He hurried to the edge of a wall bordering the open ground and ducked behind it, the dog following him.

Then he waited, the dog sensing something was happening and sitting quietly wedged against his leg. And as Davie waited, he felt that old familiar sensation rise within him and a roar grew in his ears. The dark thing was here.

He didn't wait long before he heard the crunch of footfalls growing closer and then the figure stepped into view. Davie grabbed him and jerked him behind the wall. He saw the object in his hand was a telescopic umbrella. He really hadn't expected it to be anything more dangerous. Not from him. The other guys were a different matter.

'What the hell are you doing?' He hissed.

Michael Lassiter overcame his initial shock and answered, 'Following you.'

'Why?'

Lassiter shrugged. 'I don't take no for an answer.'

Davie glared at him, but this was not the time for a debate. 'You alone?'

'Yes.'

'Where's Mannie?'

'Back in the hotel...'

'Shit,' Davie whispered then jerked the actor to the side, placing himself between him and the street. He could hear the double footsteps speeding towards them. He handed Lassiter the dog's lead. The actor took it without a word and Davie flattened against the brickwork. Lassiter began to speak but Davie held up a hand. They were coming. They had been waiting for a chance to come for him and the move to the waste ground had been Davie's gift. He was confident they would think like him, would not want to risk witnesses. It was late, but anyone could peek through a window and see. Davie also wanted to control the situation, choose his ground. Lassiter was a complication he didn't need, but the American had something he could use. Davie snatched the umbrella from Lassiter's hands and waited.

They rushed round the corner of the wall too fast. They should've taken their time. They should've split up. Big mistake.

The one nearest Davie had an automatic pistol in his left hand, the other unarmed. Davie went for the gun first, slamming the hard wooden handle of Lassiter's expensive umbrella hard onto the wrist. When the gun didn't drop, he whipped the umbrella upwards, cracking the handle onto the bridge of the guy's nose.

The man's head snapped back, blood erupted and he staggered, his mate stepped forward so Davie swung his makeshift weapon again, jammed the curved handle into the man's eye. The second man yelped as Davie lashed out again with the umbrella, hitting him so hard on the temple that the thin alloy connecting the handle buckled. The man spun around, stunned, and Davie dropped the brolly, his attention reverting to the gunman, who was the most dangerous at this point. The man's eyes were streaming with tears and his nose gushed, but he was bringing the gun up again. Davie stepped in close, gripped the wrist, pivoted, then jerked his free elbow up into the man's face. The nose was already broken, another blow would have been excruciating. A third loosened his grip on the gun but his mate was closing in again. Davie kicked out and cracked the heel of his boot into the man's knee. He grunted but kept coming, so Davie did it again. This time the leg gave way and the man went down. Davie's elbow connected with the gunman's nose for the fourth time and he felt the hand relax enough for him to jerk the gun from between the fingers and throw it to Lassiter who, to his credit, caught it without thinking. Davie pushed the man backwards, spun and slammed his boot into his balls. The breath exploded from the man's lungs with an audible groan and he slipped on the snow. Davie whirled again, because the second guy was getting to his feet, a knife in his hand, edging forward, cagier now, knowing that Davie was no pushover. The man slashed the air in front of him to keep Davie away from him. He was limping and wanted time to let the pain pass. Davie knew he would have to hit that knee again soon. He circled, drawing him further away from Lassiter but also bringing his pal into his line of vision. The guy was beginning to draw himself to unsteady feet, in pain, but still a danger. Davie would have to move fast. The man with the knife sidled closer, the blade swinging up and down. Davie kept his distance, keeping his eye on the weapon, gauging the speed and trajectory. Then, just as the knife was at its highest, he lunged, intercepting the man's arm as it lashed down again, holding it tight with both hands while at the same time sending the toe of his boot flying into that weak knee. The man's face contorted with pain, but he continued pushing with the knife, trying to reach Davie's flesh. Davie held the arm steady and kicked again, putting every inch of power from his hip, thigh and calf into it and this time the man groaned in agony and began to slump. Davie knew he hadn't shattered the kneecap, but it wasn't far off it. He held onto the arm as the man slid, twisting and pulling until he heard something pop, and only then did the guy scream. Davie threw the knife to one side and launched himself at the disarmed gunman again, catching him full in the chest, the impetus of the charge carrying him back and up against the wall. The man pushed at Davie, trying to get away, but Davie grabbed him by the chin and thrust his head back, slamming it into the hard brick. Davie bounced the man's head off the wall once more then jerked him to the side, throwing him to the ground, where he sprawled, fingers splayed on the snow. Davie wasn't finished. The dark thing was in charge now and it would not be satisfied until both men were disabled. He stamped his foot onto the hand, grinding down until he heard the snap of the thin bones. A high-pitched screech burst from the man's throat and he rolled away. Davie knew that would hold him for a time and spun back towards the other attacker, who was sitting up holding his injured shoulder, obviously in agony. That wasn't good enough for Davie, who leaped closer, swinging with his foot again, this time to shatter the man's cheekbone. The man's head snapped to one side and he slumped into unconsciousness.

Lassiter, the gun held at his side in one gloved hand, stepped forward, his eyes darting from the prone figure to the first man, who had propped himself against the wall to nurse his shattered fingers. 'Jesus,' Lassiter said.

Davie shook his head to silence him, tented a tissue he'd taken from his pocket and used it to ease the gun from the actor's gloved hand. He realised the dog had watched everything without movement. Abe would've pitched in. There was still ground to be gained between him and this dog.

He stood over the first man and stared at him. He'd never seen him before. That didn't mean anything, though. He'd been attacked many times by men he'd never seen before.

'You've broken my fuckin hand, ya bastard,' the man said, his voice thin with pain. East coast accent, Davie noted. Again, didn't mean anything.

Davie glanced at the first attacker, who was still out cold. 'Yes, I did,' he said, softly.

'Ya bastard,' said the man again, his teeth gritted against the pain. 'Fuckin bastard.'

Davie thought the man's anger was misplaced, given he'd come at him with a gun, but he let it pass. 'Who sent you?'

'Fuck off.'

Lassiter opened his mouth to speak again but Davie shook his head to tell him to keep quiet and motioned for him to stay exactly where he was. With any luck, neither of these jokers had recognised him. There was a good chance, for Lassiter's hat, scarf and high coat collar did obscure his features pretty well. But Davie didn't want him to speak.

Davie knelt and pressed the pistol muzzle against the man's thigh. The man watched through eyes heavy with pain.

'Who sent you?' He asked again, his voice even. He might've been asking him the time.

The man smiled through his agony. 'You don't do guns, McCall. We all know that. That's why only one of us was tooled up.'

Davie pressed the gun deeper into the flesh. 'You sure about that?'

The man looked very confident. 'Aye.'

Davie stared at him. 'People change.'

A shake of the head. 'Not you. You're known for it. No guns, no killing.'

Davie was immobile for a few moments. Then he shrugged. 'You're right.' As he removed the gun from the thigh and straightened, Davie was aware of the man relaxing. He hadn't been that sure, then. Good to know. He looked down at him for a few moments then held the gun towards Lassiter, handle outwards. 'Shoot him, Jim.' Lassiter's eyes widened but he took the gun from Davie's grasp and turned it towards the man on the ground. The man tried to scramble away, but Davie placed his foot on his chest. 'Jim's not got my scruples.'

Lassiter must've been shit scared, but he held the gun steady. He was playing a role. This was what he did. Davie had banked on his craft coming to the fore and he played the part to the hilt, the unwavering muzzle pointed directly at the man's head. Even in the moonlight, Davie saw the injured man's face blanche even further.

'It was Maw Jarvis,' the words came out in a rush. 'Payback for Marko.'

Davie soaked the information in. Something deep down knew all along it would happen. He was seen to be close to Rab, so he would be fitting payback for the death of her son. A proportional response. 'Okay.' He took the gun from Lassiter's hand before stooping to retrieve the knife.

The man winced as something shot through him and he pulled his hand closer, as if he could squeeze off the pain. 'We'll get you for this, McCall.'

Davie turned slowly, his face blank, his blue eyes boring deep into the man's face. 'I wouldn't.'

The man tried to hold the stare but couldn't. Few could. His head dropped. He'd heard the stories. He'd met a boy who would never walk again after he tussled with Davie McCall. This was supposed to be a quick in and out job, wait for McCall to come out on his nightly walk, then jump him somewhere nobody would see, give him a going over. But it had gone sour and now Davie McCall knew what he looked like. The way he saw it, his mate's burst face and dislocated shoulder and his own broken hand and nose were a small price to pay.

Davie retrieved the broken umbrella and told Lassiter to wipe it and the gun clean. Lassiter did as he was told. Davie turned back towards Paton Street, Lassiter followed. 'Jesus, Davie...'

'Shut up,' Davie snapped.

Davie wiped the handle of the broken umbrella with the handkerchief then threw it over the fence into the bushes beside the railway track. The gun and the knife would have been harder to dispose of, which is why he left them. There was nothing to connect them to him or Lassiter so he felt it was safe. And neither of those guys was likely to be making a report to the police.

He took the dog's lead from Lassiter's hand, looked down at the animal walking beside him. The dog was with him, but was not yet his. He was there, but not really present. He felt disappointment hollow out his chest.

Was this how Vari felt?

Lassiter was silent as they walked along Duke Street. Davie knew he couldn't let him go anywhere alone, so he took him back to his flat, made them both a cup of coffee, made sure the dog had a long drink. The coffee tasted foul, but he didn't think the actor would notice. Lassiter was trembling as he sat in the armchair nearest to the gas fire. He accepted the mug with an unsteady hand and carefully laid it on the coffee table before he spilled it. Davie sat on the couch and took a sip, watching Lassiter over the rim of the mug. Lassiter saw his look and gave him a weak smile.

'I'm okay,' he said.

Davie sipped his coffee. Lassiter had just watched him disable two men. He'd aimed a live firearm at one of them himself. He'd done well, but he was far from okay.

'That was really something, Davie,' Lassiter said. 'I mean, I've never... well, you know.'

Davie knew. Lassiter lived a world of make-believe violence. It was seldom anything like the real thing. There were no fancy moves, no exotic martial arts, no stunt men to roll with the punches. In the real world, in Davie's world, it was quick and it was sharp and the idea was to do unto others before they did unto you.

'And you...' Lassiter said, then seemed to run out of words. He took a sip of his coffee, swallowed hard, as if trying to dislodge something in his throat. He shook his head. 'You were amazing. Incredible. I've never seen anything like it. You were so... efficient. Was there no fear?'

Davie thought of a windswept harbour and saw again the blood streaming from Audrey's throat and the words in her eyes.

You could have saved me.

Fear had made him hesitate that day. He had vowed he would never hesitate again. He banished the image and said, 'Fear cripples.'

'And what you said to that guy, when he said they'd get you –

"I wouldn't".' Lassiter's accent had changed into a passable Glasgow as he repeated Davie's words. He shook his head in admiration. 'I mean… wow. So simple. Economical.'

Davie sighed and set his mug down. 'This isn't a movie, Lassiter. You could've been killed out there.'

Lassiter shook his head. 'No,' he said, 'I saw the way you operated, the way you moved. You knew what needed to be done. Fast. Single-minded. And your face was calm all the way through it. Like it was frozen. There was nothing there, no emotion. No hate. No fear. No rage. Nothing.' Lassiter had leaned forward, his hand chopping the air in front of his face for emphasis. His trembling had stopped, replaced by eagerness. 'You had a job to do and you did it. I don't think I was in any danger at all tonight. Not with you there. That's why I need you for this project. I don't want this to be just another Hollywood movie, designer violence, style over substance. I want to do something real. I want it to be like that out there.' He gestured towards the window. 'This is my chance to do something with real meat. Okay, we've still got a story to tell and we've gotta get asses on seats, but I feel I've got a shot here. I can show them what I've got, inside me, you know? But I need you, Davie.'

Davie shook his head. 'Lassiter, listen to me. What you saw there was nothing. A boy died the other night, stabbed to death. Another died today, shot. It's not going to end there. I'm going to be in the middle of it. I don't want to be, but that – out there – means I'm in it whether I like it or not. Stay the hell away from me, understand? I'm not good for your health. I'm not good for anyone's health.'

But even as he spoke, he could tell that he wasn't getting anywhere. Lassiter had said it himself – he didn't take no for an answer. He wasn't used to people saying no. Davie sighed. It was a deep sigh, filled with resignation. *A man should always know when he's beaten, accept with grace and move on.* That's what Joe used to say.

'Okay,' said Davie with as much grace as he could muster. 'Here's the ground rules. One – you never come here again. I'll come to you.'

'Agreed.'

'Two – I give you one week. We'll go through the script, I'll point out what's bollocks. We don't discuss any real life situations, I don't introduce you to anyone. And you never – *never* – mention what you saw tonight to your friends, lovers, agent, shrink, whatever.'

'Agreed.'

'Three – you'll pay me £10,000.'

Lassiter's eyes widened at that. 'For one week's work?'

'And it won't be a full week – it'll be one meeting, once a day. You have any more questions after that, tough.'

Lassiter's eagerness was evident, but he was no pushover. 'Five grand.'

Davie gave him a thin smile. 'Fifteen.'

Lassiter paused, a smile beginning to grow. 'You'd do well in Hollywood. Ten it is.'

Davie nodded, satisfied. 'And four – you *never* come here.'

'That's the same as number one.'

'I know, that's how important it is. Deal?'

Lassiter stared at him for a second, an amused look on his handsome features. Then he pulled his coat from the back of the armchair, found the inside pocket and produced a chequebook and pen.

'Cash,' said Davie.

'I don't carry that kind of cash around with me.'

'It's okay, I trust you.'

Lassiter put the chequebook away then stood and held out his hand. Davie reached over the coffee table without standing and shook it. The actor's grip was strong and dry, but he held it for a moment longer than Glasgow propriety demanded. 'I want you to know,' he said, 'I would've paid you double.'

Davie laughed and wondered if he should say that he would've done it for free just to get the guy off his back.

TUESDAY

First thing in the morning, Davie went to The Black Bird to tell Rab of the previous night's events. Such matters were never discussed on the phone. Rab was on a war footing already and had arranged for one of the other boys to drive him to work. He didn't want the two of them to be in the same vehicle from now on. Davie spotted the guards in the street easily, which was fine, because they were supposed to be visible. There were more inside, all drinking coffee and tea because Rab had decreed there was to be no booze. Fat Boy McGuire and Choccie Barr sat in the corner, and Stringer, of course, off on his own, reading a Robert Ludlum novel. Kid Snot wasn't there, though. Davie was disappointed. He wanted a word with him about Lassiter.

There were no customers, not that day. Anyone who fancied a drink was told to try elsewhere. The Black Bird was closed for the time being. No explanation was given, it was all very polite. Unless someone turned stroppy, then politeness went the way of the dodo.

Rab was in his office. He listened quietly as Davie told him what happened, including Lassiter's involvement. The big man's face grew darker while Davie talked, then he launched himself from his chair and paced around the small office, a stream of invective flowing from his lips. Davie waited until the first gush of anger dried. Rab fell silent and sat back in his chair again.

'Come stay with us, Davie,' Rab offered, 'till it all blows over. You know you're welcome. Place is like a fuckin fortress, so it is. And Bernadette will be glad to see you. The kids, too.'

Davie knew he would be safer in Rab's Bothwell home. He knew it would be guarded round the clock and the layout of the cul-de-sac in which the expansive detached house sat made it hard for strangers to get by unnoticed. But he couldn't be that close to Bernadette, even though he'd turned a corner. He shook his head. 'I'm fine, Rab, thanks.'

There was a pause and Davie knew Rab was building up to something. He stooped to stroke the dog's head, then he looked around the room as if there was someone else to overhear and said quietly. 'I heard about Vari. You okay?' Rab was never good with personal matters. It took a lot for him to ask and, despite the growing distance between them, it showed they were still mates.

Something tightened in Davie's chest. He didn't know whether it was the mention of Vari or Rab's obvious concern. 'Aye. Happier on my own, you know that.'

'Okay.' Davie smiled at the relief in Rab's voice. 'This thing last night. You know this means you're in it, right?'

'I know.'

Rab nodded, satisfied. 'Okay. Good. C'mon, let's rally the troops.'

Davie grabbed the dog's lead and followed Rab into the bar. 'Right, lads, the Jarvis clan made a bid on Davie last night. That's two of their boys won't be coming out to play for a wee while.'

A chuckle rippled round the room. Everyone except Stringer, who kept reading.

'So,' Rab went on, 'we know they're coming after us. We all need to be on our guard, right? We...' He stopped as he scanned the room. A face was missing. 'Where the fuck's the Kid?'

'Said he had to see a guy,' said Fat Boy.

Rab frowned. 'He's no on his own, is he?'

'Well,' Fat Boy said, his bulk shifting in his chair, 'I don't think the guy's a guy, know what I'm sayin, Rab?'

'What the fuck did I tell you lot?' Rab's voice exploded round the bar. He was a big man and he had a voice to match. Even Stringer looked up. 'We don't go anywhere on our tod. We go somewhere, we take a coupla lads with us. Fuck's sake – everyone in this room is a target. Where is this guy who's no a guy?'

Fat Boy looked ashamed. He glanced at Choccie for help but he looked away, telling him he was on his own. 'Dunno, Rab...'

'So you're telling me the Kid's out there, on his own, God knows where?'

Fat Boy defended himself. 'It's no my fault, Rab. I'm no his faither.'

Rab opened his mouth and closed it again. Fat Boy was right, the Kid was a big boy and he should've known better.

Davie said, 'He's been seeing someone in Cumbernauld – the wife of Jojo Donnelly.'

Rab nodded. 'Stringer, find him, get him back here. And don't none of you move from this bar unless I say so.'

Rae Donnelly was in her thirties and lived in a split-level terraced house in Ravenswood, one of the older areas of what used to be the new town of Cumbernauld. She had a head of thick, black hair that the Kid longed to run his hands through. A raven-haired beauty, his dad would call her, which fitted with her neighbourhood. If she was a redhead, she'd be a flame-haired beauty to his old dad. Blondes were golden-haired beauties. Even if none of them were that beautiful. But she was raven-haired and it was luxurious, long and lovely.

The Kid had said he'd get over to see her that day. He didn't think it would do any harm, he'd only be gone for an hour or so. He'd been working on her for weeks. Her man was doing five for punting weed and wasn't due out for another year. The Kid had been doing her wee favours – taking her shopping, picking her boy up from school, doing odd jobs around the house – all designed to ingratiate himself. He even managed to control his sniff reflex when he was around her. That morning, she'd complained she hadn't seen him for a few days, so he took that as a good sign. He said he'd get over that day. He was as good as his word.

It looked promising when she met him at the door wearing her dressing gown. It was half eleven in the morning and she was still in her nightie under it. At least that's what he assumed. Then he thought, *what if she's no wearing nothing under it? Hey, what if this is it, finally?* The Kid had to admit he felt a slight *frisson* at the thought, even though he hadn't the first clue what the fuck a *frisson* was. He'd seen the word in a book and he assumed it meant the electric tingle that spread from his groin. Maybe pretty soon they'd be *frissoning* like rabbits.

She made him a cup of tea, asked him if he wanted a slice of toast. He declined, thinking *what I want is a slice of morning glory, darling.* They sat in the living room downstairs, sipping the tea, an electric fire burning between them doing its best to heat the room. Her boiler had packed up, she said, as usual on the coldest night of the year so far. Not that the year was all that old, right enough.

They talked about the snow and how she had got her son to clear the pathway outside the front door. He was only fourteen, she said, be a man before she knew it.

The Kid soon realised, with great disappointment, that she had no carnal motive. Sometimes a dressing gown is just a dressing gown. Rae was no skank, she was just lonely. She missed her man. Her son was growing up before her very eyes. She was getting older. She enjoyed the attentions of a younger man, but she had no intention of doing anything about it. The Kid realised all this while he sat and politely nodded as she talked about her son, the snow, the dodgy gas boiler and, for all he knew, the price of fish, because he stopped listening halfway through.

The doorbell rang and she looked flustered. 'That'll be the gas man about the boiler. Do me a favour, let him in. I can't open the door to someone like this.' When he nodded she added, 'Let me nip upstairs and get dressed, will you?'

He let her slide past him in the hallway, enjoying the fleeting sensation of her body brushing his, then she darted up the stairs to the mid-level where the front door stood and on up the second flight of stairs to the bedrooms on the top level. The Kid followed her, his disappointment weighing him down. He really thought this was the day. Maybe it was time he gave this up as a lost cause.

He could see the smudged outline of a man through the frosted glass and the lacy curtain. He heard Rae's bedroom door close and then he turned the lock, sniffing as he did so.

The first thing he saw was the over-and-under barrels of the shotgun staring right at him. Then he was aware of the bloke behind it, his face obscured by a balaclava.

'How you doin, Kid?' said a voice muffled by the thick fabric of the balaclava. The blast blew holes in the Kid's chest in an eruption of blood and cloth and bits of bone and threw him back onto the stairs. The Kid didn't see Jerry Jarvis look around him to ensure no-one saw before sprinting back along the pathway alongside the row of terraced house. The Kid was unaware of Rae rushing down the stairs. The Kid didn't get to enjoy the sight of her dressing gown flapping open to reveal a thin nightgown. The

Kid would've liked that, if he could've seen it. But the Kid couldn't
see it. He couldn't hear her scream. He couldn't feel her raven hair
gently brushing his face as she leaned over him. He wouldn't see
or hear anything ever again.

It was already noon, but Davie guessed Lassiter was not an early
riser, for he'd been waiting ten minutes and he still hadn't emerged
from his bedroom. Mannie was there, though, and Davie took the
opportunity to deliver a warning. He gave the big guy a hard look
and said, 'Never let your boss go off on his own again.' Mannie
blinked but said nothing. Davie was taciturn, but he realised this
guy had turned it into an art form. 'You understand?'

Mannie blinked again and Davie thought he saw something
like belligerence cross the broad face. Davie tensed, wondering if
the bloke would take a swing. If he did he'd move fast, pick up the
heavy ashtray he saw on the coffee table and go to work. Davie
had already identified it as a possible weapon, should he need it.
It was something he'd done almost unconsciously, along with
checking out the exits. He knew he couldn't take Mannie without
a weapon, he was too big. But Mannie simply nodded and looked
away. He knew he'd screwed up and he was man enough to admit
it. He was silent and he admitted his mistakes. They'd get along.

The door to Lassiter's bedroom opened and Davie had a glimpse
of a big bed and Coco's naked back as she slept on her stomach.
It was tanned and smooth and delicately muscled. So she assisted
the actor in that way, too. That's showbiz.

'Davie,' said Lassiter, his voice hoarse. He coughed, trying to
clear it, not managing. 'Come for the script?'

Davie nodded. Lassiter moved to the table by the window and
lifted an inch-thick bound sheaf of paper. He crossed the room,
holding it out. As he got closer, Davie could see his eyes were
red-rimmed, as if they'd been sewn in with red thread. And his
hand trembled slightly. He'd had one hell of a party, right enough,
probably came back the night before and hit the medicine. Fair
enough, Davie thought, we all unwind in different ways. In Lassiter's
case it was drugs and, Davie assumed, sex with Coco. For others it

would be drink. For himself, after Lassiter had left, he had listened to music, let Nat King Cole's smooth voice sooth him. It was a greatest hits album and it worked, particularly 'Nature Boy', a song Davie found hauntingly beautiful.

During one of their many nights playing chess and listening to music, Jos Klein had once told him that the singer had a rough time in the entertainment business, thanks to his colour. Cole himself thought the executives were 'afraid of the dark.' Davie did not understand prejudice, whether racial or religious, but he knew all about fear of the dark.

'Have a read, let me know,' said Lassiter, his voice still scraping like a match on sandpaper. Davie nodded, flipped through the pages. It had a strange format, all 'INT: CITY STREET – NIGHT' and the dialogue was centred under character names, but he'd get the hang of it.

'I appreciate you doing this,' the actor said. 'It'll make all the difference, you know?'

Davie didn't know if he would make a difference or not, but he'd made a deal and he'd see it through. 'I'll come back tomorrow,' he said.

Lassiter said, 'Take a coupla days. Read, digest.'

'I'll come back tomorrow,' Davie repeated. He'd made a deal, but he wanted this done quickly. 'There's something else you need to give me, too.'

Lassiter looked puzzled, then he recalled their bargain. The money. 'Sure, Coco'll get it for you today. Tomorrow then. We'll make a start.'

DCI Bolton didn't ask Knight to sit down. Knight would've found it funny if it wasn't so pathetic. All this over a bit of fanny. The thing was, old by-the-book hadn't even been married to the cow when Knight was shagging her, so what the hell was he getting all bent out of shape for? She knew the score, knew he was a bit of a lad – truth be told, that was what she'd liked about him, Knight was certain of that. But here was Bolton, keeping him standing in front of his desk like a cadet about to get his arse felt, nose buried in some file or other. Knight had been in Stewart Street the day before but Bolton had been 'too busy' to see him. A smile teased Knight's lips. It was all a game. Knight may be a DI, but Bolton was a DCI and this was a show of power.

'Something funny, Knight?' Bolton was looking at him, having finally lifted his face from the file.

'Naturally jovial, Scotty, you know me.'

'Yeah, you're just a ray of sunshine. And it's DCI Bolton or Sir. Keep that in mind.'

Jumped up wee shite. 'Understood.' He paused before he spoke again, just to show Bolton what he thought. 'Sir.'

Bolton sat back in his chair. 'Let's get something clear right away – I don't want you here. I think you're trouble. Jack Bannatyne might think the sun shines out of your jacksey, but I don't.' He leaned forward again. 'But I'm lumbered with you, nothing much I can do about it. So I'm warning you, Knight, I don't want any of your shit here, right? You'll do things my way, or not at all. Is that clear?'

Knight smiled at him. 'As the proverbial crystal.' He fell silent for a couple of beats again, then said, 'Sir.' He hoped he made the single word sound like *and I hope your next shite's a hedgehog.* 'So, what would you like me to do? Sir?'

If Bolton caught the disrespect in Knight's tone, he didn't show it. 'The vagrant who'd been dossing in the alleyway. We're drawing a blank. Not surprising really, these people don't tend to leave a trail. All we know is his street name is Scratchy. I think he saw something and he's making himself invisible. You're well acquainted with the low lives of Glasgow, Knight, so I want you to bring your particular skills to bear. Find him. Find him fast.'

'You've got two bodies already. You think some jakey will add anything concrete?'

'An eye witness is always good, Knight.'

'What about the lassie and the junkie?'

Bolton shook his head. 'She's in no state. Under sedation. She was as pissed as a fart anyway. She says she can't ID anyone. As for the junkie…' Bolton gave the notion a dismissive shrug.

'This guy you're looking for is probably out of it most of the time, too. And he might not even have been there.'

'We won't know that until we find him, will we? And I'm not looking for him, Knight – you are.'

Knight tilted his head, giving in. 'You're the boss.'

'Yes,' said Bolton, 'I am.'

Davie sat in what had once been Rab's bedroom in the Sword Street flat, but had now been given over to Joe the Tailor's record collection. The old man had loved crooners – Sinatra, Martin, Crosby – and Davie had developed a taste for them, too. But he had also come to enjoy the swing music of the '30s and '40s. Joe's extensive collection contained a number of albums, all lovingly cared for, by the likes of Tommy Dorsey, Duke Ellington, Stan Kenton, Benny Goodman and the rest. He was listening to Artie Shaw's version of 'Stardust' and the plaintive horn was ideal for his mood. He was staring at Audrey's face, drawn from memory. It was a skill he'd discovered while inside. Now he sketched whenever he was alone. He'd sit in this room, music playing on Joe Klein's old stereo, wishing that the old man's voice would echo from the speakers. He had hundreds of sketches, all hidden away where no-one would find them. It relaxed him. He'd draw faces he'd seen during the day, faces – like Audrey's – from the past. Landscapes, some of the city, others of vistas he'd only seen in photographs.

He laid the pencil portrait on top of the wide arm of the armchair and looked at another drawing. Vari, drawn from life. She was the only person who had ever sat for him, the only person who had seen his work. He'd not shown Rab, who would have thought it poofy. He'd not even shown Bobby. He looked at Vari's pretty face and remembered it in the flesh, her blue eyes smiling at him, always trying to draw him out of himself. And he recalled other things. The feel of her cool lips. The touch of her hand on his body. Her fragrance. Her taste.

All she had wanted was for him to let her in. He'd wanted it, too. But there was always something holding him back. And he'd been too willing to succumb to Bernadette. Sure, he'd stopped it before it went too far, but still...

Vari was a nice person, despite the troubles of her past, and she deserved better. Davie knew he was not a nice person. He was the bad guy and no good came of growing too close to him. So he had kept her at arm's length. It was the right thing to do. At least, that's what he told himself.

The doorbell snatched him from his thoughts and he carefully placed the drawings into the centre of the double album of 'Frank Sinatra: A Man and His Music,' one of Joe's favourites, and gently slid the album back into its place on the shelves lined with precious vinyl. The rest were spread throughout Joe's old records, where no-one would ever look. As he moved into the hallway he heard someone stamping their feet on the stone floor outside, dislodging snow from shoes.

He opened the door and a face he hadn't seen for five years looked up. Davie was speechless for a second.

'Davie,' said Sammy.

'Sammy,' Davie said, a grin spreading, 'when'd you get out?'

They shook hands, but he noticed Sammy wasn't smiling back. He looked a lot older, the lines around his eyes deeper, his body slimmer, more stooped. They'd spent a lot of time together in the Bar-L, where Sammy had kept him from his own stupidity when the system turned harsh, helped him see that being a troublesome prisoner was self-defeating. You couldn't beat the system, it was too big. Sammy had told him to do his time, get out and don't let the bastards grind you down. The old guy hadn't taken the place of Joe Klein, but he came close.

'Coupla months ago,' said Sammy. 'November.'

Two months. 'Why'd you not come see me? Phone?'

Sammy didn't answer the question. Instead he said, 'You gonnae invite me in, son, or keep me standing here like a fuckin milk bottle?'

Davie apologised and stepped back. He watched Sammy's face as he passed. He'd seen that look of grim determination before. Davie had barely stepped into the cell they shared for the first time before Sammy began a lecture on the stupidity of fighting the system. He sensed something similar was coming. He offered a cup of tea but Sammy declined. He didn't take off his thick coat. He didn't take off his gloves. He stood in the living room and Davie could feel the older man was on edge.

'What's up, Sammy?'

Sammy was silent for a moment, but his eyes continued to betray him. Something was worrying him. He needed help. But he was finding it hard to ask.

'Sammy,' said Davie, 'it's me. What is it?'

Sammy swallowed. 'You mind when we was in the jail and I told you about your dad?' Davie nodded. Sammy had known his father in the old days and had given him some insight. Not enough, though, for the man Davie finally faced was not the Danny McCall Sammy had known. 'Mind I told you that when the devil came knocking...'

'And you either let him in or told him where to go? Sure, Sammy, I remember it all.'

Sammy stared straight into Davie's eyes. *Here it comes*, Davie thought. 'I didn't come see you before now because I've heard a lot about you since you got out. The devil came knocking, didn't he? And you let him in, didn't you, son?'

Davie felt his breath freeze. After Joe the Tailor, this man was the one person in the world he looked up to and he knew now that he had let him down. Sammy was an old lag, he knew the score – he wasn't inside for going through a red light – but he had warned Davie about the dangers of the dark thing. He'd told him that it would consume him if he let it, just as it had his father. Davie had vowed it would never happen to him. And it hadn't. Not yet. But it was close.

'So, you asked me why I never got in touch when I got out. I'll ask you something – why'd you never come see me while I was still inside?'

Davie shifted his feet like a schoolboy caught with his hand in the biscuit tin. Sammy nodded, knowing the answer to his question.

'You didn't come to see me because you knew I'd spot it in you.

And I didn't come and see you because I didn't think I'd find the young guy I knew inside.'

Davie sat down on the couch. He didn't know what to say. Sammy watched him then seated himself in the nearest armchair. 'I've heard the stories, son. Lots of stories. Blokes would come in the jail, talk about the outside. Your name would be mentioned, how you did this fella or that fella. One bloke told me what you did to him, beat him down, battered fuck out of him, kicked him. Broke his arm, fractured three ribs. Knocked him cold.'

Davie's voice was flat. 'What was his name?' Sammy told him. Davie tried to remember, but he couldn't. There were so many.

Sammy watched him trying to recall the incident and coming up with nothing. He exhaled in disappointment. 'I heard what happened with your dad, terrible business, right enough. But you've let what lives inside you take over. You've let Danny take over.'

Davie looked up then, some heat returning to his voice. 'I'm not like him. I'm nothing like him.'

Sammy conceded the point with a tilt of the head. 'Maybe no. Not yet. You still follow old Joe's rules and that's something, at least. But you've hurt people. For Rab. For the business.'

Davie glanced away. 'I didn't hurt anyone who didn't deserve it.'

Sammy shook his head and Davie knew he'd said the wrong thing. He'd hurt people simply because Rab had wanted him to do it. He still followed the rules – no women, no children, no civilians – but anyone else was fair game. That was his world now. He understood why Sammy had stayed away and he didn't blame him. He'd been a handy bloke in his day, an armed robber, a hard man. Until he was banged up for killing an old man during a bank raid. He hadn't pulled the trigger, but he'd been there all the same. Even so, he'd kicked against the system in the jail – attacking the screws, waging war with dirty protests. When Davie met him he'd calmed down, but he was no pushover, as some boys found out when they stepped over a line. But Davie knew that all he wanted to do was complete his lengthy sentence, get out and get back with his family. With Davie being the way he was, Sammy would not have risked being drawn back into The Life.

'So why are you here, Sammy?'

Sammy's jaw clenched and he began to blink rapidly. Davie could tell this wasn't easy for him. 'I need your help.'

'With what?'

'My grandson – I told you I had kids?' Davie nodded, glad the focus was away from him. 'He's in trouble.'

'What kind of trouble?'

Sammy hesitated. 'He's basically a good lad, but he's got into the wrong company. You know how it is.'

Davie nodded. He knew how it was. To some, he was the wrong company.

'My lassie, she's done her best,' Sammy went on. 'Tried to keep him out of trouble, him and his wee brother both. Her man's away most of the time, works the rigs.'

Davie said softly, 'What kind of trouble is he in, Sammy?'

The old man looked away, ashamed. 'They've charged him with murder. They say he's killed one of your mate Rab's lads. In some club down the town.'

The Dickie Himes murder. 'Which is he, Bonner or Moore?'

Sammy closed his eyes, took a deep breath and said. 'His name's Martin Bonner. But he didn't do it, I know him, he couldn't.' Sammy opened his eyes and Davie saw the anger and defiance he'd seen back in the jail. 'He's being fitted up, Davie.'

Jimmy Knight's Uncle Charlie had been a copper, spent thirty years in the blue, walking the city streets, never made it out of uniform. Knight had seen photographs of him in uniform, a big man, a powerful man, the kind of man you wouldn't want to cross. However, his memory of him was of a man who had been eaten away by cancer, lying in a scabby hospital bed in striped flannel pyjamas, talking about the old days in a voice coarsened with disease and medication. The young Jimmy wanted to be a policeman when he grew up so Uncle Charlie told him stories of the glories of the Force. He also told him about the 'bonuses' he got on the beat – bottles of whisky here and there, the occasional couple of quid from reporters looking for some tip or other, a freebie from a tart up a back close.

'But that was nothing,' the old man rasped, his hand gripping the boy's wrist, the bones shining white through the dying flesh, 'nothing to what some of the CID boys could make. Listen to me, son, if you want to get ahead, get a hat, get a hat...'

He was talking about the then Head of CID's insistence that all his plainers wear a hat of some kind. To hear Uncle Charlie talk, there wasn't a straight cop in CID, they all had their nose dipped in some trough or other. When Knight joined the Force and eventually got into CID, he found that wasn't the case. There were strokes pulled, certainly, but only the occasional bad apple. Knight, though, had decided that he would not end up like Uncle Charlie. Cancer aside, the old guy died with barely a pot to piss in – and that was owned by the NHS. No, Jimmy Knight would not die in some hospital bed in a cheap pair of pyjamas. When he went, he'd be wearing silk with a shapely blonde by his side. Maybe two. The Job paid peanuts, but he was no monkey. So he kept his eyes and ears open, always on the lookout for the main chance. He'd spotted Rab McClymont early on, recognised a kindred spirit, forged an alliance. It had proved mutually beneficial over the years. There were others, for Knight had more strings to his bow than a paranoid archer. He did not kid himself, though. He knew he was corrupt. He didn't try to justify it to himself, didn't analyse it. He was a crooked cop and that was the way he liked it, because it brought him money, it brought him the recreational stimulants he enjoyed during his off hours and it brought him women. A certain type of woman, sure, but that was what he liked. He had a wife at home and a daughter heading into her teenage years with his dark looks but too much weight. He'd married because it was an aid to upward mobility on the Job – the bosses liked to see a man settled. The missus was a quiet girl, didn't ask too many questions, accepted that he was away from home a lot. *Pressures of the job, dear.* She had a nice house in Milngavie, two foreign holidays a year, her own four-wheel drive, enough money to buy nice things. He threw her the occasional shag, strictly missionary position, never forgot her birthday or Mother's Day or their anniversary. She was happy. The fact of the matter was, she was none-too-bright, but that suited Knight right down to the ground. He was able to juggle his work life and his home life and his real life with ease.

The thing was, he was a good copper. He'd risen to DI because he brought in the bodies. Sure, sometimes it was thanks to Big Rab and his other associates steering info his way for their own reasons, like the two Jarvis busts he'd dutifully passed onto the drug squad. But he actually had a talent for detective work. He was not afraid to do the footwork, to hit the cobbles and dig around in the gutters.

So when he embarked on his hunt for the vagrant called Scratchy, he was confident that, sooner or later, he'd find him. In addition to not doing sentiment, Jimmy Knight didn't do self-doubt. That was for losers, the going nowheres, like Frank Donovan.

He'd grabbed a couple of hours sleep earlier and it set him up for pounding the streets that night. It was cold, but that didn't bother him, for he had a thick coat and a hip flask with some single malt, the rest of the bottle waiting in the car. He liked it cold, the weather anyway. Cold and dry. Unlike his women, who he liked hot and wet. The thought raised an image of the blonde waitress he planned on visiting later. He'd told his wife he'd be out all night working and it was partly true. He'd be out all night, but he wouldn't be working all that time. Not police work, anyway. The blonde lived up Balornock way and after a few hours' spade-work, he'd head up there and unwind. Some whisky, some blow and so to bed. The lassie was very inventive and fond of a wee bit of kinkiness. His kinda gal.

He hit the Great Eastern Hotel first. He always smiled when he thought of the suffix 'hotel' for this massive, imposing building on Duke Street. He used to pass it when he was a boy, as his parents drove into the city centre, and he'd see the grey men hanging around outside. They all looked the same, the men. Ragged and lost. The building was grey, too, but even the young Knight could tell it had been impressive once. He'd asked his dad why those men were always lurking there and was told it was their home. Little Jimmy thought about that and said, 'They live in a hotel all the time?'

'It's not a hotel, son,' his dad said. 'It's a doss house. Those men are homeless. Tramps. They don't live there all the time, they move around.'

Then his father told him the building used to be a cotton spinning mill, but it became the hostel before World War One. He said the Molendinar Burn, which was part of the Dear Green Place that St Mungo found when he settled way back when, ran down beside it. Knight's dad loved his bit of history. Knight himself couldn't give a toss.

As a cop, Knight had been in the hotel many times. He hated to return. It always reeked of disinfectant, but then, that was necessary, for personal hygiene was not top of the residents' agenda. He'd been in one of the rooms upstairs, only once, but that was enough. A dosser had died suddenly and he'd been part of the police team called in. There was nothing suspicious about the death, the guy's body had just given up the ghost, but they still needed to attend. Knight had stood in the centre of the room, unwilling to let any part of him touch anything in it. He swore blind he could see lice crawling up the walls and the unmade bed was stained with who knew what. The first thing he'd done when he got home was throw off all his clothes and shower.

Now, as he stood outside the arched doorway of the bleak six-story structure, he could feel his skin crawl. He didn't plan to get any further than the entrance. He'd talk to the bloke in charge, ask about Scratchy and move onto the other moadels – as the hostels were known – in Minerva Street, the Gallowgate, Abercomby Street, London Road. He planned to hit them all over the next couple of days and nights. He'd find Scratchy. He knew it.

But not that first night. He met blank stares or shaking heads. Sometimes just a defiant silence. But was he discouraged? Was he hell. He'd find the guy. Only a matter of time.

He was bright and chirpy as he drove out to Balornock, some whisky in his system, a cigarillo in his mouth and thoughts of kinky fuckery in his head.

WEDNESDAY

'How did you get the scar on your face?'

Davie felt the wound burn when Lassiter asked the question. 'Occupational hazard.'

He would never tell him how he got the scar. He had another one on his chest, not as deep as the one on his face, but there all the same. There was a third on his thigh, all left there by his own father. Even so, his mind flashed to the carpet knife and the sting as his flesh was ripped.

He pushed the memories and the voices out of his mind and tapped the script on his lap. 'The guy that wrote this has never been to Glasgow, has he?'

Lassiter sat back in the luxurious armchair in his hotel suite and shook his head. 'Coupla times, maybe. It was originally written for Seattle, but I wanted to give it a fresh background, one that's never been used in the movies. Does it show?'

Davie nodded. 'To me. To anyone from Glasgow. Maybe not outside it.'

He'd already pointed out some errors in the script, including mention of the Crown Prosecution Service, which did not operate in Scotland, and coroner's inquests, which did not apply either. 'You've got too many guns. They're still not that common here.'

That was changing, though. There had been too many guns around before, as far as Davie was concerned, and now it was even worse. Rab was ensuring his guys were tooled up after Kid Snot's death. He imagined the same was happening over in Possil, where Maw Jarvis lived. Guns, too many guns – and some in the hands of boys who should never be near a cap pistol, let alone a real firearm.

'And your fight scenes – too long, too drawn out. The idea is to put the other guy down, as fast as you can. And keep the punching to a minimum. You ever punched someone?' Lassiter shook his head. 'It hurts, even if you land it right. Use your feet, use whatever comes to hand, bounce heads against walls.' Lassiter nodded and Davie knew he was recalling the fight from the other night. 'And when you know someone's got a weakness, use it. If you've damaged a knee, keep going for it, damage it some more. It's not fair, it's not nice, but you fight to win. There's no Marquis of Queensberry rules on the street.'

Lassiter was scribbling Davie's thoughts on the pages of his own copy of the script. He nodded as he wrote. 'Yeah, yeah, great.'

Davie closed the bound copy of the script he had been reading and dropped it on the low coffee table between them. He hadn't spoken that much in one go in a long time. It felt alien to him.

Coco was sprawled along the couch, the latest issue of *Cosmopolitan* propped up on her stomach. When Davie looked at her he found her watching him over the top of the pages, as if she was assessing him. She smiled at him, then focussed on her magazine again.

Mannie was filling one of the armchairs, making it look like a piece of childlike furniture. He still hadn't said a word and Davie was impressed.

'Okay,' said Lassiter, re-reading his notes. 'This is all great stuff, Davie, really great stuff. I think a lot of this will play, make that script better. What do you think?'

Davie shrugged. He didn't know whether the script was good or bad. All he knew was that its contents were as close to his reality as *The Lion King* was to life among the lions.

'Could we run through some ideas for the fight scene between my character and the heavy? Maybe using some of the moves I saw the other night?'

Davie gave him a stone-faced look then flicked his gaze to Coco once more. Lassiter's expression was open, he didn't realise he'd mentioned something he shouldn't. He followed Davie's eyes and then understood. 'It's okay, Coco's cool. She knows what happened. Mannie, too.'

Davie wondered what part of not telling anyone Lassiter didn't quite grasp, but it did explain why Mannie accepted Davie's instruction the day before so easily.

'Yeah,' Coco said, lowering her magazine and looking right into Davie's eyes. 'Thanks for looking after Mickey. Thank God you were there.'

If Mickey hadn't been following me, he would never have been in any danger, Davie thought, but he didn't say it. He sighed, wishing he'd never become mixed up with this actor in the first place. God knows what else he'd told his assistant.

'So what do you think, Davie? You and me, go through a few moves? Then I can present them to the fight arranger?'

Davie nodded. He'd been paid, after all. The money sat in a brown paper bag on the table in front of him. 'Tomorrow,' he said.

Frank Donovan sipped his drink as he waited for Davie McCall to arrive. He'd selected this pub near St Enoch Square because it would be quiet, even at lunchtime. When Davie phoned him, saying he needed to talk, he knew it would be something important. Davie McCall didn't contact him otherwise. Davie wouldn't like a crowded place, so Frank suggested the pub.

Davie McCall. He often wondered about their relationship. They weren't friends, they weren't enemies. Davie was not a tout. Donovan was a cop, McCall was a crook, but over the years their paths had crossed more than once. Trust is what it boiled down to. Donovan trusted McCall and he believed that trust was reciprocated.

He took another sip of his whisky and water. He'd intended just having the water, but changed his mind at the last minute. He'd been drinking too much, far too much. He thought it would take the edge off his worries, but it didn't. He recalled a line he'd seen on a mug once – *I tried to drown my troubles, but the little bastards learned to swim.* He had a few days left to find the cash to pay off his debt, otherwise Bang Bang Maxwell would do his thing. The problem was, he didn't have all the money. He'd slammed another 50 on a horse the day before, which had romped home at 8–1. He was still short by 600, at least. He hadn't slept properly for days, what rest he'd had was fitful, troubled. He had taken to avoiding Marie altogether now, because he couldn't look her in the eye. He knew he was looking rough, Knight hadn't been wrong. Bolton had been looking at him strangely, too, which only added to his worries. He was a good boss, but if he ever found out he'd got himself into hock with a moneylender, he'd have him bounced out the job quicker than he could say Police Federation. He had to find the rest of the cash, somehow, somewhere.

Davie McCall pushed through the pub's doors, followed by an older man with thick white hair and prison pallor. Donovan could spot an old lag a mile off. There was something about the way they moved through their space like it was a gift. McCall spotted Donovan at the corner table and nodded. As he neared the table, Donovan saw his eyes flick from the half-finished whisky to the clock on the wall and thought, *that's right, the sun's not over the yardarm yet.* McCall didn't say a word, though. He jerked a thumb in the older man's direction. 'This is Sammy. He's an old friend. Sammy, Frank Donovan.'

Donovan held out his hand, Sammy took it, then sat down in the wooden chair across the small round table from Donovan. Davie walked to the bar, leaving them alone. Donovan felt he had to say something. 'So, how do you know Davie?'

'The Bar-L,' said Sammy, without hesitation, and Donovan mentally complimented himself. Barlinnie jail. Now, if he could just find a way to make money out of spotting former prisoners, he'd be a happy man. Sammy went on, 'We shared a peter.'

Peter, old slang for any kind of lockfast place. It could mean a safe, hence the term *Peterman* for a safe blower, or a prison cell. *You're a mine of information, Frankie,* he told himself, *none of it profitable.*

Donovan saw that McCall was still waiting to be served, the barmaid being busy taking a late lunch order from two young guys who looked like students. Donovan drained his glass and asked, 'What's this about, Sammy?'

'Martin Bonner is my grandson.'

Donovan couldn't help but feel ambushed. His voice was calm but cold when he said, 'I can't help you.'

'Hear us out...'

'No, I'm investigating your grandson's case.'

'What I've got to say can be part of your investigation.'

Donovan thought about it. Maybe there was something he could learn from the grandfather. One of the other detectives had spoken to Bonner's mother and got nothing out of her. Maybe this guy had something to say. Davie came back carrying a pint of Guinness for Sammy and two Cokes, one of which he laid down in front of Donovan. The cop looked at the glass and then at McCall's blank face. Donovan almost smiled. McCall didn't look much like anyone's guardian angel. Davie sat down in a chair against the wall, right in the corner. Donovan had chosen the table specifically with Davie in mind. He knew he'd take that seat, for it gave him a clear view of the rest of the bar. He'd come to know the man quite well.

'Your pal here just told me he's Bonner's granddad,' said Donovan. 'You should've told me that on the phone.'

'You wouldn't have come.'

'I'd've liked the choice.'

McCall gave a little jerk of his head. Donovan didn't know if it was dismissive or apologetic, McCall being a hard bastard to read. 'You're here now. Listen to us.'

'Why?'

'Because we may be able to help.'

Donovan looked from McCall to the old man. 'Were you in the alley that night?'

'No.'

'Have you spoken to your grandson about it?'

'No.'

'Then how can you help?'

Sammy's face was stony as he said, 'He didn't do it, Mister Donovan.'

'We've got evidence that said he did.'

'You've got evidence that says he was there, maybe. But he didn't stab that guy.'

Donovan picked up his glass and took a mouthful. He couldn't help but agree with the old man. 'Let's say that's true. How can you help?'

McCall spoke. 'We can speak to people who won't speak to you.'

Donovan shook his head. 'It's an open and shut case, Davie. Bonner and his pal did it.'

'You're not interested in the truth,' accused Sammy, his voice sharp.

'The truth is whatever the evidence supports.'

'Fuckin shite, that.' There was a fire burning in Sammy's eyes now and Donovan could tell this old guy had been something in his day. Donovan felt pity for him, even though he didn't know him. The vehemence in his tone drew a glance from the barmaid. She watched them to ensure they weren't going to cause a disturbance. Donovan smiled at her and waved, telling her everything was fine.

Sammy asked, 'What led you to my boy from the start?'

Donovan sighed. 'Look, I can't discuss this...'

Davie cut him off. 'We heard you found a blade with Marty's blood on it.'

Donovan wasn't surprised Davie knew. Things like that had a way of leaking. 'That's right.'

'How'd you find it?'

Donovan sipped his drink and gave Davie a half-smile. 'A tout of Jimmy Knight's.'

'Knight? He's on this?' Davie was even more alert. He'd had dealings with the Black Knight in the past, none of them pleasurable. 'If Knight's bringing evidence, you know it's dodgy.'

Donovan sighed. Davie had put into words what he'd felt from the start.

'I take it there were no eye witnesses?' Davie asked.

'Young girl, but she said she didn't get a clear view. She was out there with her boyfriend. He was the second victim. We think he tried to stop them as they ran away. The girl's a mess, too traumatised to talk sense. But we're going to run her past an ID Parade soon as we can. There's a junkie, too, but he's as much use as a chocolate fireguard.' He paused, wondering now if he had said too much. Then he thought, *to hell with it – I've gone this far.* 'We're trying to trace a homeless person who'd been dossing in the alleyway for a while. We don't know for certain he was there, but we need to trace him to make sure. Problem is, all we've got is a nickname.'

'What's that?' Davie asked.

'Scratchy. He's not been seen since the night of the murders. He might've seen something, but we've hit a dead end. Can't find him.'

Davie nodded. 'That's where we come in, then.'

Scratchy was on the move again. He had to keep moving. Couldn't sit still. He'd been going from one place to another, never felt safe, never felt secure. So he kept moving.

And there was that big cop. He knew he was a cop. It was in his eyes, in the way he held himself. Scratchy had seen him the night before, at a moadel. Asking questions. Asking about him. But Scratchy was clever. He kept on the move. Kept out of reach. Scratchy knew the city, knew his way around, knew the dark, secret places. The cop wouldn't know them, couldn't know them, because he'd never been street. Only those who were street knew them.

Scratchy was under the iron bridge stretching across the Clyde from Central Station. There were other people like him there too, but he was uneasy. He could see the water. He did not like the water. The water made him remember and he did not want to remember. But as he lay on the narrow spar, he could hear it gurgling away beneath him, flowing to the sea, and it was on the sea that it happened.

Scratchy heard the screaming again.

Scratchy heard the agony of the dying men.

Scratchy could smell the flesh burning.

His flesh.

He could feel it now, his skin shrivelling, drying, contracting on one side of his face, down his neck and over his shoulder where it was bouldered with scar tissue. Scratchy closed his eyes and heard the *crump* of the Exocet slamming into the hull, causing the fire, and the smoke that choked and blinded. Scratchy rubbed at his eyes, feeling it again, smelling it again. Scratchy felt the panic and the fear and the pain build up within him again. Scratchy needed to get away from the water, had to get away, back to land. It was dangerous here.

'What's up, pal?' A hand on his shoulder. It was Ayrshire Larry. A friend. A mate. Scratchy's pal. He was kneeling beside him, perched on the walkway. Scratchy looked down. Saw the water flowing beneath him.

Heard the screams...

'Scratchy needs to go,' he said. 'Scratchy not safe.'

'Wait till morning, friend,' said Larry.

Scratchy shook his head. 'Scratchy needs to go. Back to land.'

He saw concern in Ayrshire Larry's face. They had shared skippers in the past, Scratchy had been glad to see him under the bridge. But he couldn't take the water. Not safe near water.

'C'mon then, we'll go to the church,' said Larry. 'No water there. You'll be safe there.'

Scratchy didn't look down as he and Larry descended from the precarious position under the bridge. If he didn't look at it, it couldn't get him. As soon as he hit solid ground he shuffled away at speed, trying to put distance between him and the river, between him and his memories.

THURSDAY

Knight watched Donovan as they drove from Stewart Street to Barlinnie. Knight had been hitting the streets on his own, looking for the homeless man from the alley, and he'd not had much sleep. But Donovan looked like shit. His skin was pasty, his eyes red. Knight recalled as kids how he and his pals would shade the backs of pennies with pencil and then press them over their eyes, leaving black circles. He saw the same thing on Donovan. He looked even more unkempt. Sure, he'd shaved but he'd missed bits, for bristles stuck out above his collar.

'Jesus, Frankie boy,' he said, 'you look like you've been ridden hard and put away wet.' Knight thought he'd appreciate the horsey reference, given he was a follower of the sport of kings. Too much of a devotee, he'd heard. But, hey, everyone had their vices, and Knight was not one to point the finger. Unless there was a profit in it.

Donovan's eyes didn't leave the road, but his fingers tightened slightly on the steering wheel. 'Not sleeping.'

'Things on your mind?'

'None of your business.'

The corners of Knight's mouth turned down as he shrugged slightly. If Frankie boy didn't want to talk about it, then it was fine with him.

He already knew, anyway.

Davie had given further views on fight scenes, Lassiter taking more notes. They were alone, Mannie and Coco having gone shopping. There was a silence for a moment, then Lassiter said, 'Let me ask you something.'

As if you've not been asking me something for three days, Davie thought.

'What's it like, being a man like you?'

Davie's face could have been carved from stone as he returned Lassiter's gaze. He knew a question like this would come, it was one of the reasons he'd been unwilling to embark on this relationship. He was uncomfortable enough talking about what he did, even in an abstract sense, but he knew the actor would not stop there, could not stop there. He wanted to know what made a man like Davie tick. But Davie didn't want to know. He was too afraid of what he'd find.

Lassiter decided to keep talking. 'Okay, I know you're always aware of your surroundings. I've seen you, checking what's around. You know what's to the left of you and what's to the right, what's behind. The first night we met, you were standing against that wall, near the door. Now I know why. Even now, look at you...'

Davie resisted the urge to look around. He already knew what Lassiter was going to say.

'You've taken the one chair in the corner of the room. You're not sitting beside the window, you can see all the doors. You never relax, always on edge. But you can't be like that every minute of every day, can you? So, what I'm asking is this – what's the real Davie McCall like, the one behind all this?' He waved his hand up and down in Davie's direction. 'Come on, Davie. I know you're not a great talker, so just give me one word that you think describes the real you. One word – the first one that comes into your head.'

Davie kept himself very still, fearful that any movement would betray his discomfort. His mind was turning the question over. Finally, only one word came to mind, but he would never share it.

Lassiter smiled. It was a knowing smile, one that was unsurprised by Davie's lack of response. 'I'll tell you, then. I'll tell you what I think. I think the one word that describes you is lonely.'

Davie felt something flinch inside him. Lassiter either saw something or sensed it, for he smiled again, a broader smile this time. 'I knew it. I'm right, aren't I? I told you before, I know people. I know you, Davie McCall, I mean I really *know* you and that's the essence I want to capture in this picture.'

Davie's mind filled with images, faces, voices. Unwanted memories that were never far from the surface.

Vari, touching his face tenderly, her voice low with sadness.
You're not here.

His father, his words being carried away by the wind.
You can't protect your women, can you?

Audrey, dying in front of him, her throat open and streaming blood, her eyes accusing.

You could have saved me.

And Joe's voice, soft, kindly, sad.

Your world is not her world.

You could hurt her.

Lassiter kept talking. 'The idea of a man alone, struggling with his nature. A man who has good in him, but finds his life makes him do bad. Does that resonate with you?'

Resonate. An actor's word. Davie didn't answer again. He couldn't. The voices from his past were mixed together in his head now. He knew Lassiter was right. He was a boozed-up, drugged-up, sexed-up pretty boy from LaLaLand, but he was no fool. Davie realised then that the actor had been studying him and even in just a handful of meetings, he'd already got his measure. Mostly, he didn't like that. But there was a part, down deep, that was glad someone understood him, even a little.

'You know why I know so much about you, Davie? Because we're alike, you and me, not just physically.' The grin was sheepish this time. 'I know, what the hell does a hard man from Glasgow have in common with a milque toast from the coast, right? But like you, no-one really gets me. They see this,' this time he waved his hand in an up and down motion in his own direction, 'and they think they know me. I'm rich, I'm privileged, my dad gave me everything. But here's the thing – I worked for everything I've got. Sure, my dad's money bought me an education, but he never once got me a part. Everything I did, I earned. I studied, I learned, I auditioned. If I thought even for a nanosecond that my dad had pulled strings, then I walked. I've turned my back on great projects, good parts, just because I suspected they were being offered as a favour for my old man, or as a way to get to him. I exist because he's my father, but I am what I am because of me – no-one else. There's part of him in me, but the rest is all me, baby.'

He paused and stood up, began to walk around the room. Davie had seen this during their meetings. Lassiter liked to walk and talk while he thought. He was warming up to his subject and

Davie was fascinated, even though he didn't want to be. The words resonated more than Lassiter would ever know.

'Then there's the stuff the tabloids like,' Lassiter said. 'They love the drugs and the girls, fills their pages. I'm a bad boy and I play it to the hilt. They think they know me, but they don't. They think that's me – a spoiled brat who never heard the word no. And I enjoy playing that part. But that's what it is, a part. It's not me, not really, fun though it is. But that's all because of the old man, too. He's one of the world's genuine good men, you know that? I know he made his name playing tough guys, bad guys even, anti-heroes. But the reality is, he's a goddamn saint. Been married to the same woman for forty years, you know that? Never stepped over the line. That's not me. He's not me. I'm not him. I've got his blood, I've got his genes, his DNA, but that's where it ends. He's not me. I'm not him.'

Lassiter filled the pause with an embarrassed smile. 'You heard the album *Who's Next*? The Who? Know the song "Behind Blue Eyes"?'

Davie nodded. He knew the song, knew where Lassiter was going.

'I'm gonna get the rights, use it in the picture. I think it'll be my guy's theme song. The bad guy behind blue eyes that no-one really knows.' He leaned forward. 'But we know him, don't we, Davie? You and me. We know him.'

Yeah, thought Davie, we know him.

His name was Patrick Fowler and he had something to tell them. But he was a crook, so information didn't come free.

They were in a small room in Barlinnie reserved for interviews with lawyers or police officers. Fowler was in C Hall, the remand wing, and Donovan and Knight knew there was a lot of loose information flying around the cells. Guys came in, sometimes wanted to talk about what they'd done, establish their credentials, as it were. Or they talked about what was going on outside the prison walls.

They already knew Fowler was due to appear on an assault charge.

'Didnae dae it,' he had assured them, but neither of the cops believed there was a miscarriage of justice pending because Fowler was a vicious little scroat.

'So, what have you got to tell us?' Knight asked.

Fowler drew on a thin roll-up and squinted at them through the smoke. 'Need you to know that this doesn't come easy, you know? I mean, I wouldnae be talkin here if I didnae think what they boys did to that lad was bang out of order.'

Knight grinned. 'Aye, you're a public-minded citizen, Patrick. So you don't want anything in return?'

'Didnae say that, Mister Knight. I mean, quid pro quo and aw that...'

'Quid pro quo?' Knight nudged Donovan in the arm. 'Classical scholar here, DS Donovan.'

'Or he's seen *Silence of the Lambs* once or twice, DI Knight.'

'Oh, aye! That right, Patrick? You fancy yourself as a Hannibal Lecter? Don't let him near the nice Chianti, for God's sake, DS Donovan.'

Fowler's eyes flicked from one to the other across the scarred wooden table. There was no confusion there, just a weariness with their patter. 'Guys, if I want a double act I'll watch *Morecambe and Wise*. You want to hear what I've got to say or no? No skin off my nose if you don't.'

'But it is, Patrick. Cos you want some kind of deal in return. You're facing a hefty sentence for banging that boy over the bonce.'

'Allegedly, Mister Knight, allegedly. No been heard in a court of law yet. My brief says I've got a good chance of walking free.'

'Patrick, you've as much chance of walking out of that court a free man as I have of shagging Elizabeth Hurley. So, let's cut the shite here, eh? Tell us what you know and we'll mention to the PF that you've been helpful. Best we can do. No promises.'

Fowler took a drag on his cigarette and considered Knight's words. He'd been hoping for better, both cops could tell that, but the bird in the hand principle applied here. 'Okay,' he said, stubbing the butt out in the small tin ashtray on the tabletop. 'So I was in the dog boxes with these two boys, okay? And they was talking about how they'd stuck this lad. Behind that club down the town, the Corvus?'

'You asking us, or telling us, Patrick?' Knight said.

'Telling you. They said they did it, Mister Knight, heard them clear as a bell.'

Donovan leaned forward. 'And it's taken you three days to come forward.'

'Wrestlin with my conscience, so I was, Mister Donovan. It's no easy turnin grass, you know? But what they did was bang out of order. Bang out of order.'

Donovan leaned back and gave Knight a look that told him he didn't believe a word of it. But he saw Knight's expression and knew that he was not about to look this gift horse in the kisser.

They stayed in the room after Fowler was taken back to C Hall. Knight lit up a cigarillo and paced the small space like a caged tiger. Donovan was tired just watching him.

'For Christ's sake, Jimmy, will you sit down?'

'We've got the wee bastards, Frankie boy. We've got them.'

'You're not believing a word that scroat said, are you? He's so crooked they'll have to bury him in an L-shaped grave.'

'Doesn't mean he's not telling the truth,' said Knight, still pacing. 'He goes on the record, it means we have the blood, Bonner's wound and an admission. We've got them, Frankie boy.'

Donovan knew cases had been won on less, but he didn't believe a word Fowler said, while a good QC would gut him in the witness box and leave him like a chippy's haddock. The blood and the knife were good, but that just placed the two lads there. They didn't have the actual murder weapon, which puzzled him. Why was the dead boy's knife the only one they found? Donovan was suffering from stress and lack of sleep but he was alert enough to sense there was something wrong here. Knight just wanted a conviction and he didn't care who it was. Donovan wanted to get the right man and his gut was telling him these two boys did not actually stab Dickie Himes, though they knew who did.

'Let's get one of them in here, have a chat,' he said and Knight stopped pacing to stare back at him.

'They didn't burst in Stewart Street, what makes you think they'll burst now?'

Donovan shrugged. 'Three nights in C Hall might've made them sit up and take notice. We bring one of them up here, apply pressure, maybe we'll get a result.'

'We've got enough, Frankie boy.'

'Can never have enough, Jimmy. And what are you worried about? The worst that can happen is that we get nothing. Best case is one of them bursts and we get an admission.'

Knight took a deep breath while he thought about this. Then he nodded. 'Which one?'

Davie was a patient man. He could sit for hours, alone, waiting for something to happen. He was comfortable on his own and the work he did often required him to be inactive, waiting for someone to turn up. He'd been waiting for Sammy for fifteen minutes, while he'd gone to visit his daughter. He didn't ask Davie into the four-storey tenement in Castlemilk, but Davie wasn't insulted. He did not like meeting new people.

The South Side scheme had been transformed over the years. Davie could remember the lines of flats, uniform grey in their discoloured pebbledash and sometimes streaked with damp. Now a housing association had taken over the running of the former council housing and had systematically converted the drab, prison-like '60s architecture into something more attractive. The facings had all been replaced, woodwork painted, windows replaced and interiors refurbished. They had done a good job and there was a new spirit about the place.

But the underbelly was still there and no amount of paint, timber and architectural sleight-of-hand would hide it. Davie knew that among the many honest straight arrows there was still the criminal element burrowing away under the surface, making a buck. Davie had dealt with them. Davie had hurt them. Davie was one of them.

Sammy emerged onto the street with a youth of around fifteen at his heels. He was typical of lads his age – gangly, pale, hair short, wearing jeans and a short but thick padded jacket. He said something to Sammy, who turned, replied. Davie wound the car window down a touch so he could hear what was being said.

'But I can help,' said the boy. 'He's my brother.' He pronounced it 'bru-er', his accent too lazy to tackle the dipthong.

Sammy shook his head. 'Naw, Jimsy, son. I need you here, lookin after your maw.'

They both looked up at a second floor window and Davie followed their gaze to see a plain, thin-faced woman of around 40 watching them. Even from the street, he could see the raw eyes and blotchy skin of someone who had been crying for days. He saw Sammy's face in her features, which was a shame. Any woman deserved better.

Jimsy turned back to his grandfather with defiance in his eyes. 'You cannae stop me, neither you can. It's a free country.'

Sammy sighed. 'You're right, son, I can't stop you. But I'm hopin you'll step up here, be the man of the house. Marty's already in trouble, we don't need you droppin yourself in it, too. What I need, what your brother needs, is for you to look after your maw. Can you do that?'

Jimsy glanced back the window just in time to see his mother step back into the room. He angled his gaze down to his feet and reluctantly nodded. Sammy gave him a soft punch on the shoulder, the Glasgow equivalent of a hug, and walked round to the passenger seat of the car. Jimsy looked up and his eyes met Davie's. Davie saw sadness and confusion. And he saw anger. He hoped that young Jimsy was a man of his word, for if he gave into his rage and tried to do something about his brother it would not end well.

Sammy glanced at the dog lying in the back seat but said nothing. He settled himself in, buckled up and nodded to his grandson through the windscreen. The boy nodded back. Davie fired up the engine and pulled away. Jimsy watched them all the way.

Stewie fidgeted. He didn't like being in this room. He didn't like being taken away from the hall, eyes on him, especially Marty's. Made him feel like a grass and he wasn't no grass. He didn't like the way the two cops were looking at him, that big dark bastard, Knight, smiling at him and smoking his wee cigar. The other one wasn't smiling. He looked ill, right enough. Maybe he had the flu or the skitters. Good, Stewie hoped he was dying.

'How you getting on in the Bar-L, Stewie, mate?' It was Knight talking, breathing a cloud of smoke across the small wooden table. Stewie hated cigar smoke, made him feel sick. Maybe that was what was wrong with the other bastard, sick to his stomach because of his mate's cigar. Serves him bloody well right.

Stewie gave them a twitch of the shoulders. 'This legal? Should my lawyer no be here for this?'

'It's just a wee chat, Stewie, friendly like. Nothing to worry about.'

'Aye, right.' They must think his head buttoned up the back. Polis didn't have friendly chats. Well, if they thought he was going to say anything without his lawyer there, they were on to plums.

'It's no nice here, is it, son? I mean, the politicians say prison's like a holiday camp these days but it's hellish, really. Mind you, I've been in some holiday camps that felt like prison, right enough.'

Did this guy think he was some kind of dickhead? Did he think this pally stuff was fooling him? Jesus, cops were stupid, so they were.

Knight leaned forward, both hands clasped on the tabletop, the cigarillo clamped between his teeth. 'I'll get right to the point, because maybe I'm keeping you from a glamorous granny contest, or whatever activities the screws have got lined up to keep you entertained. We've just had a wee natter with a guy who says you and your mate admitted to stabbing Dickie Himes.'

Stewie felt the shock tingle throughout his body. His mind raced, trying to think who would say such a thing. He drew a blank.

'And see this guy?' Knight was talking again, his tone still reasonable, like they were discussing football. 'He's willing to say it in court. He's going to say that you and your mate Marty told him you did it. He's going to say that Marty held Dickie down while you stuck him.'

'That's shite, that is!' Stewie was on his feet now. He was up before he knew it. The two cops didn't even flinch, though.

'Calm down, Stewie,' it was the other one now, Donovan. 'Take it easy.'

'Take it easy? Take it easy? I'm getting fitted up here and you're sayin take it fuckin easy?'

'Sit down, son,' Knight again. Stewie remained standing, a nerve in his thigh making his leg jiggle. Knight's voice hardened. 'Sit down, son, before I sit you down.'

Stewie sat down. He placed his hand over his thigh and squeezed to keep it still. This was bad, this was really bad. He tightened his grip, trying to keep the panic in.

'No-one's fitting you up, son,' said Donovan. 'Look at it from our side. We've got a knife we know was Dickie Himes's covered in your pal's blood. Your pal's got a face wound and doctors say it was left there by a knife just like Dickie's. You say you were with him all night on Friday. And now we've got someone who says you've been bragging about doing it.'

'That's shite, I've no said nothing.'

'We know how it is in here. You've got to show you're a hard man, show the guys what you're made of. Lets them know where you stand in the pecking order. Most of they guys in the hall? They're in for theft or possession, maybe assault. Murder's really something, Stewie. Makes you a big man, right?'

'I never plunged that boy.'

Knight said, 'Evidence tells us different.'

'Your evidence is shite. You're shite. You've got it all wrong.' Stewie was talking tough, but even he could hear the tremble in his voice. He knew he wasn't fooling them. He slumped in his chair.

Donovan leaned forward now, speaking softly. 'Then put us right, Stewie. Tell us what happened.'

Stewie stared at the tabletop, the fingers of his hand still biting into the flesh of his thigh, but he didn't notice it now.

Donovan was still talking. 'You're right – your lawyer should be here. But it could help you if you tell us what happened that night. I don't think you did it, DI Knight doesn't think you did it, but with what we've got on you, a jury will think different. You're facing life, Stewie, you need to realise that. Just tell us what happened and we'll do everything we can to help you.'

Stewie shook his head and when he spoke what fire had been there before was quenched. 'Cannae say.'

'Yes, you can, Stewie. I know you don't want to grass but this is self-preservation we're talking about here. Why should you go down for something someone else did?'

Stewie looked up, his eyes floating with tears. 'They'll do me.'

'Who'll do you?'

Stewie shook his head, dislodging a single tear. 'Cannae say nothing.'

'We'll protect you, you'll be safe. We'll get you on protection. No-one will get to you.'

Stewie looked up. He wanted to believe them, he really did. But still the street rules held him back. You don't grass, simple as that. You certainly don't grass a headbanger like Scrapper Jarvis. But if he didn't, he would go down for life. If he didn't stand up for himself, who would? He swallowed hard, feeling something bitter dislodging in his throat. Scrapper was a menace, so he was, shouldn't be on the streets. Him and Marty were just ordinary blokes, they didn't even carry blades, for Christ's sake. Why should they go down for something Scrapper did? And they said they could protect him. He'd need to say it court, or at least in front of his lawyer, before it was binding. Maybe if he told them, he'd feel better, then he could deny it later. But he needed to get them off his back for now, give him time to think, time to talk it over with Marty. That's it, Stewie, buy time...

'We didnae do it. I cannae say who did, though. No yet. Let me talk to my lawyer.'

Bobby Newman's brow furrowed as he thought about what Davie and Sammy had told him. They were in the cosy living room of the home he'd made with Connie, a former council house Bobby had bought years before and had fixed up. It had been completely remodelled inside, with the living room and kitchen now converted into one big room, separated by a dark wooden breakfast bar. It had a new roof, the dampness that had attacked it after years of neglect eradicated and it was warm, comfortable and tastefully

decorated, thanks to Connie. But even through the double glazing
Davie could still hear the traffic whizzing past on the Edinburgh
Road.

Connie held her three-month-old baby as she listened to them
talk. She was a tall woman, dark-haired, dark-eyed, attractive in
the kind of way that it takes a while to notice. She had been good
for Bobby, had prompted him to leave The Life behind, become a
straight arrow. He'd gone to work in his uncle's hardware business
on Duke Street. When his uncle died of a heart attack two years
before, he'd taken it over. He was doing well enough to hire people
to enable him to spend time at home on a weekday.

But it wasn't hardware Davie and Sammy had come to discuss.
And Connie wasn't pleased.

Bobby was pouring the coffee he'd brought in from the kitchen
when she said, 'I don't want Bobby involved, Davie, simple as.'

Bobby said, 'Connie...'

Connie cut him off. 'Sammy, I'm sorry, I know you need to help
your grandson and I sympathise, but Bobby's left all that behind.
You must know what I'm saying?'

Sammy nodded and accepted the coffee cup from her wordlessly. He knew to keep out of this.

Bobby said, 'Connie, I'm not going to go back to The Life.'

'Bloody right you're not.'

Davie decided it was time he said something. 'Connie, all we're
asking is that Bobby steer us in the right direction.'

That was all they wanted. Bobby had always had a bulging
contact book, even if only in the figurative sense. For as long as
Davie had known him, Bobby had always 'known a guy'. Whatever
was needed, he knew someone who could provide it. He was not
in The Life any longer but he still had the contacts.

Davie had asked him if he knew anyone who could help them
find a homeless guy called Scratchy. All they knew of him was that
he dossed in the lane behind the Club Corvus.

'Skippered,' Bobby had corrected him.

'What?'

'They don't call it dossing, it's skippering.'

But the mention of the Corvus had worried Connie. She'd read about the murders, knew about the Jarvis Clan and did not want her husband anywhere near either.

'Take it easy, darling,' Bobby assured her. 'We're no getting the band back together, honest. There's no way I'm being drawn back in.'

'Aye,' she said, 'that's what Michael Corleone said, too.'

Bobby smiled. 'That's a film, pet. This is real life. All I'm gonnae do is steer the boys in the right direction, introduce them to a guy...'

Connie glared at him, but Bobby broadened his smile and rubbed one hand up her arm. She exhaled deeply and audibly and looked down at their child, sleeping peacefully in her arms, then turned to Davie. 'You let him get hurt, David McCall, and you'll have me to answer to, understood?'

Davie nodded. He'd take on any number of Glasgow neds before he'd want to face up to Connie. She was the toughest of them all. And she was a primary school teacher. He looked to Bobby. 'So, who's this guy?'

'Bloke called Lester, but for fuck's sake don't call him that. He prefers Lenny, for some reason. Ex-paratrooper, but you won't believe that when you see him.'

'How'd you mean?'

'Cos he's the answer to one of the greatest mysteries of all time – who ate all the pies?'

DCI Bolton listened to Donovan's account of the interviews with both Fowler and Stewie without interruption. Donovan was thankful for that, because his lack of sleep and excess of stress made it difficult for him to retain any kind of flow. When he'd finished, he sat quietly, waiting for his boss to say something.

Bolton thought over everything, staring at his desk as he pushed items around the surface. Finally, he said, 'So what do you think, Frank? We got the wrong guys here?'

'They were there, boss, no question. But I've never bought into the notion that they actually killed Himes.'

'If not them, who?'

'We know they run around with Scrapper Jarvis. We know Himes was punting gear at the Corvus, we found it on him. We know the Corvus is a Jarvis place. We know Scrapper's a dangerous wee shit and if he's coked up he could be lethal.'

'We don't know he was there, though. Maw Jarvis swears blind he was at home with her all night Friday.' Donovan grimaced to show what he thought of Scrapper's alibi. Bolton smiled, then said, 'Okay, this lad wants to talk to his lawyer, let him. We'll see if he comes back, if not you go see him again. What does Knight think, by the way?'

'You know Jimmy Knight. He doesn't care either way. He knows this pair were there, that's good enough for him, they'll still go down unless they make a deal with the PF to give evidence about who actually did do it.'

'Where is he now?'

'Grabbing some kip before he heads out again tonight, still looking for that dosser.'

'He's dogged, I'll say that for him.'

'Aye, once Jimmy gets his teeth into something, he doesn't let go. Especially if there's something in it for him.'

Lenny Malloy had obviously been a powerful individual, but he'd let himself go to seed. Bobby had told them he'd been with the 2nd Battalion of the Parachute Regiment. He'd been one tough bastard back then, seeing action in the Falklands. Operation Corporate, they'd called it, and 2-Para had been deployed as part of 3-Commando. Lenny had been one of the first to land on Blue Beach, as San Carlos Water was known. After that, he'd fought at Goose Green and Wireless Ridge before helping recapture Port Stanley. He'd been wounded in the hip, invalided out. He had a walking stick and it tapped along the corridor of the building on the Clydeside near the Saltmarket as he led them to what he called the mess hall. Bobby had said he didn't need the stick, he just liked to carry it.

In addition to being a fit bugger who liked nothing better than throwing himself out of planes, Lenny had always been a genius with figures. When he came home he finagled a job in the financial sector and made a good living helping the city's well-off become even more comfortable. And as he put his old life behind him, he cast off his powerful build. He was a big man and at his peak he was all power and muscle. As he kept figures on paper looking good, he allowed his own figure to vanish under a layer of flesh that would've made a whale blush. He ate well and he drank well and he not only lived off the fat of the land, he became it.

But one January night two years before, when the mercury had taken a nosedive, he found a man dead and frozen on a bench on the Clydeside. The man had been a Gulf War veteran and an Iraqi bullet had taken off part of his thigh. His return to civilian life had not been glorious, but he found drink and drugs. He'd been on the streets for a year when Lenny found him.

The words 'by the grace of God' were uppermost in Lenny's mind and he realised that he had allowed his life to become one of excess and privilege. He resolved to do something about it. He set up the Soldier's Rest Hostel, forged out of a derelict building near the Saltmarket. He even sketched the logo he wanted, an infantry-man sitting against a wall smoking a cigarette, although an artist refined it. The logo adorned a sign at the front of the building and also on the black sweatshirts worn by the volunteers who worked there.

He'd made some canny investments and he had enough saved to bide him over, so he jacked in his job, although he still carried out some lucrative freelance consulting for those with the readies. He spent most of his time helping those on the streets, not just the former military personnel. He'd lost some of the weight he'd gained, but when Davie was introduced to him, he was reminded of the line that inside every fat man is a thin man wondering how the hell he'd just been eaten.

A young volunteer, a stick-thin teenage girl with long dark hair pulled into a ponytail, brought them all coffee and left them to talk. They sat in a corner, well away from the street people who were being served food and drinks by four other volunteers. Nothing fancy, Lenny had explained, just basic stuff, but it helped keep

them alive in this weather. Davie scanned the faces of the customers, seeing men and women, young and old. He wondered how
they ended up here. He wondered if he could ever end up here.

When he looked back, he saw Lenny watching him as he sipped
his coffee. Something had come into his eyes when Bobby had
introduced them and they had rarely left Davie's face since. Bobby
had explained they were looking for a street person called Scratchy
and he'd told him why. Davie and Sammy knew Bobby would tell
the man everything, it was the best way.

'And if you find Scratchy, what will you do with him?' The
question was directed at Davie

Bobby answered. 'We steer him to a friendly copper.'

Lenny's eyes bored deep into Davie's. 'That right?'

Davie nodded. This guy knew him, or knew of him at least.
Sometimes that was good, sometimes bad. It was difficult to say
what it was on this occasion, because Lenny gave nothing away.
The big man stared at Davie for a few moments then gave a satisfied bob of the head.

'Okay,' he said. 'I know Scratchy, you'll find a lot of the street
people do. He's one of those kind of men, people know him, people
like him. He used to be in the Royal Navy, was sent to the
Falklands. He was on the *Sheffield* when the Argentinian Exocets
found it. He was badly burned and sometimes it itches, which is
why he's called Scratchy. Suffers from PTSD, which is not uncom-
mon out there. MOD doesn't fully recognise it because the shit-
licking civil servants don't have a form for it. Not yet, anyway.'

Bobby asked, 'And now he's homeless?'

'Yes, lots of ex-servicemen come back, mind and body screwed
up to buggery, can't keep things straight. Hit the bottle, hit the
needle. Hit the streets.'

Sammy leaned forward. 'Can you find him?'

Lenny thought about this, but when he spoke, he spoke to
Davie. 'I've heard of a Davie McCall. Bad bit of goods, I'm told.'

Never fails, thought Davie.

'The way I hear it, Davie McCall is a cold bastard, wouldn't go
out of his way to help a mate.'

Bobby cleared his throat. 'Lenny, that's...'

Lenny raised his hand. 'But Bobby here vouches for you – and I'm not inclined to pay much heed to rumour.' He switched from Davie to Sammy. 'I can find him... Sammy, is it?' Sammy nodded. 'I can find him.'

'Cops have been looking for him since last Friday, Lenny.'

Lenny smiled. 'The street people won't talk to the cops. But they'll talk to me.'

Jimmy Knight was pissed off. Three nights now he'd been hitting every bothy, hostel, dosshouse and skipper he could think of and had come up with bugger all. He didn't like that. He wasn't used to it. When he set out to find somebody, he found them, but this bloke Scratchy was proving harder to catch than a fish in the desert. If tonight's search yielded nothing, he'd have to admit defeat and that didn't make him a happy bunny.

The Christian Street Mission was his final throw of the dice. They were a bunch of happy clappers who went out into the streets to bring food and succour to the down and outs and street walkers. Soup, hot rolls, blankets, a tip for a bed for the night if they needed it. Of course, they threw in a word or two about God and Jesus, but that was a small price to pay. Knight didn't know how many souls they saved, but he'd often picked up a line or two from their customers. They had a converted ambulance that they parked up at various locations to act as a beacon to bring the street people gathering round.

He found them near the archway at Glasgow Green opposite the High Court, the ambulance's blue light flashing. A crowd of the city's homeless and a few working girls hung around on the pavement, clutching plastic cups filled with soup or munching the rolls. It was a cold night, well below zero, and their collective breath frosted in the air like ectoplasm in a ghost story. That's how it looked to Knight – some of these people were already dead, they just hadn't lain down yet.

One of his great strengths was his memory. He remembered names, dates, details, faces. And one of the faces in the crowd was

familiar to him. He hadn't seen it in eighteen years but he knew it
right away. The man was nearing forty now, but he still had the
glasses, the longish hair, although it was thinning. He'd lost weight
since Knight had last seen him, across Court Number Two over
the road, but Knight knew him.

'Well, well – Lowry-like-the-painter,' he said, forcing the man
to turn around, a startled look on his face that took Knight right
back to another freezing cold night all those years before, back to
Firhill Basin where Knight found him hiding behind a rubbish
skip. 'When'd you get out?'

Lowry pushed his glasses up his nose – *Christ*, thought Knight,
he still has the same mannerisms – and his eyes became hunted.
Knight had seen that look before, when he'd bumped into men he'd
lifted in the past. Generally it was guys like Lowry, not criminals,
just blokes who had made a mistake. In Lowry's case, that mistake
had led to a life sentence. 'Coupla years now, Mister Knight,' he
said. His voice had changed, though. Still posh West End, but it had
matured. He'd grown up in the jail. Knight would've taken even
money that he'd not had an easy time of it inside. 'Out on licence.'

Knight jerked his head at the ambulance beside them. 'You
with this lot?'

Lowry nodded. 'Volunteer. Felt I needed to do something.'

Knight lowered his head and said softly, 'Lowry-like-the-painter
– you get religion inside?'

The man looked almost embarrassed for a moment, then nodded
his head. 'I did wrong, Mister Knight. I was punished by the law,
but a greater punishment lies ahead.' He sounded as if he was
repeating what someone else had said.

'Trying to get a wee bit on the credit side of the balance sheet,
that right? Do a bit of good?'

Lowry nodded again. 'It won't bring that girl back, though.'
He looked at the ground, his shame apparent. He'd killed a girl
he'd fancied back in '77, battered her, strangled her, almost killed
the boy she'd been humping on the canal path. Knight and
Donovan had been in uniform then, guarding the body until the
brylcream boys arrived to take charge. Lowry had done the return-

to-the-scene-of-the-crime thing, giving his real name. 'Lowry – like the painter,' he'd said, and that was how Knight still thought of him. He'd tried to get away, but Knight ran him down to Firhill Basin and that skip. A wee tap on the napper with his baton and Knight was on his way to plainclothes.

Knight asked, 'You been doing this long?'

'A year or so, started a few months after I got out.'

'You'll have got to know some of the regulars, then?'

Lowry became wary. 'A few.'

'Know a dosser named Scratchy?'

Lowry pushed his glasses up his nose with his thumb again, his brow wrinkled. He shook his head. 'Why you looking for him?'

'Routine inquiries,' Knight said. It was his go-to answer when he didn't want to expand further.

'Sorry, don't think I've ever heard of a Scratchy.'

'You sure?'

'Positive. You get to know some of the names, faces mostly though. If you had a picture?'

Knight said, 'Naw, no picture. Not even got much of a description. Average size, long hair, wears a long brown coat, uses one of they stretchy things to keep luggage safe on a car roof rack as a belt, you know what I'm talking about?' Lowry nodded to show he did. 'That's about it. Ring any bells?'

Lowry searched his memory, but came up with nothing. 'Sorry, Mister Knight.'

Knight felt irritation rise. This was not proving to be his finest hour and it was getting his goat. Still, wasn't Lowry-like-the-painter's fault. He took a final look around the people milling about on the pavement, saw no-one else he recognised or who would help him. 'Not to worry, son,' he said. 'You keep out of trouble, okay?'

'That's my plan, Mister Knight.'

Knight gave him a hearty clap on the back, propelling the young man's slight frame forward. 'Good man.'

Knight lit up a cigarillo as he walked away, thoughts of the waitress's tidy frame perking him up. He'd failed to find Scratchy, so what? Can't win em all. And he really doubted the boozed up vagrant had anything to say. He was only looking for him because he wanted to show off to by-the-book Bolton. He'd had uniforms and plainers from Stewart Street swarming everywhere trying to find the man and Knight would've liked it if he could've shown them all up. Anyway, *c'est la vie.*

As he walked away, he didn't see the small, wizened face watching him intently from behind the converted ambulance, the eyes thoughtful.

FRIDAY

Jerry Jarvis had one thing in common with Davie McCall, but he
didn't know it – he was used to waiting. He was a patient man,
unlike his brothers. Marko had been all go, a bundle of nervous
energy that found release in shagging. Andy was also full of life,
always moving, having to be doing something. Scrapper was a
walking punch, little more than muscle and threat galvanised by
cocaine and a low boredom threshold. But Jerry could sit still for
long periods of time, just waiting for something to happen. It didn't
mean he lacked resolve, it just meant that he appreciated those quiet
moments when he could lose himself in his thoughts.

It wasn't easy with the two Welsh brothers rabbiting in the front
seats of the four-wheel drive. Owen and Gwynfor Jones, bickering
about something or other. Jerry had long ago lost interest. They
were big men who made a brick shithouse look like a prefab and
they were well used to meting out punishment, which was handy,
because that was exactly what Jerry was about that day. But, my
God, they didn't half get on his tits. They never agreed with each
other, always found something to pick at, like an old married couple.

He was about to tell them to shut the fuck up when he saw a
battered old van pull up outside the workshop across the road.
Jerry watched a small man with thinning grey hair climb out of the
driver's seat, unlock the workshop door and go inside. Jerry gave
him a moment then got out his four-wheel drive. He told Gwynfor
to stand guard and he and Owen pushed the door open.

The small space was dominated by a workbench on which lay
four wood panel doors. There was raw timber piled up against every
wall apart from one, where a series of old shelves was filled with
a variety of tools. The man they had come to see was called Ron
Hobbs. As they entered he had his back to them and was hauling
on a pair of overalls. He was a carpenter by trade, but a crook by
choice. Jerry knew the man had a lucrative sideline in punting
smack, courtesy of Big Rab McClymont. In fact, Ron was one of
the big fella's oldest customers, having bought stuff from him since
the very early days. He wasn't a big player, but he was a player
nonetheless. He'd regret it.

Ron turned round, his eyes instantly suspicious when he saw Owen Jones wedging the door shut. He knew who Jerry was, of course, but he feigned nonchalance as he thrust his arms into the overalls and buttoned them up. 'What can I do for you?'

Jerry walked over to the doors on the workbench and ran his fingers along the grain. 'Don't need doors, if that's what you're offering. Mind, these are nice, right enough.'

Ron let the compliment pass and backed slowly towards the shelves. Jerry saw the move and he nodded to his man, who sprang forward just as Ron stretched beyond some tins of woodstain to reach the handle of a sawn-off shotgun. His fingers brushed the weapon just as he was jerked away and spun towards the bench, where Jerry waited, one hand leaning on the new door. Owen stayed close to Ron, his face impassive.

Ron gave the burly Welshman a look up and down then watched as Jerry sauntered over to the tool shelves. Ron swallowed and said, 'I don't know what you want here, Jarvis, but I cannae help you.'

Jerry's eyes roved over the tools on display. 'Your man McClymont has done us a bit of damage this past few days and we want to repay him. In kind, you know what I'm sayin?'

Ron knew what he was saying well enough. 'I told you, cannae help you.'

Jerry smiled. 'Ron, Ron, I think you undervalue yourself. I think you can help me big time.'

Ron glanced again at Owen, then looked back at Jerry. 'How?'

Jerry reached out and plucked a nail gun from its place. He hefted it in his hands. 'Nice tool, this. Handy thing to have. Save a lot of effort, does it?' He didn't wait for a reply. 'Bet it does. Saves all that banging with a hammer. Just a couple of dunts with this and the job's done, I'll bet.'

Ron swallowed hard again. He knew about Jerry, about his reputation, but he was determined not to show fear, even though he could feel his knees weakening and his guts seethed. He hoped he wouldn't lose it, hoped he wouldn't throw up. Ron was a crook but he wasn't a hard man. 'I don't know what you're after, but I'm telling you, there's nothing I can do for you.'

'Tell us a wee bit about Big Rab's operation.'

Despite his growing terror, Ron smiled. 'Do you know how Big Rab has stayed ahead of the game all these years? Because he doesn't tell guys like me anything. There's only him and maybe one or two other blokes who know what he's up to. You heard the sayin "the left hand doesn't know what the right hand's doin"? Well, Rab's left hand doesn't know what the left hand's doing. I'm just a buyer. I take some smack and I punt it around the town. That's it. I don't know where he gets it, I don't where it comes from, I don't know fuck all.'

Jerry nodded. This was what he'd expected. *Ah well*, he thought, *such is life*. There were more dealers on his list to see, maybe he'd have better luck there.

'Sorry to hear that, Ron,' he said and then nodded to Owen. The man moved fast again, pinned Ron's arms to his side and bent him over the workbench. Jerry moved back to the bench and began to loosen the clamps of the vice that jutted from the edge. Ron struggled but was held down easily.

'You see, Ron old son, if you'd known anything, it might've saved you a shitload of pain,' said Jerry as he grabbed hold of Ron's left hand and thrust it into the vice. He spun the metal lever to tighten the jaws, clamping Ron's hand in their grip. 'Who really cares what Rab's left hand's doin, eh? Cos we know what yours'll be doin, pal. Hold your breath, cos this is gonnae smart...'

He twisted the handle again, tightening the vice on Ron's hand. Ron tried to jerk free but both Jerry's man and the vice held him steady. And as the unyielding metal crushed his fingers, he began to scream.

Marty watched Stewie chewing on his lunch and waited for the right moment to say what he had to say. He knew his mate would burst, but now he had to rein him in. Marty hadn't touched his own food, because he'd felt like throwing up all morning, ever since his brief conversation with Andy Jarvis up on the gallery. As soon as he saw the bloke heading his way, he knew it wasn't good. He was right. Now he had to pass the message on to Stewie.

He waited until there was no-one within earshot, but he still kept his voice low. 'Don't do it, Stewie.'

'Don't do what?'

'Tell the law about Scrapper.'

Stewie's jaws stopped moving and his eyes took on a wary look. *Oh Christ*, Marty thought, *he doesn't even trust me.* 'Don't know what you're talkin about, Marty.'

Marty looked around, leaned forward, dropped his voice to a whisper. 'Stewie, mate – they know. The Jarvis clan. They know you've been talkin. They know you're thinkin about burstin.'

Denial sprang in Stewie's eyes, but died a swift death. Marty knew he couldn't lie to him. 'How'd they know?'

'Fuck knows, but they do. Andy Jarvis had a word. They said I was to explain the situation to you.'

Stewie's voice turned hard. 'I don't give a fuck, Marty. I'm facin life in the jail here for something I didnae do. They can do what they like to me. If my lawyer says it's a good idea, I'm going for it.'

Marty shook his head. 'It's no you they'll do anything to, son.'

Stewie's eye narrowed. 'What do you mean?'

Marty took a deep breath. This was what had sickened him. 'They said if you spoke out of turn, you'd never see your maw again.' Stewie blinked, but for Marty, there was worse to come. 'And they'd do Sonya, too. My Sonya. So I'm askin you, mate, for your maw's sake, for Sonya's sake, keep your mouth shut.'

Stewie blinked again and Marty thought he saw tears welling up. Stewie looked down at his half-eaten lunch and pushed the tray away. When he spoke his voice was hoarse. 'They're bastards, so they are.'

Marty saw Andy Jarvis watching them from another table, a broad smile on his lips.

'Aye, son, so they are...'

Bernadette sipped her coffee and listened to her husband rage. She knew to let him vent without interruption, although she wished he wouldn't use such language so close to the kids. They were tucked up in bed upstairs, but Rab's voice could carry, especially when he was in full flow.

'Fuckin bastardin shitehawk Jarvises,' he said, his voice just a bit too loud, but then, he'd had a few whiskies since the news came in. 'Dirty fuckin scumbags.'

Six of Rab's best customers had been hit that day, each one badly injured. Two had been shot in the legs, one had his hands crushed in his own vice and nails driven into his knees with a nail gun, one had been beaten with an inch of his life, one hit by a car and another had both kneecaps drilled with a power tool. They had also nailed his hands to the chair for good measure. It was brutal and barbaric and it horrified Bernadette. They were used to violence, but the level of reprisal shown by the Jarvis clan had shocked even Rab. The upshot was that many of Rab's dealers were laying low, fearful they might be next.

Rab's tirade finally ran out of steam and he stared at his wife, knowing she would have something to say. She waited to make sure he was finished, then she laid her mug of coffee down on the small table beside her armchair and leaned forward.

'You knew there would be repercussions, Rab,' she said, her voice soft.

'Yeah, I know – but this? Torture, just for the sake of it? I mean, Jesus...' He shook his head. He had done many things in his life but this kind of viciousness was beyond even him. He was confident none of the injured men would have been able to say anything, but it was still damaging to the business. Other dealers would think twice about coming to him for product if they thought Jerry Jarvis was going to pay them a visit. 'Fuckin butcher, right enough.'

Bernadette said, 'This has to end, you know that.'

'Yeah, but Davie was right, we've opened up a can of worms.'

'Then we close it again.'

'How?'

Bernadette sat back in her chair. 'How do you kill a snake?'

The first night of their search had revealed a new world to Davie. He knew the city had multiple personalities. To straight arrows, it was a home and a playground. To those in The Life, it was a money-maker. To the homeless, it was at once a refuge and a prison.

Lenny took them to the places that did not appear on tour guide schedules, showed them things that councillors in their polished offices in the City Chambers liked to pretend didn't exist. They visited shelters, parks, abandoned factories. Under Lenny's direction, Bobby drove them from an old hospital in the north to a railway embankment in the south. Many of the homeless were middle-aged, with the wraith-like flesh of the user, the drinker, the living dead. There were young people, male and female, fleeing abusive homes, Lenny said. He saw a young girl standing against a wall, smoking, her eyes older than her years, her face thin and pale and a stranger to a smile. She was Vari in an alternative universe. This could've been her life, Davie realised. But she'd been stronger, found a job, set up on her own before she'd ever met him.

Others he could see had obvious mental problems. He watched one woman clutching an old teddy bear and muttering to herself, being coaxed into eating something by charity workers on an empty stretch of dockland on the Clydeside. Care in the community at its worst.

Davie had always known there were homeless people in Glasgow. As a boy, he'd seen men in rags sitting on the pavement in the city centre, looking for handouts. He'd once been on the Broomielaw with his mother, he would've been about eight years of age, and she'd pointed out a group of men sitting in a group sharing bottles of cheap wine. She told him they sometimes drank meths mixed with milk. He didn't know if that was true, but the sight of the men with nowhere to go haunted him. He had a fear of being without a home ever since.

He recalled Audrey showing him addicts waiting for their dealer to arrive. He'd not been long out of jail and he hadn't really understood how his city had changed in the ten years he'd been inside. The sight had sickened him. He felt the same as he watched this parade of human misery. He felt uncomfortable, ashamed somehow, that he had a decent flat in which to live and these people were freezing on the streets or depending on charity to keep them alive.

But he forced the feeling down, squeezed it into the deepest, darkest part of himself. It was crowded in there, but he knew he had a job to do. Scratchy had to be found. Lenny had heard Knight was on the trail and they had to get to Scratchy first. They knew the big cop was striking out but that wouldn't last long. Someone along the line was bound to give him a steer, it was inevitable. They had known when they set out they were against the clock but now the countdown had accelerated.

'Hey…'

The voice was ragged and sounded female, but when Knight turned he really wasn't sure what sex he was looking at. The figure was small, bundled in layers of grimy clothing, hair cropped close as if someone had been trying to get to the nits nestling there and the face was round and streaked with dirt.

'I heard you speaking to that young fella last night,' said the creature. Female, decided Knight, definitely female. 'The Holy Joe.'

Knight sensed a breakthrough here. 'That's right.'

'I ken him, the guy you're looking for. Scratchy. I ken him. So does the Holy Joe; no matter what he says. '

So Lowry-like-the-painter had lied. How about that? Knight considered finding the speccy wee bastard again and exchanging a pointed word or two, but then thought better of it. He couldn't blame the man for holding a grudge but it did prove that turning the other cheek wasn't high on his new agenda. Knight looked back at the figure before him. 'You know where Scratchy is then?'

The woman's expression changed to one Knight recognised even under the layers of grime. Greed. Didn't matter who you were, rich man, poor man, beggar man, thief or whatever the hell it was he was looking at, they all had it. 'Aye, well, info like that doesn't come cheap, ye ken.'

Knight suppressed a grin and dug in his pockets, pulling out two fivers. He held them out but the sharp eyes merely gave the notes a disinterested look. 'It's no the Christmas sales, son. Way I sees it, you need to find this Scratchy bad, otherwise why would you be oot here in the cold at this time of night, ye ken? A tenner's no gonnae quite cover it, like.'

Knight was not offended. This was business and greed was something he could understand. He added another £10 note to the bid. 'How's that?'

A manky hand snapped out and snatched the notes away before Knight was aware of it. Must've been a magician in a previous life, Knight thought. 'So where is he?' Knight waited but she said nothing more. 'Well? You going to tell me or do I guess?'

'Keep your shirt on, big man. Just building up the suspense…'

Knight exhaled sharply through his nose, resisting the temptation to grab her by her throat and slap her around. It was only the thought of what he might catch that prevented him. *Where are rubber gloves when you need them*, he thought.

After what seemed like ten minutes, but was probably more like ten seconds, she spoke again. 'I've known Scratchy for years, ye ken. Been here and there with him, skippered up thegither. Before I tell ye anything, I need to know – is he in any trouble?'

'Does it matter?'

'It matters. You're polis. I'm no tellin ye where he is if you're gonnae bang him up, ye ken.'

'How do you know I'm polis?'

She gave a little snort that passed for a disdainful laugh. 'Gimme a break, big man.'

Knight shook his head. 'Just routine inquiries.'

'Aye, heard you say that to the Holy Joe back there. Routine inquiries, my arse. Why you want him?'

'He's maybe a witness, that's all. I just need to talk.'

She stared into his face and he saw there was a bright look to her eyes. Down and out she may be, Knight realised, but there was one sharp cookie underneath all the grime. She nodded, satisfied he was telling the truth. 'There's an old church, up Roystonhill way? You could try there.'

Knight checked his watch. It was after midnight, he was dog-tired, but he really wanted to find this guy. His self-respect demanded it.

He gave the woman a curt nod and said, 'That's a great help. Thanks, hen.'

Ayrshire Larry straightened, clearly insulted, 'Here, who you callin "hen", ya cheeky bastard?'

The church sat on the crest of a hill. Somewhere over to the right, the M8 carved its furrow through the city, although at this time of night it was little more than a brightly-lit stretch of empty road. Knight stopped on the pavement and looked up at the dark stone spire and a clockface that had long since frozen in time. There were buildings like this all over the city, he realised, and they could all be used by the men and women like Scratchy. He'd concentrated on the hostels and well-known sites where the dossers set up. He now knew that if he hadn't lucked into that guy earlier, the chances were he'd never have found Scratchy. But Larry – he'd given him his name, his street name at least – said this was where he'd be. The main door, a tall gothic arch, was firmly fastened, with planks nailed across it and a warning painted on one saying: BUILDING DANGEROUS – DO NOT ENTER. Knight stepped off the pavement and onto the rough ground, pulling a small torch from his coat pocket. He shone it over the walls of the church, looking for another way in. The narrow beam picked out large, arched windows but they were securely barricaded with heavy wood. The snow crunched underfoot as he moved and his breath frosted like the manifestation of the Holy Ghost. He wondered why the congregation had abandoned the church, why it now lay empty. He decided it had probably shrunk to such numbers that keeping a building like this proved unviable. A cat shot out from behind a mound of rubble and darted towards the street. It gave Knight a jolt and if he could've moved fast enough he would've given the wee bastard a kick. He resumed his circuit, eyes probing the shadows for an open door.

He found it at the rear, the wooden barrier that had once been nailed in place now sitting slightly off to one side. He slid it away and stepped into the gloom. He found himself in a small entrance-way that led to the main church through an open doorway. When he swung the torch beam beyond that doorway, he could see that anything of value had been ripped out. The pews, the font, the altar were all gone. Boards had been ripped up from the floor, leaving gaping holes. Mounds of snow piled where it had fallen through the missing slates on the roof. Part of that roof had caved in, and there was a mountain of wooden beams and slates jutting from the hole to the floor. The structure looked somewhat rickety, he could see it swaying in the slight breeze from the open roof. One good push and the whole lot could come down, so Knight decided to keep well away from it. He allowed the torch beam to roam around the walls, his body turning with it, but he saw nothing to suggest that anyone had been sleeping rough. He wondered if Larry had been spinning him a yarn. Then he saw another door, half hidden behind a mound of detritus. He lowered the torch beam to the floor so he could see where he was placing his feet, and stepped gingerly towards it. He feared some of the boards underfoot were so rotten they would snap under his weight but they held. He stepped round the mound of rubble and found himself up against the door. Knight paused then, listening at the old wood, trying to hear sound from beyond but there was nothing. Okay, so maybe Scratchy didn't snore. He turned the heavy metal handle and shoved, expecting there to be resistance but the door moved inwards easily.

Knight's small torch lanced through the darkness beyond, motes of dust dancing as if enjoying the light. He traversed the room, finally lighting on a pile of old blankets and a ratty-looking sleeping bag. But no Scratchy. He looked closer, saw a few candles and a box of matches. He carefully stepped closer, knelt and touched the sleeping bag. He grimaced as he slid his hand inside. He couldn't be sure, but he thought it was warm. He straightened. Had Scratchy heard him? He hadn't exactly been in silent mode. Or had he simply gone walkabout? These guys did that. Maybe in search of something to eat.

Whatever, he thought, my work here is done. He pulled his mobile phone from his pocket and made a call.

Jerry snapped his mobile phone shut and looked across at Maw Jarvis. She hadn't so much as cracked a smile since Marko's death, which did not surprise him. However, his police contact had told him something that may make her feel better.

'Got a line on that homeless person,' he said.

'Finally,' she said, as if finding one homeless person in Glasgow was the easiest thing in the world. 'Find out what he saw, get it sorted.'

Jerry nodded. Getting things sorted was his speciality.

They waited in Bobby's car beside a stretch of open ground in the Gorbals while Lenny spoke to a tall, impossibly thin man with a lank combover who hugged himself to keep warm. It was no wonder, for he was wearing only a thin windbreaker and ragged tracksuit bottoms. His feet were encased in a pair of manky old trainers with holes in them.

Lenny held a hand out to the man, telling him to stay, and limped back to the car. He leaned in towards Bobby in the driver's seat. Bobby rolled the window down. 'He says he knows where Scratchy is.' An apologetic tone crept into his voice. 'But he wants some dosh.'

Davie already had a £20 note in his hand and he stretched past Bobby from the passenger seat. Lenny took it, held it in his hand as if he was reading it. 'It won't take that much,' he said.

'Give him it,' said Davie.

Lenny leaned down lower to get a better view of Davie. There was a different look in his eye now. 'He'll just drink it away.'

Davie stared through the windscreen at the man waiting a few feet away. 'Give him it.'

Davie could tell Lenny was seeing him in another light, maybe even beginning to think the stories he'd heard weren't true. *They're true*, Davie thought, *but they're not everything*. Lenny nodded and walked quickly back to the man. He handed him the twenty. The man stared at it as if he'd never seen one before. Then it was folded up and thrust in his pocket with a speed Davie never thought possible. One second it was being studied, then it was gone. He said one sentence and then turned away to walk across the waste ground.

Davie could see a few cardboard boxes at the far end, some old pallets and sheets of plywood brought together to create some semblance of a shelter. There were once tenements on this site, the remains of the old street grid and pavements and even signs on street lamps still there. But the buildings had been cleared away as the city reinvented itself. The only homes now were the flimsy cardboard and plywood shelters that would any day be cleared away by council workers and whoever was living there dispersed. Or some street gang would come along and set fire to the makeshift structures to brighten up a dull winter's night.

Lenny was back in the car, rubbing his hand against the cold. 'A church, up by Roystonhill...'

Donovan wished Bang Bang Maxwell would stop creeping up on him. Bastard walked very quietly for such a big man. It happened at almost the same spot, too – a car park near Stewart Street, Donovan heading for the bus to take him home and no doubt another bollocking from Marie. She'd found out a bit more of their financial situation and was far from happy. He couldn't blame her. He'd screwed up pretty badly all round.

And here was Bang Bang again. It couldn't be good.

'You're early,' said Donovan, the harshness in his voice belying the soft feeling in his gut. 'I've got a few more days yet.'

'There's been a change in our working relationship,' said Maxwell, forcing Donovan to stop and face him.

'What kind of change, exactly?'

'In that we don't have one anymore.'

Donovan searched the broad face before him for some sort of clue. He dredged up a quick smile. 'What you saying? Someone paid off my debt?'

Bang Bang's face remained immobile. 'In a manner of speaking.'

Donovan's smile withered and slid away. 'Spit it out, Bang Bang.'

'Your obligation to Ray has been acquired by a third party.'

Donovan felt the queasiness in his belly sharpen into pain. Someone had bought his debt. That means someone else knew he owed cash to a loan shark. That was bad news. 'Who?'

A look that was almost apologetic crossed Maxwell's face. 'Not at liberty to say. All I've to tell you is that our current arrangement with you has been terminated. Thank you for your business and I wish you a pleasant evening.'

Maxwell turned away but Donovan grabbed him by the arm. 'Hang on...'

Maxwell stared at the hand on his arm. 'You don't want to be laying hands on me, pal,' he said, the previously pleasant tone being replaced by pure Bridgeton Cross. It had slipped Donovan's mind that Bang Bang Maxwell did not like to be touched. He removed his hand, raised it in supplication.

'I just need to know who's bought the debt, that's all,' he said.

'I told you, not at liberty to say,' said Maxwell, his tone still hard as an East End pavement. Then he sighed and Donovan saw his body relax slightly. When he spoke again, the voice was softer, quieter, as if he didn't want anyone to overhear. 'But I'll tell you this – and you didn't get it from me, okay? The party who has taken on your obligation is not as soft-hearted as Ray and me, you understand? My advice? Get the cash, pay them off. Because you really do not want them on your back.'

Maxwell stepped away and turned the collar of his thick coat up. 'There's more snow coming, I hear. Just what we needed, eh? If I was you, I'd get home sharpish, cos they say it's going to be a bad one.' Then he turned and walked in the direction of Port Dundas Road, leaving Donovan listening to the sound of the traffic and the worried nagging of his own thoughts.

The first flecks of snow were beginning to drift down from a pitch-black sky as Bobby brought the car to a halt about a hundred yards away from the church. Davie had told him to stop there so he could study the street. He ignored the twin lines of homes bright with squares of light where people lived their lives bathed in the glow of electric bulbs and TV screens and focussed instead on the parked cars. His gaze settled on a dark van sitting in the darkness of a faulty street light at the top of the hill, exhaust fumes rising like steam in the cold air from the tailpipe. Could be perfectly innocent but instinct told him it was trouble.

'You guys better leave this to me,' said Davie.

'No, I'll come with you, Davie,' Bobby said.

'Me, too,' said Sammy.

Davie shook his head. 'Bobby, you have to stay out of it. You're a straight arrow now and Connie'd kill me. Sammy, you're on licence. We don't know what's waiting in there for us and you can't get involved. They'd haul you back inside.'

'There's not going to be any trouble from this guy,' Bobby protested.

'No, but you know who else is looking for him.'

Jimmy Knight. Davie had sensed for some time that one day there would be a face-off. Maybe tonight was the night. When it happened, it wouldn't be pretty.

'Davie's right,' said Lenny. Davie nodded his thanks. He handed the dog's lead to Sammy.

'Keep him here. Any sign of trouble, get the hell out of here. I mean it.'

There was no answer and Davie decided to take it as a yes. He climbed out and began to walk up the street towards the church. The gentle advance guard of snowflakes had been joined by an army. He hunched against it, his hands thrust deep into the pockets of his woollen coat, his fingers clenching and unclenching.

The spire was a solid dark mass against the sky, the blackened stonework of the church itself a sorry sight, abandoned, forgotten, unloved. Except perhaps by Scratchy. Davie hoped they weren't too late. His gaze flicked to the van further ahead. The windscreen wipers flicked, just once, brushing the snow from the glass. He couldn't see anyone in the driver's seat, but someone would be there. He walked straight past the church without a glance, head buried deep in his upturned collar as if he was trying to shield his face from the snow, but in reality he didn't want to risk being recognised. He tried to put a little unsteadiness into his gait, just a bloke heading home after a long day and a few pints with his mates. He passed the van without breaking his pace but did catch sight of one man in the front, the face turned his way as he trudged by. He'd seen him around before, knew he was bad news. There wouldn't be anyone in the back, of that he was certain. Just the one to deal with for now.

Davie kept walking, knowing the guy would be eyeing the side mirror, but just as he reached the back of the van, he ducked suddenly to the side and out of sight. That should get his attention, he thought. Now came the tricky part.

His name was Pauley and he was glad he'd been told to stay in the van with the heater running. He never liked old buildings and he didn't like churches, so it was double jeopardy. He knew he wasn't a good man and the vestige of the old faith his maw tried to instil in him told him he would not be welcome. He wondered if churches remained holy when they weren't used, but he was glad he didn't have to take the risk. Maybe he'd vomit pea soup, or something. That wouldn't have looked good, him puking his guts up in front of the boys. Never live that down.

So he sat in the toasty van and waited for them to come back. They hadn't been away five minutes before he saw the fella weaving towards him. He clicked the wipers on to clear the build-up of snow and get a better view. White flecks covered the bloke's hair and the shoulders of his coat. Couldn't see his face, but he looked as if he'd had a couple, way he was walking. Pauley watched him pass, then kept tabs on him in the nearside mirror.

Then the guy ducked in behind the van. Pauley froze, wondering what the fuck he was playing at. He checked the offside mirror but all he saw was the side of the van, the empty street and the falling snow.

Fuck.

His head swivelled as he looked from mirror to mirror but there was no sign of him.

Fuck. Fuck.

He pulled the lever and shouldered the heavy door open. A blast of cold air and a flurry of snow surged in as he leaned out and squinted the length of the van. What was the guy doing back there? Having a slash? Pauley thought, *better no be pishing against the motor*. If he catches him he'll tie a knot in his tadger. With a final glance at the offside mirror, just to make sure the guy hadn't made his way back to the pavement, Pauley slid down from the driver's seat and walked briskly to the rear.

But there was no-one there.

Three or four steps and he was on the pavement, peering through the thickening snow, but there was no sign of the guy. Pauley frowned. Must've missed him. Maybe he was just crossing the road behind the van and he didn't see him. He smiled as he retraced his steps to get back into the warmth of the van. Thoughts of his head swivelling on his shoulders in the church were making him jumpy.

The guy was waiting for him on the far side of the van. Pauley rounded the corner and a pair of hands grabbed him and threw him up against the side, his head banging off the bodywork. His ears whined with the impact and then he was being pulled away again. Pauley was stunned, but he wasn't about to let whoever this was away with it. He pushed back, but the guy had already kicked his legs from under him. Pauley went down heavily, the fall knocking the air from his lungs. He tried to get up, but saw a boot heading straight for him. He felt the impact, the bone-crunching pain and the whine in his head reached a crescendo. Then there was only blackness.

Davie opened the rear doors of the van and bundled the prone man inside. He closed the doors again, checked his surroundings to ensure he hadn't been seen, but saw nothing through the heavy snow. He couldn't even see Bobby's car, the blizzard was so thick. Satisfied, he walked quickly back towards the church. There would be more men in there, although he did not know how many. For an instant, he thought about going back to the car and getting the others involved, but he dismissed it. Too risky for them. Anyway, this is what he did.

He found his way into the derelict building round the back and was grateful to get out of the blizzard. He stepped lightly, knowing that the floor would be covered with debris, not wishing to alert whoever was inside. He came to a halt, listening. Voices, coming from beyond a doorway. Guttural. And someone whimpering.

Then there was a sharp thud and the whimpering rose to an agonised shriek.

Davie took a deep breath and closed his eyes. The familiar sound of rushing wind whirled in the convolutions of his ears. He could feel his heart beating steadily, echoing in his temples, and he took another deep breath. The wind died, the beating subsided. He was ready.

He saw them as soon as he eased the door open. Five of them, standing round someone on the floor. Scratchy, Davie presumed. And he was hurt, his body writhing as he screamed. The movement seemed constricted, though, one arm stretched to the side, as if he couldn't move it, the other arm flailing, twisting, trying to reach it. Jarvis stood over him, one leg on either side of Scratchy's torso. He was smiling. They had never met, but Davie knew him. The other four looked on. Davie recognised faces but couldn't put names to them, apart from one – Owen Jones, a big Welshman whose broad shoulders, thick neck and broken nose was testament to his rugby playing days. There was a squat fellow with similar features to Owen – without the broken nose – who was doing his best to melt into the far wall. Davie assumed this was his brother. He looked sick. He didn't like what was going on. The third man kept his distance, too, also uncomfortable with what Jarvis was doing. The fourth was less squeamish, for he was positioned just behind Jarvis, a slight smile on his face.

None of them were aware of Davie's presence as he carefully picked his way among the rubble. There was a precarious column made up of a wooden beam that had crashed from the ceiling and other items of debris which would offer some cover if needed, so he made for that. He took a careful note of his surroundings as he did so, all the while keeping tabs on the men, waiting for one of them to spot him but they were too focussed on Jarvis and what he was doing.

'Just tell us what you saw, man.' Jarvis's voice was reasonable and calm.

Scratchy shook his head furiously, still trying to pluck at something in his other hand. Davie could see what it was now. A nail, driven through the palm, pinning the hand to the rotting floor. From his new vantage point he could just see the nail gun held in Jarvis's right hand.

Davie examined the fallen beam to his right, his eyes following it up to the ceiling and then down to the floor. Heavy snow drifted through the large hole in the roof, frosting the space below like an uneven cake. The beam itself was hazardously positioned and it wouldn't take much for it to come crashing down. Good to know.

Jarvis's face creased with a mixture of disgust and irritation. 'Grab his other hand.' It was Owen Jones who moved to obey, seizing hold of Scratchy's free arm as he frantically tried to dislodge the nail piercing his flesh. Scratchy cried out as Jones forced the arm against the floor and Jarvis ducked down, swinging the nail gun up from his side and laying it against the flat hand. The man struggled but Jones held him firmly. Jarvis smiled again and pulled the trigger.

The thunk of the nail being driven through the hand and into the floor below seemed very loud – but not as loud as Scratchy's scream. Davie was no stranger to violence, but he could feel something bitter churning in his gut. This was unnecessary. This was fun to Jarvis. It reminded him of Danny McCall, his father, who had reputedly nailed a man to the floor himself. Davie didn't know if it was true, Joe the Tailor refused to talk about it. Davie knew his father, though, and knew he was capable of it. His face that day would have mirrored Jarvis's.

'See, you say you saw nothing, mate,' Jarvis said, his expression back to neutral again. 'But I ask you – can I really take the chance? Should I take the word of some boozed-up lowlife?'

Tears streamed down Scratchy's face as he writhed, spread-eagled now. His head twisted back and forth, spittle spraying his lips. 'Scratchy never saw nothin. Scratchy's telling you the truth.'

'Scratchy could be a lying piece of shite, though.' Jarvis rested the nail gun on Scratchy's forehead. 'And either way, I'd be putting Scratchy out of his misery…'

'That's enough, Jarvis,' said Davie, his voice loud in the hollowed-out building. Jarvis whirled, his men looked round. Scratchy didn't react, his head still shaking, a low mutter dribbling from his lips.

Jarvis narrowed his eyes, focussing through the gloom and the snow piling in from the fractured roof. Finally, he recognised Davie.

'Fuck off, McCall – this doesn't concern you.'

Davie didn't reply. He knew the less he said, the better. He stepped forward, placing his feet carefully on the sagging floorboards, keeping his eyes on the men before him. They wouldn't rush him, not on this dodgy surface. They were spaced out, which was good because that meant he could take down a couple before the others reached him. He'd never handled five at once, though, and he wasn't sure he could. But he couldn't walk away either. Jarvis stepped away from Scratchy, the nail gun dangling in his right. They called him the Butcher, but he was only a big man with his lads at his back and a weapon in his hand. In Davie's mind, he was a craw – a coward – and he'd enjoy damaging him.

'I said, fuck off, McCall. This is none of your business.'

Davie was committed now. He would have preferred this encounter to be outside, where there was more room to manoeuvre, but he couldn't just turn and leave. Jarvis meant to kill Scratchy and he'd do it here. Davie unbuttoned his coat, held the sides out. 'I'm not armed, Jarvis.'

Jarvis's mouth tightened into a thin smile. 'You think that matters a tinker's fuck to me?'

Davie didn't think it did. He'd only unbuttoned his coat because it was too constricting. When he moved, he'd have to move fast, and he couldn't be bound by buttons. He studied the men before him. Owen Jones was to his left and already moving, sliding an automatic pistol from his coat pocket, his brother was far to the rear, still unhappy with the savagery of what he'd witnessed. The other two were watching Jerry for instructions. Davie couldn't be sure if they were armed, although he'd bet good money they were carrying something. So far, they hadn't produced anything, and it would take valuable time for them to do so. Jarvis had the nail gun, but that was only good at close quarters. Jones had a gun, so that made him the bigger threat. Glasgow neds were far from crack shots, but that didn't mean he couldn't get lucky.

Davie needed an equaliser.

He tilted his head towards the snow falling through the hole in the roof. At least, that's what he let them think. In reality, he was having another look at the towering beam that stretched from the punctured roof to the uneven floor. He knew what he was going to do, knew it was a gamble, but in such a situation, a gamble is the only thing left. He gave Jarvis one more look and smiled.

Jarvis's forehead lined. 'What the fuck you grinning at, ya bastard?'

Jones was closing in. It was now or never, Davie thought, and dodged to his right, putting the beam between him and the gun, then threw his shoulder against the heavy wood. He felt it give immediately, but not enough, not nearly enough. He heard Jarvis swear and then the sound of Jones's pistol, but the shot must've gone wide. Davie glanced round the beam, saw Jarvis moving towards him, the other three still far enough away with Jones closing in from the left, gun at arm's length. That wouldn't help his aim, Davie thought, as another round went wild. A third shot thudded into the wood just above Davie's head and as he strained against the beam, he saw Jones had stopped and was trying to take careful aim, using both hands like he'd seen in the movies. Davie planted both feet firmly and heaved, straining against the beam. It shifted, bringing some slates crashing close to Jarvis. Jarvis jerked back and looked up. Davie rammed his shoulder against the beam again, heard the base rasp against the boards beneath. He continued to shove, feeling the weight of the beam itself begin to help him, more material tumbling from the roof as the top dislodged and began to topple. A section of wood lanced down and battered into the floor in front of Jones, who threw himself out of the way. Jarvis backed away, his eyes on the loosening roof, and the other three men also retreated. They all wanted to get away from the beam as it first rocked then descended, bringing with it a shower of debris. Jarvis dodged a thick plank of wood that shot his way then spun, jerking the nail gun in the direction he'd last seen Davie, but couldn't see him through the blizzard that now raged through the widening hole in the ceiling and the dust thrown up by the collapsing wood and slates. The beam finally crashed to the

ground, sending more particles of dirt and shattered slates flying
into the air. Jarvis waved the cloud away from his face, squinting
for Davie. Jones picked himself up and slouched into a crouch,
peering through the mixture of snow and dust.

Jarvis didn't see Davie closing in on him from his blind side.
Davie hadn't stopped moving as the beam fell, he'd circled round,
and came at him from the darkness. He rammed into Jarvis,
grabbed his right wrist with his right hand, looped his arm round
his head and wrapped his fingers round his chin. He gave Jarvis's
head a sharp tug, heard a pained groan, and twisted the arm
holding the weapon until it was folded behind the man's back. He
jerked on the shoulder, fingers digging into the flesh of the wrist
and he leaned into Jarvis's ear. 'Drop it,' he breathed.

Jarvis may have been a craw, but he wasn't going to give in
easily. 'Fuck... you...' he managed, before Davie forced his arm even
further up his back, putting more strain on the shoulder ligaments.
The nail gun slid between them to land on the floor. Davie kicked it
further way, then shot a look over Jarvis's shoulder to see his men
had gathered again and were moving towards them from all sides.
Jones was already just a few feet away, gun raised. Okay, he'd
disarmed Jarvis, but he still didn't have Scratchy – and he was the
object of the exercise. He looked down at the man, nails poking from
his bloody hands. He'd stopped writhing but was still muttering.

'What you gonnae do now, McCall?' Jarvis sounded trium-
phant through his pain.

The truth was, he had no idea. He could stun Jarvis, take Jones
down, grab the gun and start blasting, but the thug Jarvis had sent
to kill him the other night had been right – he didn't like guns, had
never used one. He twisted Jarvis in front of him, hearing a satis-
fying grunt of pain, and backed away, keeping Scratchy and the
far wall behind him and all four men in his eyeline. With Jarvis's
body shielding him for now, Davie's mind raced again. Fine, he
had Jarvis, they were away from Scratchy, but what now?

'It's not too late, McCall,' said Jarvis, his voice showing the
strain of Davie's grip. 'You can just turn and go, no harm done.
It'd be like you'd never been here...'

Sounded reasonable, but Davie knew Jarvis didn't mean a word of it. There'd be a bullet in his back before he reached the door. No – the dice had been thrown, now Davie had to wait to see whose number came up.

Jarvis, though, lost patience. 'For God's sake, shoot this fucker, will you? He's breaking my arm here.'

The men fanned out, encircling Davie and Jarvis, leaving him open to attack from any side. One of the other men had a gun out now, which complicated matters. Davie jerked Jarvis from side to side, trying to keep them all in view. He would've preferred the solid wall directly behind him, but he was a good six feet away and had very little idea how solid the flooring was between him and it. He'd had no firm plan from the start, which was a mistake. Never go in blind, Joe used to say. Know the ground, know the exits, know the strengths and weaknesses. But Davie had come in blind and he'd been forced to act sooner than he expected and now he was paying the price. His mind galloped through various scenarios, but none of them ended well for him. His best bet was to wait, see how it played, then seize any chance he could.

He was barely aware of the movement to his left, just something surging across the empty church, a blur, a growl and then Jones turning towards it, a curse on his lips and shock in his eyes. He didn't know what had hit him until he was falling back, the dog's paws on his chest and its jaws snapping at his face. He tried to bring the gun level as he pitched backwards, but the dog twisted, sank its teeth into his hand. Jones screamed, hit the floor and tried to roll away, but the dog held on, his head shaking his prize back and forth. There was blood now – and screaming, lots of screaming.

Davie threw Jarvis away from him with force and darted forward, trying to reach the nail gun. Jones' brother remembered why he was there and moved just as quickly, trying to get to the weapon first, but Davie snatched the tool up and rolled to the side. The man tried to follow but Davie stretched out, pressed the gun against his leg and pounded a nail into his calf. The man dropped to his knees, his screams mixing with his brother's, who had managed to jerk his hand free, losing a chunk of flesh in the process. The gun lay at the dog's feet and he stood over it, teeth bared in a bloody snarl, as if daring Jones to try to snatch it away. Jones backed away, never taking his eyes from the animal.

Davie pulled himself to his feet and looked across the space to see Lenny pinning the other gunman by the throat against the wall. The man's feet were a good inch from the floor and his eyes were bulging. Lenny gave him a rap on the forehead with his cane, let him drop like wet washing then retrieved the gun from where it had landed and expertly slid the magazine from the grip, jerked a live round free and checked the chamber was completely empty. Bobby held the last man in an armlock and was dragging him around the room, firing punches at his face as he moved. He darted one final blow then let his opponent go. The man's knees buckled and he slammed onto the floor. 'Oops,' said Bobby.

Jarvis had hauled himself to his feet and he watched his men being bested as he rubbed his shoulder. He made no moves to help them or go for Davie. He knew when he was beaten.

Sammy strode between them all and knelt beside Scratchy. When he laid a hand gently on his chest, the vagrant cried out and his head jerked up. Sammy shot back like he'd been burned.

'Easy, son,' Sammy said, his voice soothing, 'we're here to help.'

Scratchy's head sank back and he resumed his muttering. Davie stepped to Sammy's side and stared down at the vagrant's wounds. The palms were slick with blood, which pooled and soaked into the boards beneath them.

Sammy looked up and Davie saw the horror in his eyes. 'Jesus, Davie…' He tried to say something else, but the words wouldn't come. Instead, he shook his head and looked back down. *Jesus indeed,* thought Davie. Scratchy had been crucified for other men's sins.

Davie turned back to Jarvis, who was giving him a dark, hate-filled glare. 'I'll not forget this,' he said.

Davie stepped closer to him and stared directly into his face. 'You played, you lost. Live with it.'

Jarvis blinked, tried to hold Davie's cold gaze, but couldn't. He looked at Bobby, then Lenny and finally Sammy. Davie realised he was memorising faces and when he spoke, his voice was so quiet that only Jarvis heard it. 'Don't even think about it.' Jarvis swallowed, unnerved by Davie's quiet manner. Davie held his gaze for a moment more then said, 'Pick up your rubbish and get home to your mammy.'

Jarvis hesitated for as long as he could, then looked away. He looked for Jones and jerked his head towards his brother. 'Jonesy, see to Gwynfor.'

'Fuckin mutt near tore my hand off, Jerry!'

'Man up, for God's sake. Give your brother a hand.' Jones cradled his hand as he haltingly went to help Gwynfor, who was tentatively touching the nail still protruding from his calf. He was crying. Jarvis turned to the man Lenny had pinned to the wall earlier, who was coming round and dragging himself to his feet, an ugly red welt already formed between his eyes. 'Tommy, lift Craig up, get him out of here.' Tommy crossed somewhat unsteadily to his mate and hauled him to his feet as Jarvis backed away from Davie. The wider the gap became, the more his courage returned. 'I don't care who you are, McCall. You've shoved your nose into something you shouldn't. I won't forget this, any of this, I won't forget any of you.'

Davie contented himself with a long, hard look as Jarvis continued to back away, his men limping or being helped after him. Then they were through the door and out of sight. Bobby shook his head as he moved closer Davie. 'How come these boys always have to have the last word?' Davie shrugged as he watched Sammy trying to comfort Scratchy, Lenny now at his side. Bobby didn't want to get any closer.

Davie knew there was little he could do to help, so he moved to where the dog sat, still guarding the gun. He knelt, scratching it behind one ear.

'You should've seen him go, Davie,' said Bobby behind him. 'Like an arrow, right for that guy, soon as he was off his lead.'

Davie looked into the dog's eyes, willing the animal his thanks. The dog's tongue rolled out one side of his mouth and he leaned forward, sniffed Davie's face. There was no attempt to lick, for which Davie was thankful, but they had turned a corner. Maybe there was a future for them after all.

He was still looking at the dog when he said, 'You shouldn't have got involved, Bobby.'

Bobby's face looked hurt. 'We heard the shooting, Davie. No way we were letting you face it alone.'

'You're out of The Life, Bobby, you took a risk.'

'I'm out of The Life, mate, not out of yours.'

Davie felt something nip at his throat and he turned back to the dog to cover up his blinking eyes. Bobby was the closest thing he had to a brother. It would remain unsaid, though. It always would between them.

'Do me a favour, though,' Bobby said and Davie raised his head again. 'For God's sake, don't tell Connie about this.'

Marie was in the square hallway of their Shawlands flat, a new red notice in her hand. Donovan didn't know where it was from, it didn't really matter. She had been waiting for him, he realised, the fury building inside her, which was why she was in the hallway, not even giving him the chance to take off his coat or step into the living room. She didn't scream, for their daughter was sleeping in her room a few feet away, but her voice seemed deafening.

'What the hell is going on, Frank?' He could see the tears in her eyes, hear the strain in her voice. He couldn't answer. He just stared at her. 'This says we're behind in the Council Tax,' she said. 'The Council Tax, Frank. What the hell is going on?'

He opened his mouth, about to say that he'd sort it, but the words wouldn't form. The truth was, he couldn't sort it, not this time. It had gone too far. He was still reeling from the revelation that his debt had been bought out. Now this. He couldn't answer. He couldn't cope.

That was when his mobile rang. Marie's eyes dropped to his coat pocket, where she knew the phone nestled, then raised back to his face. Her mouth was set in an angry line, her eyes glistened with moisture and rage and confusion. The ringing didn't stop, but Frank still did not move.

'You'd better get that,' Marie said, her voice flat. 'Maybe they'll get something out of you, because God knows I can't.'

She turned away, her shoulders hunched, and walked into the living room. Frank watched her go, the phone still ringing, then turned into the kitchen. He took the mobile from his pocket, clicked the green button. 'Hello.'

'We've found him.'

Frank Donovan hadn't expected Davie and Sammy to find Scratchy at all, let alone this fast. But then, as they'd said, they had access to sources closed to the police. He'd given Davie his personal mobile number, feeling it was best not to have contact through the Force's phones. He'd thought it was a good idea then, now he thought it was a great one, for it had got him away from the accusing eyes that had cut through him like lasers.

'Where?'

'Abandoned church in Roystonhill.' Donovan had worked Baird Street for a few years, he knew the church. 'Frank,' said Davie, 'he's in a bad way. Jerry Jarvis got to him first. You'd better call an ambulance.'

Donovan understood immediately. Davie and his friends couldn't call the services because that would leave them open to questioning. 'Okay. I'm on my way.'

He left without a word to Marie. There was nothing he could say.

Davie got back to his flat in the early hours of the morning. They'd waited a distance down the road from the church until the ambulance arrived, closely followed by a police patrol car with two uniforms. Donovan finally pitched up about ten minutes later. They gave him a rundown of what had happened and then they left. There was nothing more they could do here and they knew Donovan would keep their names out of it.

There was a message waiting for Davie on his machine. An impatient Lassiter, wondering where the hell he was. Davie realised he hadn't seen him that day, then resolved to call him tomorrow. He was tired and he needed sleep. He glanced at the dog, who was already curled up on his duvet in the living room. Davie left him there, went into his bedroom, dropped fully clothed onto the bed and closed his eyes.

Five minutes later, he heard the dog padding into the room and felt his weight landing on the bottom of the bed.

SATURDAY

Maw Jarvis was, to an extent, a creature of habit. Her boys knew there were certain constants in her life. One was that they always – *always* – had chicken for Sunday dinner. They longed for the occasional bit of roast beef or lamb, but no, she liked chicken on a Sunday. Wednesday night was pasta night, Friday, a Chinese carry-out. Similarly, every Christmas she baked a clootie dumpling, just like her mum and her gran had. The heavy fruitcake would last well into January and they'd be expected to eat it as dessert, as a snack and even fried with their breakfast. Her habits extended to her own routine. She had her hair done on the first Tuesday of every month. She put flowers on her dead husband's grave every Saturday afternoon.

And every Saturday she went to Safeway for the weekly shopping.

Jerry had asked her not to go, but she was damned if she was going to let Big Rab have the satisfaction of upsetting her life. She had done this every week, except when they were away in Spain on holiday, and she would do it this week.

She had a couple of boys waiting in the car, because she wasn't stupid, but the shopping she did on her own. She doubted if anyone would try anything in the supermarket. She hated anyone trailing along behind her as she pushed her trolley up and down each and every aisle. She had a list of what she needed, but she also kept her eyes open for something new or on offer. It was one of the few moments she had to herself, so she took her time doing it. Living in a house full of men was tiring for her, but this day she wished she had company. Marko was dead, Andy was on remand, Scrapper still confined to the house. Only Jerry was out there – and he had screwed up last night. He should've done that tramp no problem, but he had to be creative about it.

He was her eldest and she loved him, but he worried her. Maybe it was her fault – she had overlooked his nature since he was a boy, when she found him torturing a kitten with a lighter. Paw had said he'd grow out of it so she had let it go, but part of her knew that it wasn't true. There was something not right in

Jerry's head. Oh, he hid it well and occasionally it was useful to put the fear of God into someone, but Maw knew Jerry was a banana short of full bunch. But he was her son and she loved him, just as she loved them all. Still, he should've done that Scratchy fella clean. Now the police had him and God knows what he's saying. Jerry said not to worry, he had that covered, but she still worried. That's what mothers did.

The girl on the checkout looked familiar, but Maw couldn't place her. Her badge said her name was KIRSTY but it didn't ring any bells. But the girl knew her, for as Maw paid for her messages she said she was sorry for her loss. Maw thanked her, it was nice of her after all, and wheeled her trolley away from the checkout, still trying to figure out how she knew the lassie. Maybe she just knew who she was and was just paying her respects. Maw Jarvis was hardly unknown between Maryhill and Springburn, after all. A few other folk nodded to her as she left, more faces she knew, and she nodded back. She did not smile, for she didn't have one in her. Her Marko was dead, murdered by that bastard McClymont. She wouldn't smile until he was in the ground.

And that was in hand.

The two boys were waiting beside the car, a black Ford, the motor running. One sprung the boot, then helped the other load the plastic bags inside. Maw supervised, making sure they packed the things away correctly. If she got home and found any of the eggs cracked or smashed, there'd be trouble. It was cold in the big car park, no snow, but there had been plenty the night before and sections of the car park were still blanketed. The sky was gun metal grey, the air ear-bitingly sharp, so they moved fast, eager to return to the heat of the car.

They should have been paying closer attention to their surroundings, but they weren't. They shouldn't have both helped with the storage, or Maw should've kept watch, but they didn't. So they didn't see the men coming towards them from three directions, faces hidden under dark ski masks, each of them armed, each of them blasting from a few feet. One of her men was hit right away, a bullet ripping away part of his shoulder. He spun away from the car and another battered into his spine. He went down, his legs twitching. The other boy sprinted for cover and they let him go. He wasn't about to turn and fight, they could tell by the frightened scream as he ran and also by the way he tossed his gun away as soon as the shooting started.

That left Maw Jarvis.

She saw her man fall and the other one turn tail. She'd heard the bullets thud into the bodywork of the car and shatter windows. But none of them hit her. Running was not an option – they'd come for her and wouldn't let her go. Even if she got into the car, there was really nowhere to hide. She didn't have a gun, wouldn't know what to do with it even if she had. She'd never liked guns, abhorred the need for them in The Life these days, so she'd left them to Jerry and his lads.

After the first volley of shots, the silence was a relief. The three men stood very still, staring at her, as if waiting for something. Their guns were trained on her but she didn't feel fear, which surprised her. She knew she was going to die, right here in this cold, snowy car park, but she felt nothing. She did feel the chill, though, so she pulled her black coat tighter to her neck.

'Come on,' she said, 'what the fuck you waiting for?'

One of the men, squat but muscular, she could tell even under his thick parka, stepped forward, his gun held at arm's length.

'What's the delay, eh?' She said to him. 'No wantin to shoot an unarmed woman? That it? No thought this through? Eh? Come on, mastermind, you've started, so get it fuckin finished.'

The man was immobile as he stared at her through the slits in the mask. She wondered who he was, what he was thinking. She wondered if he would go through with it. Shooting at her boys was one thing, but this was a different, this was cold-blooded.

The bullet hit her before she even registered the report of the gun. It burrowed through her left cheek and shattered teeth as it carried on out the back of her neck. She felt the sharp pain as it entered and then something like a blow to her head as it exited. She slumped back against the rear of the car and the man fired again, twice, the first one exploding into her chest, the second tearing off a slice of her thigh. She slid to her left, coming to rest against the rear bumper. The agony raged through her body and she felt her left hand jerking, but she couldn't do anything to stop it. She tried to talk, but all she could produce was a gurgle as blood filled her mouth and drowned her tongue. She saw the gunman standing over her, his weapon at his side now, his head cocked to one side as he watched her. She heard sirens, far off still but coming. She slithered further down until she was on her side and the world went sideways. Then, like someone using a dimmer switch, the sirens faded into silence and the chill, grey day eased into black.

Jack Bannatyne knew he should've stepped into the investigation before now, but he hadn't wanted to tread on Scott Bolton's toes. But with the murder of Marko Jarvis and now the shooting in the supermarket car park, he had little choice. Scott would still lead the investigation, but now he had the full support of the Serious Crime Squad. It was bigger than the murder of some small-time pusher in a city nightclub. This had erupted into a full-scale gang war, something Bannatyne had feared for years.

He sat beside Scott Bolton in the briefing room at Stewart Street police station, a mixture of his own men and the local strength seated at tables in front of them. He saw Frank Donovan at the back, a pale shadow of the man he'd known years before. And there was Jimmy Knight, right at the front, a cigarillo smouldering between his teeth. Jimmy had passed Donovan as he walked in, clapping him on the back. If looks could kill, the one Donovan shot Knight would've had the undertaker getting out his tape measure. Bannatyne knew something grated between those two but now it had developed into unmasked hatred on Donovan's part. He wondered if it was something to do with what they were going to discuss with him later.

When Bolton stood, the steady murmur of conversation stilled. Every face turned to him as he took up a position in front of three white boards covered in photographs and notes. Dickie Himes' picture was there, as were mug shots of Kid Snot, Marty Bonner and Stewie Moore, Andy Jarvis, Marko Jarvis and now their mother.

Bolton took a deep breath then said, 'You'll have seen that DCS Bannatyne is here and you'll know why. Serious Crime Squad are now on board with our investigation, thanks to the escalation of violence. Sir?'

Bannatyne nodded and rose. 'Things are out of hand,' he said, deciding to get straight to the point. 'And we need to put a stop to it.' He moved to the first white board and tapped the shot of Dickie Himes. 'What started out as a typical Friday night knifing has blown up into the kind of gang war we've not seen here for years. I won't have that, not in my city. And I want it stopped. I want you out there, in the streets, tapping every tout, tart and toe-rag you know. I want stones turned over and anything we find wriggling underneath poked with a stick. I want these gunmen in the cells before Monday morning. I want Strathclyde Police to be able to tell the taxpayers that we're on the case. Because right now Mr and Mrs Public are wondering just what the hell we're doing with ourselves. These morons are running around the streets, firing off guns and we're sitting in the station with our thumbs firmly up our backsides. That ends now. If I don't see the will to crack down on this bloodshed then it'll be my boot up your arses and not your thumbs, understood?'

Bannatyne waited a moment, flicking from face to face to make sure his message had sunk home, then he sat down again. Bolton stepped forward again. 'So what have we got so far?' He turned to the white boards and provided a verbal rundown of what had happened since the previous Friday night, tapping each picture in turn as he mentioned their names. When he turned and mentioned Scratchy's name, he asked, 'How is he, DS Donovan?'

Frank cleared his throat and said, 'Not good, virtually catatonic. Docs say it's shock.'

'So he's saying nothing, right?'

'Nothing you'd understand.'

Bolton sighed. 'So, no eyewitnesses, just blood, DNA and Bonner's wound. It'll do to put him and his pal away for a long time.'

'I don't think they did it, boss,' said Donovan.

Bolton looked irritated, but it was Jimmy Knight who stood up. 'They did it, Frank. I'd bet my pension on it.'

Bannatyne saw Donovan fire off that dark and deadly look again, but his voice was calm when he spoke. 'They were there, but I don't think they did Dickie Himes. I almost had Moore talking...'

'But he's not, is he?' Knight gave the rest of the room a big grin.

Donovan paused, his teeth clenching. He was holding something in, Bannatyne could tell. 'No, someone got to him, put the fear of death into him. I wonder how they found out he was talking to us, Jimmy.'

Jimmy Knight caught the tone and turned round to face Donovan across the room. The smile was still there, but something frosty crept into his tone. 'You got any ideas about that, Frankie boy?'

Donovan held Knight's eyes with his own. 'A couple.'

There was a silence then, as if everyone was holding their breath. The antipathy Bannatyne had sensed was now out in the open and they all knew it. It was Bolton who broke the spell.

'Then until we get some firm evidence, Bonner and Moore it is. But that's not the immediate problem. As DCS Bannatyne said, this is out of hand. It's up to us to stop it. You all know what to do. Hit the streets, bring us something that will lead to convictions.' The collection of cops stared back at him, expecting him to say more. He waited until they realised there was nothing further to be said and they began to file out. Knight gave Bannatyne and Bolton a nod and sauntered towards the back of the room. Bannatyne had often thought the big cop was the only person who could swagger while sitting down. Knight stopped as Donovan rose to meet him, his body language that of a man with a mind to take something further. Bolton saw it, too, because he shouted, 'DS Donovan, can we see you for a moment?'

Donovan tore his eyes from Knight's grinning face and looked towards Bannatyne and Bolton. 'Yes, sir,' he said. Knight gave Donovan a grin, lodged his cigarillo between his teeth again and stepped round him. Donovan swivelled his head to watch him leave, and saw a sharp-suited man with the look of a Pitt Street smoothie walking towards him, a slim but expensive briefcase in his hand. He stopped and gave Donovan a nod, waving a hand in front of him.

'After you, DS Donovan,' he said, his voice strong and cultured. Cologne wafted from him like a calling card and his tan was deep, even and not the product of a sunbed. Donovan preceded him down the aisle to where Bannatyne and Bolton waited.

Bannatyne kept his seat while Bolton gave the white boards another look, then perched on the edge of the table. Donovan took a seat in the front row, the newcomer did the same, but on the other side of the aisle. Donovan waited for someone to speak.

'DS Donovan,' Bolton began, then tried to adopt a less formal tone. 'Frank, we've had some... erm... disappointing information steered towards us.' Bolton paused. 'About you.'

Donovan shifted slightly in his chair. 'What kind of information?'

Bolton coughed, clearly uncomfortable with the situation. It was the suit to Donovan's right who spoke next. 'Personal information, Detective Sergeant Donovan. You owe people money.'

Donovan said nothing, but he felt his breath freeze in his chest. He looked at Bolton then at Bannatyne and saw concern on their faces. Then he looked at the third man and saw nothing but business. Right then, he pegged him as being from Complaints and Discipline.

'This is DCI Oxford,' said Bannatyne.

'The Rubberheels?' The words were out before Donovan knew it. He saw a flicker of annoyance on Oxford's face, but he didn't rise to the bait. Donovan regretted his lack of control. This was no time to poke the bear.

Oxford said, 'We've been made aware of your situation and are extremely concerned.'

'Who made you aware?'

'That doesn't matter. All you need to know is that we know.'

Donovan opened his mouth, then closed it again. He paused. 'Do I need a federation rep here?'

'This is off the record, Frank,' said Bolton. 'Between us.'

'For now,' said Oxford, and Donovan caught the heavy tone. This was serious. Oxford got right to it, pulling a file from his briefcase like a rabbit from a hat. 'It appears you have a gambling problem, DS Donovan, and thanks to that you owe money to the wrong kind of people. People you should be putting away.'

Donovan blinked rapidly, licked his lips, swallowed. 'I like a punt now and then, sure...'

'It's more than that, I think,' said Oxford, looking at the file. 'You play the horses, you play poker, you play the gaming tables at the Corinthian Casino. And you lose heavily at them all.'

Christ, they've been digging around. 'Sure, I've had a bad run, but that happens. It's under control.'

'No, it's not,' said Oxford, his voice even, measured. 'You're a drowning man going down for the third time. And the Chief Constable doesn't want you taking the Force with you.'

'Look at you, Frank,' said Bannatyne, 'look at the state of you. You've lost weight, you're like a walking corpse, for God's sake. And now you're into the Jarvises for almost two grand.'

Donovan leaned forward. 'The Jarvises?'

'DS Donovan, please don't treat us like idiots. Certainly we've only been aware of your problem for a day or two, but we've done a thorough job. We know how much you owe and to whom you owe it.'

The Jarvis clan, thought Donovan. Shit – that's who bought it over. And now he knew why. And two grand – they'd added interest.

'I'm being set up,' he said and that raised what passed as a smile from Oxford. 'No, listen,' said Donovan, desperation creeping into his voice. 'I know it was Scrapper Jarvis who killed Himes and they want me out of the way.'

Bolton said, 'We've been through this already, Frank. There's nothing to link Scrapper to the killing...'

'Yeah, but they know I'm not going to stop until I find a link. They're not taking any chances, boss.'

Oxford exchanged glances with Bannatyne and Bolton. Donovan knew they weren't buying it. Oxford exhaled heavily and closed the file. 'As we said, this is an off-the-record chat. However, the Chief Constable does want you to take some time off, take some sick leave. You've been under some stress of late, I'm sure.'

'I'm okay...'

'We need you off this, Frank,' said Bolton. 'We need you out of the building until the Himes case and all the rest is cleared. We can't have you involved or in a position to contaminate the investigation.'

Donovan stared at him. 'Contaminate? That's what I am now? Some kind of virus?'

Bannatyne leaned forward. 'As far as this case is concerned, yes. Look at it from our side, Frank – we've got an officer involved in a high profile murder investigation who owes a substantial sum of money to known criminals who also happen to be targets in that investigation. First Moore was, as you said, scared off from talking. Now, who told the Jarvises that the boy was thinking of talking?'

'It wasn't me.'

'I'm not saying it was, I'm just saying how it looks. Then there's this Scratchy individual. You knew we were looking for him, but someone got to him first.'

'Everybody knew we were looking for him...'

'Not everyone gets an anonymous tip to where he is lying injured.'

'Jimmy Knight found him before I knew where he was.'

Bolton sighed. 'I don't like Knight any more than you do – less, probably – but he phoned me immediately and told me where this individual was. I'd arranged for uniforms to swing by, but it all went down before they could get there, thanks to an urgent shout elsewhere.'

Donovan shook his head. 'This doesn't make sense.'

Oxford spoke. 'We're talking about how it looks, DS Donovan, and this situation could be made to look very bad for us. A half-decent lawyer could create reasonable doubt without breaking a sweat. And there's no getting away from the fact that you owe moneylenders cash. That's a disciplinary offence right there. And you've been drinking a lot lately, people have seen you. And then there's the gambling. It doesn't look good, does it?'

Donovan had to admit it didn't look good at all. He felt dizzy, it was all happening so fast. He couldn't believe it. He ran a hand through his hair, tried to control the tremor in his fingers but couldn't. He felt sick. He felt tired. He felt like he needed a drink.

'See your doctor, DS Donovan,' Oxford said, and Frank thought he heard something like sympathy in his voice. 'Tell him you've been under a lot of pressure. Tell him you've been drinking too much, not sleeping. Tell him about the gambling if you feel you have to, but get him to sign you off on the sick.'

'And then what?' Frank didn't like the sound of his own voice. It sounded dull, lifeless.

'Then we discuss your future at a disciplinary level.'

Donovan knew what that meant. He was finished. Everything would come out, because the Rubberheels were nothing if not thorough.

Jerry Jarvis was numb as he looked down at his mother. They'd told him they'd done everything they could, but it was only a matter of time. She should have died in the car park, they said, but she was hanging on, as if there was something else she had to do. The doctor actually said that. As if she had something to do. The doctor spoke softly, as if she didn't want to wake Maw up.

Maw looked so frail in the hospital bed, a respirator helping her breathe, wires trailing from her arms, her chest, her head. Her eyes were closed, her face pale, sunken. She looked old. He'd seen her that morning and she looked the same – still in mourning, sure – but her face was full and her eyes lively. Scrapper hung back from the bed, as if he was scared to get too close. Useless wee fuck.

Jerry touched her hand, expecting the flesh to be cold, but there was heat there. He slid his fingers through hers and gave her hand a gentle squeeze. He felt the pressure returned, just barely, but she knew they were there. She knew he was there.

'We're here, Maw,' he said, his voice hoarse as he fought the tears. 'Me and Scrapper, we're here.'

He felt her fingers twitch again and he saw her eyes move under her lids. Jerry couldn't stand seeing her like this. She was his maw.

She had always been the strongest of them all. And now she was lying in a scabby hospital bed, the life all but gone. He swallowed back the grief and the anger and said, 'Can you hear me, Maw?' Her fingers closed on his hand. Her eyelids fluttered open and she looked straight at him. He saw her mouth working, but the respirator prevented any words.

'Don't say nothing, maw,' he said, 'just take it easy. Rest.'

Her eyes blazed, Jerry didn't know with what. Her grip tightened on his as she stared at him. She was trying to tell him something. He struggled to understand what she wanted, thought about buzzing for a nurse, but knew in his heart this was not a medical issue. He felt tears sting at his eyes. This wasn't his Maw, not this weak, wounded thing. This wasn't her. He saw effort crease her face as she forced her fingers to tighten further on his. That old light burned brighter as she tried to convey her thoughts. He shook his head, 'Maw, I don't…'

And then, in a blinding moment of clarity, he heard her voice in his head, clear as a bell, as if she was whole and healthy again and standing beside him. He leaned in until his mouth was at her ear. He said a few words and straightened. She nodded. He'd guessed correctly. He was her first born and there had always been something special between them. He knew there was nothing supernatural about what had happened, it was just another sign that they were on the same wavelength. Her fingers spasmed and fell away from his hand. Her eyes rolled to white before the lids slid over them. He thought she'd slipped away, but she was still breathing, a mucus-heavy rattle coming from her throat.

Jerry let go of her hand and moved to Scrapper's side. His younger brother said, 'What did you say to her, Jerry?'

Jerry took one last look at his mother and stiffened his shoulders, willing the bitter tears to dry. He was her son. He wouldn't break, not yet. There was work to do.

'Jerry?' Scrapper again, his voice pitched even higher than usual. Jerry stared into his face, saw the fear there. Jerry felt no sympathy for him, for it was his weakness that had caused all this. But he was still his brother and he would look after him. That's what

Maw would've wanted, for she believed family was everything. 'What did you say?'

'Time to finish it,' he said.

Lassiter listened to the phone ringing, his irritation growing with every ring. Jesus Christ, he'd paid the man good money for a service and now he was nowhere to be found. Goddamn it! He slammed the receiver down so hard that even Mannie jumped.

'We're going over there,' he said.

'You think you should, Mickey?' Coco said. 'Davie told you not to go there again.'

'I'm his boss, for Christ's sake,' said Lassiter. 'I tell him, he doesn't tell me.'

'Give it another day, huh? He's maybe got something on. I mean, he is a criminal... maybe he's been arrested or something.'

Lassiter thought about that. She might have something. And if he went over there, what would he be walking into? On the other hand, he was having a meet with the screenwriter on Monday in London and he needed a few more notes from Davie. They were making progress, this project was shaping up to be everything he wanted it be – but now his special adviser had gone walkabout. He shook his head. 'Don't worry, babes,' he said. 'It'll be okay. I'll just go there, speak to him or leave a note telling him I really need to see him, then I'll be back.' He saw the worried look in her eyes and he reached out and touched her cheek. Sometimes he really loved this chick. 'Hey, Mannie'll be with me. It'll be in, out, no sweat.'

She smiled but it was forced, he could tell. 'Please, Mickey, just give it one more day. Another day can't hurt.'

He saw the plea in her eyes and he relented. 'Okay, babe, sure. One more day.'

'It's over, Davie,' said Rab, smiling. 'Ding-dong, the witch is dead.'

He was behind the bar of the The Black Bird, pouring himself a celebratory malt whisky. Davie looked at Stringer, sitting at a table nearby, a lager in front of him. He'd pulled the trigger on the woman, no doubt about it, just as he'd done Marko. The man's broad face was neutral as he returned Davie's gaze, giving nothing away. Choccie Barr and Fat Boy McGuire sat at another table. Fat Boy was smiling, Choccie was serious. Like Davie, he knew this wasn't over.

'I heard she's hanging on.'

Rab dismissed the thought as if it was a mere formality with a wave of a hand

'Jerry Jarvis is still walking around,' said Davie. 'Even Scrapper.' Rab waved his hand again. 'Jerry's just a thug, nothing without his Maw. She was always the brains. As for Scrapper, there's a village somewhere looking for its idiot. We'll deal with them both, when the time's right.'

Davie knew Gentleman Jack Bannatyne himself had paid Rab a visit earlier that day. Rab, naturally, denied all knowledge of any unpleasantness – *only what I read in the paper, Mister Bannatyne. I'm just a businessman, earning an honest crust.* Bannatyne wouldn't have believed a word of it, of course, but Rab was too clever to let any of the blood splash back on him. However, he'd pull back for a while, let the heat die. Davie wondered if Jerry Jarvis would do the same.

'The Jarvis clan is finished now,' said Rab. 'What was theirs is now ours for the taking, know what I'm sayin?'

To the victor goes the spoils, Rab was saying, but Davie wasn't so sure. The Jarvis clan was down, but it wasn't out. Jerry Jarvis was a sadistic sod and he was enough like his mother to carry on where she left off. This wasn't over, not by a long shot.

SUNDAY

The pub was busy, but not with customers. Bernadette and Rab were in the office. The kids sat with Choccie and Fat Boy, young Joseph as serious as ever as he read a *Spider-Man* comic, Lucia working on a colouring book, helped by Fat Boy. She hummed a song Davie recognised but couldn't put a title to. She broke off to tell Fat Boy that he had to stay inside the lines, silly, and he grinned and apologised. Davie smiled at the sight of Fat Boy's fleshy hand trying to grip the slim crayon as he worked on the drawing, his face a picture of concentration.

Sammy had also arrived and he sat at a table with Davie, stirring at a coffee. The dog lay under the table, gnawing on a rawhide chew.

'The lawyer says there's nothing much can be done,' Sammy said, then looked towards the opaque glass facing onto Shettleston Road. Shadows passed outside, people walking by, ordinary people, going about their lives. The cough of buses expelling diesel fumes, cars, taxis and lorries edging from one set of traffic lights to another. Life went on in the city. And his grandson sat in his cell up in Barlinnie while the legal noose tightened. Finding Scratchy, getting him to talk, had been his only hope but the guy was too trauma-tised to say anything. They'd saved his life but it hadn't been enough.

'He may talk yet,' Davie said.

Sammy shook his head. 'Your pal, that cop, said it – he's too far gone. Mind's snapped. If he saw anything he'll never remember and even if he did some lawyer'd tie him up in rings. I saw Marty this morning, broke the news to him.'

'How is he?'

Sammy inclined his head. 'Resigned. Knows the game's a bogey. He's pissed off, though, that Scrapper Jarvis is getting away scot-fuckin-free.'

Davie thought about Marko Jarvis and his mother, both dead or as near as damn it. Another brother facing heavy time. Scrapper himself may still be at liberty, but the family hardly got off scot-free.

Sammy gave Davie a wan smile. 'Justice, eh?'

Davie felt he had to give the old man something but couldn't think what to say. In the end all he could say was, 'Sometimes these things have a way of working out.'

Mannie had bought the coat the day before because he needed something to ward off this country's goddamn climate. It was a big, black waterproof and when he pulled it on, it looked like he had wings.

'Jeez, Mannie,' said Lassiter, smiling, 'you're like a goddamn crow in that coat.'

Hurt flitted across the man's big face as he looked down at the expensive slicker and Lassiter instantly felt sorry. He'd not meant anything by it, but sometimes he forgot how sensitive Mannie could be. He'd been with Lassiter for years, since he was in his late teens, when his dad had told him the big fella was going to be his new best friend, and there were times when Lassiter took him for granted.

'Sorry, big guy,' he said, patting Mannie on the shoulder, 'it's a great coat, really good for this place, this time of year.'

Mannie's pained look subsided and he smiled.

The cab dropped them off right at the entrance to Davie's building. Someone had cleared the snow away from the sidewalk, but they'd dumped it into the gutter and Lassiter's foot sunk right in as he stepped out of the rear of the black taxi. He cursed and pulled his foot free as Mannie came round the rear of the hack. If he thought it funny that his boss was shaking snow from his shoe and the bottom of his trousers he didn't show it.

'Wait in the street, big guy, won't be long,' said Lassiter as the taxi rattled off. Mannie nodded and took up a position beside the doorway and Lassiter pushed the security door open. It was busted, he knew that from his first visit. He stamped the last of the snow from his foot as he made his way to the first flight of stairs. There were a lot of things he liked about this city, but jeez, it was cold. He was a California boy and he didn't do the kind of cold that made your balls shrivel. He regretted the decision to shoot so early in the year but it was necessary to get the chill into the visuals that he wanted in the story. He wanted this to be a throwback to the '70s style of movie. Thrillers today had very little grit, they were all MTV flash and no substance. He wanted a harsh, grainy feel and he knew he'd find that in a Glasgow winter.

The few meetings Davie had taken had proved invaluable to Lassiter's vision. The guy was a real find. He'd helped Lassiter turn an okay script into something special. He hadn't written a word, but his insights into the mind of the character were illuminating, even if he didn't see it himself. The character – Connolly – was becoming fully-rounded now, at least in Lassiter's mind. He knew how he was going to play him, what nuances he would bring into his performance. He'd be based very much on Davie McCall, his mannerisms, his stillness. Shit, if he did this right, he could be in line for an Academy Award. Wouldn't that be something? It'd make his dad and his brother sit up. It was a pity the character died at the end of the movie, Lassiter had a real feel for him now. Maybe they could rewrite the ending, have him survive. Maybe get a franchise out of it. No more than three movies, though – wouldn't want to milk it. What was it they said here? Rip the arse out of it? Yeah, rip the arse out of it, sure. He had too much respect for the character to do that. A trilogy. That'd be about right. He'd talk to the writer about it when he got down to –

They say you don't hear the one that gets you, but Lassiter did. He heard the crack of the pistol just as he crested the flight of stairs on the second floor. He was turning towards McCall's door when the bullet caught him. He felt something strike him on the shoulder, something hot, something heavy, and it threw him to his left to slam into the wall. Another punched him on the chest and he felt fresh heat sear through him. His legs buckled and he slid down into a sitting position. He didn't know what was happening. He couldn't understand. He saw a man stepping down the stairs from the next landing, a gun stretched out ahead of him, and Lassiter knew then he'd been shot. He dropped his head to his chest, saw the blood seeping through his coat. This wasn't happening, he thought. He tried to raise his head, but it wouldn't move. A pair of feet appeared in front of him and he knew the guy was looking at him. Lassiter tried to speak, but the words wouldn't come. He heard the guy swear and then he was running down the stairs.

Lassiter tried to call out after him, to ask him why, but all he could manage was a croak. The pain was lessening now, which was something, but he knew that wasn't a good thing. He hoped someone had dialled 911. But it wasn't 911 here, was it? It was 999. Three nines. Triple-niner. Whatever the fuck it was, he hoped someone was punching it in right now. He willed his legs to move, to strengthen, to help him rise but he couldn't move any part of his body. All he could do was sit there and wait.

Bastard had looked so much like McCall.

Same hair, same build. Even had the same blue eyes, when Jerry Jarvis got closer.

But it wasn't him.

Jarvis pounded down the stairs, eager to put space between him and the guy bleeding on the second floor landing. He looked familiar, though, but in his panic Jarvis couldn't put a name to him.

He'd waited for over an hour on the landing between the second and third floors. He'd smoked ten fags in that time, just as an excuse for being there. Anyone came up or down, he'd make them think he was just outside for a smoke because he wasn't allowed to do it in the house. That'd satisfy them. And if it didn't then they could take a flying fuck. He'd not seen hide nor hair of anyone since he'd arrived, though, which was good. He'd rattled McCall's door when he arrived but there was no answer, so he'd taken up his position on the landing. His plan was to do him as he unlocked his door, just blast away with the pistol. Wouldn't give him the chance to do anything.

But it was the wrong fucking guy.

He'd been too nervous, that's what it was. Too eager. He should've made sure before he let loose. But the nerves got the better of him. Killing Kid Snot had been easy, but this guy, Davie McCall, he was something else again. He'd shown that in the church. I mean, who the hell would've pushed that fuckin beam over like that? Could've brought the whole place down on them, but he didn't give a fuck. That was McCall all over. That was why he had to go down, just like Rab would. Had to be out of the picture because you just never knew what he was going to do. Anyway, Jerry owed the bastard. He'd made a fool of him in the church, him and his pals. He'd get them all, sooner or later.

He stopped briefly on the first floor, the fag butts he'd left strewn on the landing suddenly hitting his mind like a thunderflash. He should've picked them up. They had his prints on them, his DNA. Fuck! He thought about going back, but then he heard the sound of heavy footsteps heading his way and a huge figure loomed into view on the halfway landing. Big bastard, looked like a fuckin raven or something in that coat. The guy stopped when he saw him and Jerry put a bullet in him. It was like second nature now, pulling this trigger. Jerry saw the bullet hit high on his right shoulder and the puff of blood, but the guy barely flinched and kept coming up the stairs towards him. Jerry backed away, fired again but this one went wild. The guy was still moving and Jerry knew he had to put him down fast. He stilled, steadied his aim with his other hand and fired. It caught the big fella square on the chest and would have stopped any other man but this guy was a fucking bear. He kept coming.

The big guy was on him before he could fire again, a meaty paw wrapped round his throat and throwing him up against the wall. Jarvis tried to pull free, but he could barely move. All he could do was flail as the guy tightened his fingers round his neck, cutting off the air supply, lifting him clear of the floor. Jarvis kicked his legs, hoping to strike something vital but it was a vain hope. He jerked at the man's hand to dislodge his grip, but it was a waste of time, the fingers crushed his windpipe like it was paper.

Jerry Jarvis died staring into the face of a man he didn't know. And as he died, a name came into his head, the last name he expected to think of.

Michael Lassiter. It was Michael Lassiter he'd killed up there. Fuck me, he thought.

Bernadette was glad to see Rab so happy but she, too, thought his elation was premature. Yes, Maw Jarvis was out of the picture, but she did not underestimate Jerry Jarvis. He had a trick or two up his sleeve, she knew it, and she urged Rab to continue to exercise caution.

'Believe me, darling,' he said, putting his arm around her. 'He's done. Those two polis raids hit them hard, two of the brothers are out the game, Scrapper's no use. We'll keep an eye on him but he'll no do nothing the now. His maw's just about gone. He'll maybe pull something somewhere down the line, but not now.'

She wished she could be as certain. Her view was that they should move in, finish it for once and for all. A clean sweep. Either let the law do it or Stringer, it didn't matter to her. All that mattered was that Rab and her family were safe.

'Davie's no sure, either,' said Rab. That didn't surprise her, for Davie McCall was always sharp.

'Does he know it wasn't Jarvis who sent those men?'

Rab shook his head. 'Nah, still thinks they came after him.'

Sending Edinburgh muscle had been Bernadette's idea, of course, but she made Rab think it was his. Her visit was an attempt to avoid using them, but she knew she'd failed, which both surprised and delighted her. She was surprised because she thought he was a sucker for a woman's charms, delighted because it showed strength of will. So as she left, she nodded to the two men who waited in their car. The attack on Davie not only kept him in the game, it also served as a wake-up call for the others. If they would go after McCall, then none of them would be safe. She hadn't expected that old lag to enter the picture, though. If she'd known that, perhaps the ruse wouldn't have been necessary. Still, that's life, she supposed.

She plucked the keys of Rab's Range Rover from the top of the desk. 'You sure you won't need it today?' She was taking Lucia to Edinburgh Zoo and she felt safer driving in the big four-wheel drive rather than her own Vauxhall. Joseph had decided he didn't want to go, so Rab would have him for the day.

He shook his head. 'I had Choccie take it down the road this morning and got it a right good clean and a hoover at the valet place. It's got a full tank of petrol, oil's been checked, tyre pressure, so you don't need to worry. Joe and me'll have a great time. I'll take him somewhere, pictures maybe. Your motor'll be fine for anything we do.'

She reached up with one hand, touched his cheek and he leaned down to kiss her. He rubbed her barely blossoming belly with his palm and she laid her hand over his. 'You take care of this wee one,' he said. 'No jumping around with the monkeys.'

She laughed. 'Which ones – the ones in the zoo or the one I'm taking with me?'

He smiled, kissed her again. 'We're gonnae be okay, love, you know that?'

She crooked her arm around his neck, pulled his face into her neck. 'As long as we're together, we can handle anything.'

They held each other for a moment. She loved this man so much it sometimes felt unreal. She could not believe how deep her passion was and how ferocious she could be in defending him and her children. Of course, there was Davie, who both attracted and terrified her. She didn't know what that was all about, but she'd deal with it.

She broke away and said, 'Right, this isn't getting us to Edinburgh. Lucia's been singing "Mamma's taking us to the zoo tomorrow" for days.'

'I'm sorry you ever taught her that bloody song.'

'You only heard it for an hour or so at night – I've had it all day long! It's like a broken record.'

They were leaving the small office now and Lucia jumped up as soon as she saw them, sending her colouring books and crayons flying. Fat Boy tried to catch them, but he was not the most agile of men and they ended up on the floor.

'Are we going now, mum? Are we? Are we?' The little girl vibrated with excitement as she ran across the pub floor.

Bernadette laughed. 'Yes, darling, we're going now. We're going to take Daddy's Range Rover, won't that be fun?'

Davie, watching from his table by the window, saw Choccie look up at that. Bernadette's gaze flicked towards Davie and she gave him a little smile. He felt a stab of discomfort, but that was all. Something was different and he wasn't sure what it was. Bernadette had changed as far as he was concerned.

Rab caught Lucia with both arms and hoisted her over his shoulder. She giggled. 'Let's get you settled in, then.'

Lucia's legs kicked and her little girl giggles built as he hefted her across the pub floor. Sunlight flooded the gloomy interior as he pulled open the double doors. Bernadette took young Joseph's hands and murmured something to him as they followed. Davie couldn't make out what it was but presumed he was being warned to be a good boy for his dad. The boy nodded, but didn't say a word.

Davie stood up and craned to see through the clear glass at the top of the window beside him. Rab crossed the street to where his blue Range Rover gleamed in the winter sunshine and strapped little Lucia into the rear seats. He kissed Bernadette. Davie felt the worm of guilt squirm in his chest, but seeing them kiss also made him think of Vari. Bobby was right – he did miss her. She brought something into his life that he was lacking, something he'd never thought he'd have. There was a time he wanted it with Audrey, but deep down he knew it would never have worked out between them. He and Audrey had been too different, whereas Vari understood him.

Bernadette climbed into the driver's seat. She waved at Rab, Lucia did the same. The little girl was smiling. She was happy. Rab crossed the street and stood beside his son, one arm draped over the boy's shoulder. Davie envied their happiness and wondered if he would ever find anything close to it. Bernadette smiled at her husband through the window and twisted the ignition.

The world slowed down when the Range Rover exploded.

The vehicle itself lifted slightly then crashed down again, a bubble of flame erupting from underneath, engulfing the interior. Davie and Sammy ducked as glass imploded around them while windows shattered on the tenement opposite and nearby cars. A murder of crows flapped skyward from a rooftop, startled by the explosion. Car alarms sounded, people screamed and yelled. Davie hauled himself to his feet, saw Sammy appeared unhurt, then glanced under the table to where the dog cowered, terrified by the blast. He told him to stay and darted outside. Rab was on the ground, Joseph underneath him, but was beginning to rise again.

He looked groggy but unscathed, even though he'd obviously
shielded his son from the blast. Davie moved across the road to
the burning Range Rover, but the flames were so intense he only
made it halfway. He shielded his face from the scorching heat with
his arm and peered into the inferno. He thought he saw a figure
slumped in the front and a smaller one in the rear but there was
no movement. There wouldn't be. There was no way either of
them could have survived.

He took a few steps back from the heat and looked round. Rab
was on his feet and stumbling towards the burning vehicle but
Davie grabbed him, pushed him away.

'Fuck off,' Rab snarled, 'Bernadette's in there!'

Rab tried to move forward again, but Davie blocked him, both
hands on his shoulders. 'My wee lassie!' Rab began, but when he
looked at the flames licking out of the broken windows Davie saw
something die. 'Bernadette…'

Davie felt his friend wilt and his legs buckle. He tried to hold
him, but he was too heavy. Rab landed hard on his knees, but he
didn't notice. Davie stayed with him, holding him tight, feeling his
friend's huge body quake with sobs. He'd never seen Rab cry
before and when he heard a howl grow from deep inside his old
mate, he felt his own heart break. He looked over Rab's shoulder
and saw young Joseph staring at the fire, his face blank, but his
eyes wide and dark. The boy shouldn't see this. Not this, Davie
thought. No-one should see this.

Choccie came out of the pub and paused at the door, taking in
the scene. 'Choccie,' Davie shouted, 'get Joseph away!'

But Choccie didn't even look at the child. He watched the
flames licking out of the Range Rover for a moment, then gave
Davie a frightened look before he ran off down the street. In that
moment, Davie knew – Choccie had planted the bomb, Choccie
had told the Jarvises where they would find Kid Snot, Choccie had
been working with them all along. He watched the man merge
with the crowd forming at the corner and then vanish.

It was Sammy who took young Joseph in both arms and carried
him back into the pub, the boy's expressionless face still watching

the flames over Sammy's shoulder. Despite the heat, Davie felt something icy breathe on the back of his neck.

Another massive sob burst from Rab and Davie held his friend tightly, as the flames crackled behind them and black smoke curled up into the winter sky. He held his friend, feeling his huge body shake and tremble as the tears flowed and he said his wife's name over and over again.

MONDAY

Donovan was drunk when he fronted Knight, otherwise he wouldn't have ended up on his arse. At least, that's what he told himself, even though deep down he knew he wasn't a match for the big bastard.

He'd intercepted him outside Pitt Street. Donovan had spent the afternoon in the Griffin Bar on the corner of Bath Street, drinking whisky with money he should have used to pay bills. Didn't matter much now, right enough, way things were. He was well screwed. Marie hadn't taken it well, no reason why she should've. He'd finally told her everything – the gambling, the debt, the arrears, the job. It had turned into a screaming match, which was always on the cards considering. It only ended when their daughter came into the room and begged them to stop, her voice choked with tears and fears. The pair of them fell silent as if someone had hit a mute button somewhere. Donovan had looked at his wife with shame but saw only fury and revulsion. He couldn't blame her. He wasn't even top of his own Christmas card list.

So he'd left, hadn't been home since. He'd taken a room in a cheap hotel in Garnethill, bought a bottle of cheap whisky, tried to find solace in a drunken stupor. He'd hit the Griffin around 5pm, knew he had a couple of hours before Knight was due to leave Pitt Street. Downed a few more, fuck the money, and then set out to face him. This was it, he told himself, showdown. Been a long time coming.

Knight didn't seem surprised when Donovan stepped in front of him, making him wonder if he'd expected him.

'Frankie boy,' said Knight, softly.

'Bastard,' said Donovan. He hadn't thought about what he would say and it was the first thing that came into his head. It sounded a bit lame, now he heard it. It needed emphasis. 'Dirty, grassing bastard.'

'Careful, Frankie, you might say something hurtful.'

'Oh, I'm sorry, bastard – did I offend you with the truth?'

Knight shook his head, tried to step around. 'Go home, son, sleep it off.'

Donovan blocked his way. 'You and me, bastard. Here.' He

adopted a crouch, his fists waist high. Knight smiled. He found this funny and that pissed Donovan off even more.

'Frankie, boy – I get the impression you blame me for your fuck up.'

'Who else would've told the bosses? Eh? Who else has the contacts to know how much I owe and who I owe it to?'

Knight shook his head. 'Wasn't me, son.'

'Aye – right.'

That was when Donovan threw his punch. He thought he'd been stealthy. He thought he'd catch Knight off-guard. He thought wrong. Knight easily dodged the lunge and planted one of his own squarely on Donovan's jaw. Donovan's feet slipped on the snow and he tried desperately to remain standing but he went down, landing squarely on his backside. He tried to get up, but he found it impossible. He couldn't look at Knight, who he knew was looking down at him with a mixture of disgust and pity. The disgust he could handle, he was growing used to that, but the pity was too much for him. He couldn't take that, not from the Black Knight.

'Look at yourself, man,' said Knight. 'Look at the state of you. Jesus, you're a mess.'

Donovan had to agree. He sat in the wet snow, his eyes downcast. Mess only just began to describe him. Then he was aware of banknotes dropping between his legs.

'Take this,' said Knight, 'go get yourself truly rat-arsed. Drink yourself into oblivion, mate, because that's all that's left for you.'

Donovan tried to think of a pithy comeback but nothing came. Knight was gone anyway. He'd stepped over him and was swaggering down the street. Donovan looked at the five £20 notes lying in the snow between his legs. It was Knight's money. Dirty money, probably.

He picked it up anyway.

Knight leaned against a black Ford in the car park, smoking a cigarillo and letting the world roll on its merry way. His encounter with Donovan had set him thinking. He understood why Frankie boy thought he'd grassed him up, but he hadn't. But he knew who had. He didn't blame Donovan for suspecting him, he was never the brightest bulb in the box, after all, but he didn't know what Knight knew.

He saw DCI Scott Bolton's step falter when he caught sight of him. The car was his. Knight was waiting for him. Time to clear some things up.

'What the fuck do you want?' Bolton said, not winning any prizes for courtesy.

'A wee word, Scotty,' said Knight.

Bolton unlocked the car door, opened it. When Knight didn't move, he said, 'You're going to look stupid flat on your back when I drive off.'

Knight took the cigarillo from his mouth and studied the glowing tip. 'Been thinking about Frank Donovan.'

Bolton took off his coat, threw it into the back seat. 'What about him?'

'It's funny the Jarvises buying over his debt, just when we were sniffing around. Convenient.'

'Who says they bought it over? The way the Complaints heard it, he owed them all along, that's why he fed them intelligence.'

'The Rubberheels are wrong.'

'How do you know?'

Knight smiled. 'I know lots of things, Scotty. For instance, I know there was a copper up 'C' Division with a taste for young girls. Very young girls. He wasn't married at the time, this copper, though he did get hitched later. But he still had this taste in his mouth for fresh meat. You never grow out of it. And the wrong people heard about it – Maw Jarvis, matter of fact. Funny how things turn out, isn't it? She started providing this copper with the lassies he craved so much. And he, like the dildo that he is, took them without thinking it through. There's photos, I hear. Nasty stuff.'

Bolton kept his face impassive as he listened, then he shook his head. 'Fairy tales, Knight.'

'Maybe so, but if that copper is real then he's feeling relief beyond belief right now, with Jerry Jarvis and Maw both gone to meet their maker.' Bolton's mouth opened slightly. 'You not hear?

She died a couple of hours ago.' Knight watched Bolton's face and was certain he saw some relief there. 'So this guy, if he exists, might think he's in the clear. But here's the thing – he doesn't know who might have those photos now.'

A nerve twitched in Bolton's eye. 'There is no cop. There are no photographs. The truth is, Donovan screwed up, pure and simple.'

'The truth's never pure, and seldom simple,' said Knight. 'Oscar Wilde said that. And he knew a lot about not being pure, didn't he, Scotty?'

Irritation gave Bolton's voice an edge. 'What the fuck do you want here, Knight?'

'Frankie boy didn't steer any gen to the Jarvises, I know it, you know it. See this copper? He exists. He told them about Scratchy. He told them about that boy in Barlinnie who was about to burst. He steered the location of the knife to me, through one of my touts. The tout told me it came from a boy he knew who runs an ice cream van up in Lambhill. That boy, I recall, was a tout back in our time in 'C' Division, Scotty.'

'So?'

'So I think I'll go see that icey owner, have a wee chat, shoot the breeze, maybe even enjoy a 99 with sprinkles. And see, during our wee chat, I think he'd tell me where he got the gen in the first place. You know how persuasive I can be.'

Bolton said nothing for a few moments. Knight gave him time to think, had a puff or two on his smoke, waited. Finally, Bolton said, 'What exactly do you want, Knight?'

'Nothing. Just wanted to let you know what I thought, keeping you posted, like I promised.' He clamped the cigarillo between his teeth, flashed a grin. 'Just so we understand each other.'

'You're not going to turn this cop in?'

Knight thought about it. 'You know? I should, I really should. But then I think, why would I do that? What's the benefit to me? After all, I may need him someday.'

'And Donovan?'

'He's off to drink himself to death. Maybe even take a long walk off a short pier. I don't owe him anything.'

'I thought he was your friend?'

Knight laughed. 'Scotty, blokes like you and me? We don't have friends. Just people we can use and people we use up. That's it for us...'

TUESDAY

The drugs just weren't doing it for Scrapper Jarvis, not tonight. He'd tried sitting at home, snorted a couple of lines, knocked back some Jack Daniels, but it didn't work. He was alone now – Maw was dead, Jerry was dead, Marko was dead. Andy was in the pokey. There was just him now, rattling around the house, trying hard to get doped out of his head.

He decided it was the house that was getting in the way, too many memories, too many ghosts, so he headed out. His mates were banged up, there was no-one else he wanted to spend time with, so he went solo. Let McClymont send someone after him, he didn't care. He'd send them to hell. But he didn't think Big Rab would send anyone. He was locked away in that fortress of his out Bothwell way, grieving for his wife and kiddie. That was a shame, way it turned out, but that dickhead Choccie Barr was to blame. He should've made sure that it was Rab in the car, not his woman and wean. Aye, it was a shame.

He ended up at the Club Corvus. He'd not been back since the night he'd done that wee bastard Himes. Brought that on himself, so he did. Should never have been punting gear in a Jarvis place, those were the rules. Someday he'd get Skooshie Thompson, too. Scrapper felt no guilt over what he'd done. In the back of his mind he knew he had been the cause the misery that followed, but that's where he kept it – in the back of his mind. He forced it down, kept it locked away, surrounded now by a fog of narcotics and alcohol.

He did another couple of lines in the toilet, the same one he'd been in with Dickie Himes. He checked his face in the mirror, not good form to go out with coke all over his coupon, and then headed out. The place was busy and what he needed now was to pick up some lassie and get his wick dipped. He'd feel better after that – he always felt better after a shag.

The knife slid into his chest as soon as he opened the door to the Gents. He saw Skooshie Thompson standing right in front of him, his face tight and determined. The blade was shoved deeper and Skooshie breathed, 'This is for Dickie, ya cunt.'

Scrapper tried to say something, but he died before the words came.

ONE WEEK LATER

The dog sat up in the passenger seat, ears pricked, eyes alert as he
followed Davie's gaze through the windscreen toward the house
across the street. It was a terraced house in a street lined with
identical houses, built between the World Wars. They were small
and neat, only different coloured doors, styles of replacement
windows and varying types of curtains betraying the individuality
of their occupants. This one had a handkerchief-sized garden to
the front, nestling behind a low wall and an iron grate. Davie
couldn't see the grass through what was left of the snow, but he
knew come summer it would be cropped, as if someone had gone
over it with scissors, and lined with bright flowers.

This was where Vari had been brought up. It was where she
was now. In his hand Davie held the sketch he'd done the week
before. He didn't know why he'd brought it. With his other hand
he absently stroked the dog who waited for him to do something.

He'd thought of a name, finally. He knew one would present
itself. It had been sparked by Bobby's comment about how the dog
had flown like an arrow at Jarvis's man in the church and by the
white mark he'd found on its chest.

He'd call him Arrow.

He recalled a Harry Nilsson song from way back, something
about a dog with that name. A cartoon on the telly. He'd been a
kid then, early '70s. His mum was still alive, his dad hadn't yet
turned into the man Davie feared and dreaded. Not at home,
anyway. On the streets, in his work for Joe Klein, it was a different
matter, but when young Davie was watching the cartoon with
Harry Nilsson songs, Danny McCall was yet to bring that home.

So Arrow it was, and here he sat, still waiting for Davie to
make a move.

He'd been sitting in the car for half an hour and it was beginning to grow dark. It hadn't been the brightest of days and
ominous clouds had gathered during the afternoon to bring the
rain threatened by the bubbly weather girl on the morning news.
It would wash what remained of the snow away, she said, as if that
was a good thing. Davie liked the snow, liked the purity of it,

although in the city that didn't last. Nothing stayed pure for long, not in these streets. Not in his life, anyway.

He thought of Rab, at home, mourning his wife and daughter. He thought of young Joseph, probably sitting in his room alone, his face still the blank mask it had worn as he watched his mother and sister die.

He thought of Lassiter and Mannie. They had died together on the cold stone floor of his landing. A neighbour told Davie the big man had dragged himself up the stairs, they could tell by the blood trail from where Jerry Jarvis lay dead. They found him cradling the actor's head in his lap.

The Jarvises were done. There was only the one brother now, and he was facing time. Scrapper was found dead in the alleyway outside the Corvus, which had a kind of symmetry to it, Davie supposed. A single knife blow to the heart. He'd been done inside and dragged out. The police were hunting for the killer, but when you boiled it down, no-one much cared that Scrapper Jarvis was gone. Davie suspected that Skooshie Thompson was responsible, but the boy had vanished. Cops had the same notion, so he hoped Thompson never resurfaced. They might not care that Scrapper was gone, but they'd still make an arrest if they could, justice being blind and all that.

Choccie Barr was gone, too, which was not surprising. If he was smart, he'd stay in whatever hole he'd crawled into.

Donovan had dropped off the radar, too. Davie had heard about his problems and had tried to find him. He'd even visited his home in Shawlands, spoke to his wife – pretty lady, even with the red eyes and the dark shadows – but she said Frank had left and would not be back. Davie was saddened by this, because Donovan, his wife, the teenage girl he'd glimpsed at the window of the flat as he'd left, were all victims of the city, too. The big, bad city. Joe the Tailor had been a student of Glasgow's history and he'd told Davie something about it. For generations they'd come here, highlanders, lowlanders, the Irish, Poles like Joe, Asians, all looking for a life and for hope. Most of them found it, some didn't. They were folded into its cold embrace and were lost forever. They fell through the cracks in the pavement and were swallowed up. Drink and drugs, violence and vice. That was the world Davie was born into. He avoided drink and he didn't take drugs. One man's vice is another man's Saturday night, Joe used to say, for Joe catered to the vices – sex, gambling, greed, corruption.

But the violence…

Davie embraced the violence and it embraced him. The dark thing, Sammy called it. The thing that had taken over his father and ultimately destroyed him. But not before he had destroyed others. Davie's mother. Audrey. Audrey's husband, who killed a man, lost his job and was now God knows where. Destroyed. Lost. Eaten up by the city.

Davie didn't want to be eaten up. He didn't want the dark thing to take over. He didn't want to embrace the violence. He never had. Audrey had been a way out, he'd thought, but she was taken away from him. Vari was another. But he had let her walk away.

That was why he was here, he knew that now. Vari was his one chance to get out. That was what had drawn him here to this street, to that house across the way. He looked at the drawing again, saw her little half smile, her eyes. Did he love her? He still didn't know. He just knew that if he let her go then the city – The Life – would have won. And he would be easy prey to the dark.

'Stay here, boy,' he said as he rubbed Arrow's head. He climbed out, reached into the back and retrieved the brown paper bag that had been lying on the seat, walked across the road, his mind made up, his step purposeful. This was a game changer, right here. This is where he turned a corner.

He had his hand on the gate when he looked through the front window. Someone had switched on a standard lamp but not yet pulled the curtains. He could see in but they couldn't see him in the gathering gloom of the street. Vari was in an armchair, smiling at a young man who was seated on a long couch facing the gas fire. He was talking, his face animated, his hands moving. And then Vari laughed. Davie couldn't hear it through the double glazing, but he heard it in his mind. He'd liked her laugh. He'd liked her. And she looked so beautiful, her face bright and beaming, her blonde hair glowing, her eyes sparkling with her laugh. Davie felt something twinge inside him as he wondered who the young guy was. Whoever he was, Vari liked him and that made the pain pierce even deeper.

She was happy here. She could be happy with whoever this guy was.

He watched her through the glass. She was a few feet away, a few short feet. All it would take to bring her back was for him to knock on that door.

Vari had been thinking about Davie as she listened to her cousin, James, talk about his recent trip to New York. She had always wanted to visit the city, had said to Davie more than once that they should go, but his criminal record would've prevented it. She was playing a Gary Moore CD, which also brought him into her mind. Not that he was very far from it at the best of times. When she heard the knock at the door, she shouted to her dad in the kitchen that she'd get it. He didn't answer, probably too intent on burning the dinner.

There was a brown paper bag on the doorstep but no one in sight, although the gate was open, as if someone had left in a hurry. She picked the bag up, felt its heft, opened it. The breath caught in her throat as she saw the money. She reached in, pulled out a handful – tens, twenties – glanced inside again. There must be thousands in there, she thought, a frown puckering her forehead.

The car starting up and pulling away from the other side of the road made her look up again.

And she saw him. Davie, staring straight ahead as he drove.

It was just a glimpse and he didn't glance in her direction. She saw the dog, too, sitting in the passenger seat.

She moved to the gate, stepped onto the pavement and watched the car move away. Part of her wanted to chase after it, to catch it, stop it, to see him again, talk to him, hold him. But that was the silly, girly, romantic part of her. The grown-up, realistic Vari knew that could never be. Davie was alone now, the way he wanted to be, the way he was born to be. She looked at the money again. To the rest of the world Davie McCall was a brutal, callous thug. He was something different to her. He had been, still was, her man. The fact that he had left this money for her showed that she meant something to him. But not enough. It had taken five years, but she had come to terms with the fact that he could not have anyone else in his life, not a living, breathing person. He had too many ghosts to cope with.

The strains of Gary Moore picking out 'The Loner' on his guitar drifted from the open door behind her. Vari's lips parted in a rueful, sad little smile.

She knew she loved him. She knew she always would, at least part of her anyway. There would be someone else, somewhere down the line, but she knew she would always hold something in reserve for Davie McCall.

After all, he was the father of her son.

As soon as the stick turned blue, she knew it was a boy. She had stared at it for a long time, taking it in. Davie's son was inside her. She was going to be a mother. And right there and then, she reached a decision. She loved Davie McCall, but he wasn't ready to be a boyfriend or a husband, let alone a father. And to stay with him would run the risk of their son being drawn into The Life, and touched by the darkness that came with it. Maybe someday she would tell him, maybe not. She might not risk their son's future on a father with too much in his past.

It was a hard decision, the hardest she had ever made, but she'd made it. She couldn't go back on it. She had to remain firm. But as she watched the car vanish in the gathering gloom of the evening, she felt tears sting at her eyes and she wished things had been different, wished Davie had been different, wished he could lay his ghosts to rest, wished he could find peace.

As she turned back towards the house, she didn't see the sheet of paper being plucked from the ground by the slight breeze, the charcoal lines that made up her image already smudged by raindrops.

Author's note

I HAVE NO IDEA whether there were heavy snowfalls in Glasgow in early January 1995. This is a work of fiction, so I simply made it up. I've taken liberties with some locations, too, in order to suit the needs of the story. Further, let me stress again that the characters here are not based on any real criminals, police officers or Hollywood actors. I made them all up too. That said, the two drug busts are very loosely based on actual incidents, the major arrest beside the canal inspired by a real-life case described by Joe Jackson in his book *Chasing Killers* (Mainstream Publishing).

As usual, there are lots of people to thank for their assistance, either in reading a draft, providing information or support, assisting with promotion or simply buying multiple copies (please keep that up). I won't list the names, as I fear I may forget someone. I know who you are, you know who you are, and what you do for me is much appreciated.

Blood City

Douglas Skelton
ISBN: 978-1-910021-24-8 PBK £7.99

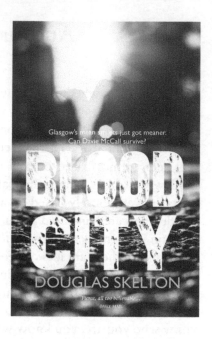

Meet Davie McCall. Beaten, bloody… brutal.

Irrevocably damaged by the barbaric regime of an abusive father, and haunted by memories of his mother's murder, there is a darkness inside him.

Enter Joe the Tailor. A sophisticated crimelord with morals, he might be the only man in the city Davie can trust. But then the bodies begin to mount…

In 1980s Glasgow, the criminal underworld is about to splinter. Battle lines are drawn, and the gap between friend and enemy blurs as criminals and police alike are caught in a net of lies, murder and revenge that will change the city forever. *Blood City* is the first novel in Douglas Skelton's Davie McCall quartet.

Fierce, all too believable.
DAILY MAIL

You follow the plot like an eager dog, nose turning this way and that, not catching every single clue but quivering as you lunge towards a blood-splattered denouement.
DAILY EXPRESS

The Glasgow of this period is a great, gritty setting for a crime story, and Skelton's non-fiction work stands him in good stead… he's taken well to fiction… the unexpected twists keep coming.
THE HERALD

Crow Bait

Douglas Skelton
ISBN: 978-1-910021-29-3 PBK £9.99

They'll all be crow bait by the time I'm finished...

Jail was hell for Davie McCall. Ten years down the line, freedom's no picnic either. It's 1990, there are new kings in the West of Scotland underworld, and Glasgow is awash with drugs.

Davie can handle himself. What he can't handle is the memory of his mother's death at the hand of his sadistic father. Or the darkness his father implanted deep in his own psyche. Or the nightmares...

Now his father is back in town and after blood, ready to waste anyone who stops him hacking out a piece of the action. There are people in his way. And Davie is one of them.

Crow Bait is the second novel in Douglas Skelton's Davie McCall quartet.

Tense, dark and nerve-wracking...
a highly effective thriller.
THE HERALD

This is crime fiction of the strongest quality.
CRIMESQUAD.COM

A gory and razor-sharp crime novel from the start, Douglas Skelton's Crow Bait *moves at breakneck speed like a getaway car on the dark streets of Glasgow.*
THE SKINNY

Skelton has been hiding from his talent for long enough. High time he shared it with the rest of us.
QUINTIN JARDINE

Details of these and other books published by Luath Press can be found at: **www.luath.co.uk**

Luath Press Limited
committed to publishing well written books worth reading

LUATH PRESS takes its name from Robert Burns, whose little collie Luath (*Gael.,* swift or nimble) tripped up Jean Armour at a wedding and gave him the chance to speak to the woman who was to be his wife and the abiding love of his life. Burns called one of 'The Twa Dogs' Luath after Cuchullin's hunting dog in Ossian's *Fingal*. Luath Press was established in 1981 in the heart of Burns country, and now resides a few steps up the road from Burns' first lodgings on Edinburgh's Royal Mile.
Luath offers you distinctive writing with a hint of unexpected pleasures.

Most bookshops in the UK, the US, Canada, Australia, New Zealand and parts of Europe either carry our books in stock or can order them for you. To order direct from us, please send a £sterling cheque, postal order, international money order or your credit card details (number, address of cardholder and expiry date) to us at the address below. Please add post and packing as follows: UK – £1.00 per delivery address; overseas surface mail – £2.50 per delivery address; overseas airmail – £3.50 for the first book to each delivery address, plus £1.00 for each additional book by airmail to the same address. If your order is a gift, we will happily enclose your card or message at no extra charge.

Luath Press Limited
543/2 Castlehill
The Royal Mile
Edinburgh EH1 2ND
Scotland
Telephone: 0131 225 4326 (24 hours)
email: sales@luath.co.uk
Website: www.luath.co.uk